THE CORRIDORS OF THE DEAD

BOOK 1 OF THE AMONG THE DEAD TRILOGY

JONATHAN D ALLEN

Maric,
thanks for the support!
Best wishes,
Jonathan D. Allen

THE CORRIDORS OF THE DEAD

A Qwendellonia Book

PRINTING HISTORY
Qwendellonia First Edition/November 2011

All rights reserved.

Copyright © 2011 by Jonathan D Allen

Cover art by Celia Chung

For more information, contact the author at crimnos@gmail.com or visit
http://jonathandallen.com

ISBN-13: 978-0615558615
ISBN-10: 0615558615
BISAC: Fiction / Fantasy / Contemporary

Every novel is a group effort; this one is no exception. Thanks go out to cover artists Celia Chung and Erwin Solbach; dedicated beta readers Aleta Best, Robert Clark, and Mary Compton; and editor Shelly Burnett for their efforts. Thank you for making this possible.

For Mary, who made this possible.
For Jeremy, who helped me believe.

Book 1: Initiation

Chapter 1

Strange Things Are Afoot

You want to know where it began. Fine. With my suffering: another shitty Friday night in a long line of shitty nights in even shittier Eureka, California, slaving away at *el supremo shitto* Circle K. At least, that's what I thought, before Delilah and the tweeker terror struck on the same night. I'd never dare bitch about a Friday night again, let me tell you.

I worked the graveyard shift. Your typical graveyard shift worker in Eureka was either a tweeker looking for something to do during the asshole hours of the night, or someone who had drawn the wrath of their boss and the boss was trying to save herself the trouble of firing your ass. I've never been one for the normal, though. I chose the graveyard shift because I hate - well, *hated* - people. I also believe I would end up a great *artiste* of some merit, but we see how that went.

My point is that even though I despised late nights, they were just what I needed: time to escape people and work on my art.

The dead of night seemed cursed, or blessed, hell, I don't know. All I know is time slowed down; everything, the demands, pressures, and expectations of the world, ground to a halt. Lack of sleep started hunting me like a hungry wolf. Mind you, I fought the wolf away, and very successfully I might add, with the aid of the Holy Trinity: Monster energy drink, Red Bull, and Mountain Dew Code Red. I always kept at least one can of these weapons in my purse, ready for rapid deployment.

Even with a good jolt of caffeine and the juice from bull balls, I told somebody - I can't remember who - that those hours were the closest you could get to understanding what it might feel like to be an inter-dimensional traveler, stuck between your world and the world of the mundanes. You couldn't help but let the weirdness guide your work. Charcoals and inks turned from tools in my hands into portals to surreal worlds, opening gates to those places. I'm talking real Lovecraftian stuff, beasts from beyond the stars.

Back to our particular lousy night, which was already drawing in on a truly shitty night, although I didn't know it yet. I had my ear buds driven as deep as I could, because they tuned in the blandest damned Sirius station they could find and God forbid if they found out you touched the dial. Michael Bolton at 3 in the morning is cruel and unusual, I say. Give me some UK Subs or even some Bowie if you're going middle of the road. I need good music - it's like oxygen.

It had been a good night so far: Babes in Toyland on the iPod, canvas pad on the counter, the charcoals *singing* under my fingers. I had started with a boring little sketch of Kristy, turning my beautiful woman into a sneering Nordic goddess, holding the severed head of her enemy in her right hand. Not my normal work, but the weird hours, right? Eh, she'd love it anyway. It was right up her alley, even if I had made it as morbid as a goth at a funeral.

I shaded the corner of her eyes, sticking my tongue out, when the front door chimed. We had the most annoying chime in the world, but it sure worked. Like Pavlov's punker girl, I swept my pad off the counter and become the most model employee the Circle K had ever seen.

Like I said, I worked the shift to escape people, so somebody coming in at 3:30 in the night was a bit...odd, you'd say. Not odd enough to anticipate the storm coming my way, but odd enough to get me a little irritated at the old woman walking through the front door.

She could be anybody's granny - had a big head of curly white hair, wrinkles around the eyes like she hadn't stopped smiling since she popped out of her mom, and bright blue eyes. It made it hard to hate on her, even if I wanted to.

She shuffled over to the Froster machine. The old biddy seemed to have a taste for the blue raspberry. I'd have gone for something with a bit more jolt myself, but maybe she just woke up? She shuffled up to the counter, and I started ringing her up.

Her behavior gave me the first clue that she might be a bit different from the old biddies that typically passed through. She didn't have anything to say about my hair color or my nose ring - how I'd be so pretty if I wasn't messing with my looks. She didn't say anything about my tattoos, either. She didn't even notice them. It made me say - and I swear to God I *never* said this sort of thing - "anything else I can get for you, ma'am?" *Ma'am!* Can you believe that?

She smiled and put a hand to her chest. "I suppose I'll need some smokes," she said.

God help me, I returned her smile. "What brand?"

"Marlboro 100s. Not the light stuff, either. Can't abide that."

I paused. Hardcore for an old lady, but it's her lungs. I bent down and got her smokes.

"It's nice to see someone's still awake," she said.

"It's kind of my job," I mumbled, chewing on my nail. I think this might have been the most I'd said to a customer in months. I'd have marveled at it, but I also noticed something going on inside me. I mean, besides transforming into Polly Prissy Pants. My chest started feeling like when you're going up in the roller coaster - you know, that building feeling? Only I never liked roller coasters, so I felt a little panicked. I went from liking the old lady to feeling in my gut that something was weird about her. Dahmer weird.

"It's still nice to see," the old biddy said. "Could just as easily sleep under there."

I forced a laugh, a little worried she would be able to tell and maybe rip my throat out. "Don't I know it? But," I said, and lifted an empty Red Bull can from beside the register, "the magic of caffeine prevails, as always."

She leaned on the counter and said. "Mmm, is that stuff safe?"

"I've never had a problem."

"Doesn't mean it couldn't start now."

"Whatever gets the job done."

"I suppose." The old biddy offered me her hand. "I'm Delilah, by the way. Delilah McKinley. At your service."

I stared at her hand.

Don't be an ass. Shake it.

I'd rather have put my hand straight up a dog's ass, but I shook it. It hadn't even occurred to me that she might be nice, warm, and soft, but she was, and it made it a little more bearable.

She expected me to give her my name, even though she could read the damned name tag. "Matty," I said. "Matty DiCamillo. At your...uh. Service. I guess."

"Good manners," she said. "You don't see that much anymore." She picked up the bag.

I faked a tip of my invisible top hat, touching my long green hair.

"When do you get off your shift?" she said.

Of course, that was it. She wanted to get some from me, and had picked up on my "family" vibe. It wasn't the first time, either. "I'm sorry. I've got a girlfriend."

"That's very sweet, and I'm happy for you, but I don't see how that's related to what I asked you."

I wondered if she was for real, or playing stupid since I shot her down. Crazy vibe or not, I had to know where she going with this. "Why do you ask?"

"Curiosity, I suppose. You look tired."

I didn't buy it for a second. She had some sort of angle, but I couldn't figure it out. "I'm fine. I get off at six. No worries."

"Mmm." She stepped away from the counter. "You take care of yourself tonight, you hear? You never know what could happen."

That *really* put the heebie jeebies in me. Dahmer weird, indeed. I shrugged, figuring the best path would be to play it cool and keep my eyes open. "I try to."

She pointed at me. "I'm serious."

Believe me, I knew she was serious. I also knew I was ready for the bat to get the hell out of my store. "Okay, okay."

The old biddy held the finger in the air a moment longer. "Good. Maybe we'll run into each other again sometime."

Not if I have anything to say about it, I thought. "Buh-bye now." I watched her wander on out the front door. Nice or not, I felt just fine getting rid of her. The rising feeling vanished, along with the need to spew.

I rolled my neck, trying to clear my mind. Even without Delilah checking in, the early morning buzz in my head was coming together, threatening to rise into the last crescendo of sleepiness that tried to pull me down right before dawn.

Caffeine. I needed more. Stat. So I wandered out from behind the counter toward the drink cases, fetching another energy drink, I don't remember which, one with a name that some marketer no doubt branded with "clever" sexual innuendo, like you were drinking down a load.

The front door chimed again.

Christ. I couldn't win. I wondered how my night could get any worse.

I've learned never to ask that question again. The shotgun leveled at my chest answered it.

The girl who held the shotgun was thin and scaly, her dyed black hair looking like a cross between a bird's nest and a tornado, makeup smeared all over her face. What we called a Eureka Tweeka, a meth head of the lowest class who usually degenerated into knocking over liquor stores or their own families, whichever was easier.

I'd encountered a few in my time at Circle K, but she was the first weapon-toting member of her tribe to cross my path. I can't say I regretted missing out on it.

"Can you control the cameras?" the Tweeka asked me, glancing at the camera over the frozen goods case.

"Sure," I lied. "Behind the counter." This just happened to be where they had plugged in the silent alarm.

She motioned toward the counter with the shotgun. "Do it."

"Your wish is my command. Stay calm." I walked

toward the counter, sure to do it nice and slow, keeping those hands in the air and visible.

She seemed to realize something might be amiss by the time we reached the counter. She furrowed her brow. I had to admit that it was a cute brow. She might have been something before the twack, but right then she had turned into pure danger and need. "Nothing f-f-funny," she said.

"I wouldn't dream of it. You've got the gun. I'm going to hit the button that turns them off, okay?"

She nodded, three rapid up-and-down bobs.

I slid my hand under the counter and thumbed the silent alarm. Pretty damned smooth, if I did say so myself, especially considering that I was ready to piss myself. "It's off."

"Open the register."

I keyed in some bullshit transaction and popped it open. She reached over the counter and started scooping out the money. You'd think it would vanish if she didn't move fast enough. I saw an opening where I could've *maybe* taken the gun, but no way would I try anything funny with a crazy tweeker.

Once she had finished emptying Circle K's coffers, she pointed the gun at me again.

"Can you get in the safe?" she asked.

"It's a time lock. I can't open it at all."

She nodded. Probably needed to fix, and had everything she needed. Except that wasn't quite it either.

I'm screwed. The bitch is smart enough to be dangerous, even with the thwack fucking her up. Hell, maybe even because of the thwack, who knows?

She had known to get rid of the cameras, and it dawned

on me real fast that she had to get rid of the only witness.

I could almost see her realize that killing me there would be bloody and make it a lot easier to catch her, as the wasteland that had once been a pretty face went blank. I'd seen this scary little tool enough to know it well: she was turning the old emotional tap clean off so she could do whatever she wanted. That, my friends, is what makes addicts the most frightening human beings you may ever encounter.

"You're coming with me," she said.

I ran into a problem here. First thing they tell you is that your odds of getting killed by a kidnapper rise when you let them take you somewhere else. Problem is, I could see this little bitch was going to kill me either way. The only chance I might have was letting her think she had control of me and getting the drop on her in some other place. I yelled at myself for not grabbing the gun when she emptied the register, but what was done was done.

"Sure, okay." I walked around the counter and toward her, heart in my throat. I wanted to think my odds of getting out of this were good, but I knew the truth of the situation. I wished I'd have had time to say goodbye to Kristy; hell, I couldn't even remember if I'd told her I loved her the last time I talked to her.

The bitch put the shotgun in my back and led me out the front door toward the most broken-down piece of crap black Cadillac I may ever have laid eyes on. It was a crime what she had done to a beautiful piece of machinery; I could have beaten her for it. Instead, I let her lead me to the trunk. She unlocked it and lifted the lid.

Ah shit, I thought, *a trunk?* I'm not one for enclosed spaces at the best of times, but the thought of getting in that thing without knowing where I was going? "Can't you at least put me in the back seat? Or up front, you can keep the gun on me there."

She shook her head, the swaying, ugly sister of her bobbing head nod. "S-s-s-somebody would see you."

"I'll get down in front of the seat so nobody can see me. I promise I won't make any trouble. Just don't put me in the trunk, for God's sake. Have a heart."

She shook her head, her hair beating her face. "Get in."

"Christ," I moaned, and believe me, I didn't mean to, but what the hell else was I going to do? I climbed in, God help me.

Chapter 2

Got No Room to Breathe

The trunk smelled like a droid died in there. Gas, dirty motor oil, filthy metal, all that good stuff. Of course I couldn't focus on the wonderful smell because panic had set my mind on fire. I could breathe, but my brain played tricks on me, telling me the thing was air-tight, and I would run out of air any second.

Calm down. You can find a way out of this. Nothing's over. She opens the trunk, you grab the gun and pop her in the jaw with the butt. No problem, right?

The little girl in my brain wouldn't listen. Too busy throwing one queen of a shit fit.

Thank God I didn't have to drag her along much longer. The next second everything went *boom*, and me and all the other crap in the trunk slammed up against the inside wall. Knocked the wind out of me. At least she hadn't bound me up or God knows, with my luck, I'd have hit my head and never have gotten to tell you this fabulous story.

Everything got quiet after I'd rolled on top of the spare tire. I lie there wondering if she was dead - would I starve to death, or would the cops figure out what happened?

Then she started screaming like Freddy Krueger was on her tail.

Something heavy hit the gravel outside the driver's side. I heard the Tweeka, clear as day.

"I didn't mean it, I swear, I'll give the money back, please, just don't-"

She never got to finish the sentence. Something made a heavy thud - I guess she got smacked over the head - and everything went quiet again.

So I laid there not knowing what the hell was going on, heart ready to explode in my chest, as I heard what I imagined was a serial killer reaching inside the driver's side, then heading toward the back of the car.

Oh shit, I thought. *He knows I'm here, and I'm next.* Hell, maybe the killer had targeted me all along. Who knew? My night hadn't exactly been full of luck.

The keys slid into the trunk and turned, sounding like God coming to get me. The trunk popped open, and everything was quiet except the killer's heavy breathing. My eyes were having trouble adjusting to the street light over the killer's shoulder, so all I saw for the longest time was an ominous shadow, standing there and weighing my life.

The killer spoke. "Are you okay?"

My brain shut down for a second. No kidding. I don't know where I went, but when I came back, I knew who spoke to me: Delilah McKinley.

You have got to be kidding me, I thought. "Please don't kill me, I'm innocent, I didn't do anything," I babbled, trying to push my atoms through the trunk wall.

"Please, calm down. I'm not here to kill you, I promise."

I wanted to buy it, but the little girl was back and ready to crap her pants. "You're lying," I panted.

"'*God never made a promise that was too good to be true'.*"

Was she *quoting* things to me? To this day I can't figure out if she was sincere or trying to calm me down. I didn't know what to say.

She touched my shoulder. "Come on, let's get you out of there."

I let her take me. I couldn't believe it myself. She put her arm around me, pulling me toward the front of the trunk like I was made of porcelain.

"Be careful," she said, and helped me climb out. I could feel every single bruise as the effects of the fear high wore off, and climbing out was pure agony.

"She was going to -" I gasped.

"I know. Thank goodness I got here first, eh? Couldn't have you going and getting killed."

I rubbed my hip. *Nearly lost it there, girl.* My death at one hand or another had been a constant reality for the last five minutes or so, and returning to a world with any other possible outcome was one bitch of a transition. "Guess not. How did you know I was out here?"

"I saw her putting you in the trunk. I followed you."

"That doesn't make any sense. She had me-"

She cocked her head. "Do you hear that?" she asked.

I'm not about to fall for that one.

I shook my head. "No, I-" I spoke too soon. I did hear it: sirens. "How the hell did they know?"

"They know because I called them." She smirked. "Now you can either come with me, or you can stay here and explain what happened to that poor girl."

I must have been a little slow on the uptake because only then did I catch on to what she had done here. Pissed at myself that I hadn't sniffed out the set-up, I shook my head. "That's stupid. How the hell am I supposed to explain where I went? Tell them the tooth fairy rescued me?"

"I don't think you understand, dear. You don't get to go back. You go with me."

Anyone else would've asked her where the hell she planned on taking them, but I didn't need to know. This *was* Delilah after all, and I didn't like the crazy gleam in her eye. Anywhere she was going was no good. "I don't think so, chief."

"You can always stay here and explain who beat that girl, but you have to make a decision soon."

She had that right. The sirens weren't getting any farther away.

She opened her mouth and made my mind up for me. "You *must* come with me," she said. "You've been chosen."

"Chosen? What the hell's that's supposed to mean? Chosen for what?"

"Something special, but come, there's no time." She took my hand, like she was my mother.

Let's say I'd never been one for the maternal type stuff. I shook her off. "Uh uh. I'm staying here."

"Are you crazy?" she asked.

Let's face it; we didn't have time to discuss the matter, because those sirens were getting closer and closer. She had to make her move now, so she started moving toward her Pontiac. Nice little black piece by the way, I'd guess the latest model G6 if you put a gun to my head. Who says insanity means you can't ride in class?

I started climbing back into the Tweeka's trunk. "Nope. I think that's you." The answer had been staring me in the face: *I was in the trunk officer, honest, no idea what happened.*

"We'll meet again," she said, like some cartoon villain.

"Let's not do that." I muttered, and closed the trunk. You

know I want to get away from someone when I'm willing to put myself into a car trunk. I laid there in the darkness for awhile, smelling the dead droid smell. She started the Pontiac and tore out of there minutes before the cops arrived. I couldn't be sure if they saw her or not, but I'm guessing from what followed, they had no clue.

The cops got there not too long after her.

Before you ask, no, I didn't tell them about Delilah. Was I supposed to tell them some granny whacked a Tweeka with a baseball bat? Sure, things might have turned out differently, but coulda, woulda, shoulda.

Instead I told them my sob story about being robbed at Circle K and tossed in the trunk. I didn't know what the hell happened because she'd knocked me out cold, and I only woke up when they opened the trunk. The cameras and my bruises backed it up.

Poof. Done. I wanted to go back to my life. It wasn't much, but it was at least *a* life.

Of course, Delilah McKinley had not disappeared from my life. Not by a long shot.

Chapter 3

Bringing the Irony

I think you might be getting the sense by now that I don't like to do what people expect of me. Hell, I *hate* doing what people expect of me. I'm sure there's some deep Freudian thing going on. No doubt my continuing attempt to piss off my mom, good old Melinda DiCamillo *if you please my dear.* She expected me to do the whole college thing and squirt out two point five kids for some bland suburban tool. Still, knowing why it happens and changing it are two separate things.

I tell you this so you understand why I went back to work pretty quick. Not the next night, but within two nights. My good buddy good pal, Daniel, took over a shift or two, before I could talk our bitch of a store manager into letting me have my shift. She wanted me to share it with Daniel for awhile, but I refused; no one would fawn over me, not under my watch. Kristy had been up my ass ever since I'd gotten out of the police station, and while I loved her to death, I needed a break.

Thank God I had been blessed with an average night. At least, until the sun started coming up. Business picked up around 4:30 in the morning, and Daniel came in around 5:00 in the morning, so we could work the shift together for a little bit. Fascinating life. Things got quiet again around 6:00; a certain type of folk got out of bed at that time, and most of the earlier crowd had cleared out. It didn't matter. What mattered was when I came out of the little cooler in the back and found myself face-to-face with none other than Delilah McKinley.

She looked different. Not just calmer, but like she'd gotten younger - maybe ten years or so. She also wore something that wasn't so…I don't know, matronly. It was a clingy blue dress, ruffled up front, and I realized for the first time that Delilah was stacked. The realization was horrifying, but the weird thing about it was that it took away the *wrongness* that I'd felt the last time I'd seen her. Maybe this was her real face, and her old face had been a rubber mask.

"Good morning, dear," she said, and even her voice sounded a little younger. Not so gruff.

"Uh, good morning." I kept my eyes straight forward in the socially awkward shuffle, heading straight for the snack aisle and I guess a Frito crucifix to chase her away.

"Please. Wait." She touched my arm. Again, it wasn't like the other night. I didn't want to rip it away; in fact, it felt pretty damned good.

"What?" I turned around, but I still wasn't meeting those eyes.

"We have to talk."

"I have nothing to talk to you about. Got it?"

"On the contrary. We got off on the wrong foot. Let me take you to breakfast and we can talk about it."

"It's about me being your Chosen One, isn't it?"

She seemed to consider the Doritos over my shoulder, her mouth screwed up. She nodded.

"What the hell's your deal? You're like the world's most persistent, murderous Mormon missionary," I whispered.

I must've caught Delilah off-guard, because her eyes

went wide right before she started laughing. "That's one way to put it, but no, dear, I don't represent any religion."

"Who *do* you represent?"

"How do I put this? A benefactor, I suppose. Someone who is very interested in your talents and would like to hire you."

"What talents? You said I'm going to be finding some stuff out…"

She looked around the store, at the other customers. "I'm afraid I can't talk about it here."

"Then I'm not going to hear it at all. We're not going anywhere together. Got it?"

"You're our only hope," she said.

"Listen, Princess Leia. You've got the wrong girl. I'm nobody special."

"Everything okay here?" That was my man, Daniel. I hadn't even noticed him creeping up on us, which is a hell of a feat given that there was about six-foot-four and one-hundred-eighty pounds of raw hipster fury to notice about him. I'm talking dark brown goatee, pompadour, and horn-rimmed glasses – chosen with the utmost of care, mind you - that coordinated with his argyle sweater. I tried to make fun of him once, tell him he was a walking stereotype. You know what he said? He said that was the point. He brought the irony, and he brought it *hard*.

I looked at Delilah. "I don't think so. She was just leaving."

Daniel looked to her. "That right?" he asked in his thick Scottish brogue.

Delilah's eyes were ready to hop out of her skull and jump down on the floor, doing a little dance for our entertainment, but she gave us one of those mean little old lady nods. "I suppose I am. But think about this, dear: a sign is coming soon." She glanced at her watch. "You'll hear about it within the hour. When you do, remember this conversation. Beware the Aetelia."

She stormed out of the place, leaving behind a bunch of baffled customers and two even more baffled coworkers.

"What was *that* about?" Daniel asked.

"Who knows? I think she's some religious fruitcake." I waved a hand. "Let's sell some coffee, shall we?"

I tried to play it off, but when a woman gets ten years younger in two days, comes into your store telling you you're the Messiah, and then proceeds to warn you about some sign...it gets your attention.

It was still on my mind when Kristy picked me up.

"Morning," I muttered as I climbed in her car. The sound system was pumping out some dubstep crap, stuff that only sounded good under the influence of heavy drugs, and in no circumstance at seven in the morning. "What the hell is this crap?"

"It's La Roux, and I *totally* love it."

"You would. Sounds like someone's attacking a parrot with a phaser."

"God you're such a bitch," she said, but she smiled and switched it to talk radio, just for special little me. Ah God, her smile could slay me. She had a wide, pale face, wide and soft, and amazing blue eyes, like safe ponds out in the wilderness. Everything about her said kindness and welcoming. The opposite of my bony, angular mess of a face, and don't try to tell me otherwise.

"It's my job." I saluted her.

"Did you score the goods?" It was *always* about the goods with her.

"I scored the goods." I opened my purse and produced: Mountain Dew Froster, package of chocolate doughnuts. We called them Polly treats.

Oh, Polly, right. It was short for Pollyanna. Look it up in the dictionary, I bet you see her picture there. It came out of me one evening when we were hanging out at the Mad Hatter's Tea Party - a tea shop on East Street, where the hipsters hung out. She tried to convince a group of us that a car crash - even one where the occupants ended up smeared on the pavement, could be a *good* thing, or at least have an upside.

Funny the things you think of, huh?

She squealed when she saw her blessed goods. Even though I must have given them to her a hundred times, it was like I produced a bag full of live bunnies just for her. "Gimme, gimme," she said, and started sucking down the Froster right away as she pulled us out of the parking lot.

With a moment's silence at last, I started paying attention to what was on the radio. "Is this NPR?" I asked. I couldn't remember the last time I had heard the President on the radio.

"It's whatever you set it to last time. I don't listen to this stuff."

I jumped, an involuntary spasm, when I caught on to what the President was saying. I held up my hand to quiet her down. I think he said something like, *"my fellow Americans, understand that this is a very serious situation. This comet is roughly the size of Texas."*

My memory of the moment's not so great. I was a little

preoccupied with trying not to puke out the window and crap my pants at the same time. A great moment, one in a million. He said some other stuff, like planet-killer. I don't remember it all, but I do remember what he said next, because it at least gave me some hope:

"Now, we've seen the movies and read the novels that told us what this means. They've shown us graphic details and the fear, but they've also shown us hope. So I would ask you, my fellow Americans, to hold on to your hope. This Administration, united with the other governments of the world, is dedicated to finding a solution to spare humanity from this catastrophe. We have assembled a task force unrivaled in the history of our species…"

I don't know what came next. I tuned it out. My brain was full of white noise. I figured I had to look pretty much like Kristy. Mouth hanging open, eyes bugging out, skin pale. What the hell do you say when the President's told everyone on Earth that they got this terminal case of dying out within the next two years?

I did all I could, and reached out to touch her. That touch reminded me of what Delilah had said. If this wasn't a sign, I didn't know what else qualified. What the hell did it mean? Was it possible she wasn't out of her mind? What would that mean for me, *was* I supposed to be some kind of chosen one?

Me. The Little Punk Girl Who Couldn't. A Chosen One. It boggled the mind.

Kristy spoke first, and thank God because I had no clue what to say. "Tell me it's not true, Boo."

I sighed. "I don't guess I can."

"I don't get it. Aren't there supposed to be, like, signs?"

"This seems like a pretty big sign. A STOP sign the size

of God."

She shook her head. "I don't think I'm going to work today. I'm feeling a little sick."

"Yeah. I bet a lot of people aren't going to work today."

The rest of the drive home was dead silent. I don't know what was going on in her head, but I thought of Delilah and her words. Turning them over like a Rubik's Cube. I never was good at those things.

Chapter 4

And I Feel Fine...

Anticlimax of anticlimaxes, we went to my place, er, abode. My trailer. In an, uhm, community of mobile estates, I believe is what we called it. Fancy, right? But what do you expect when you work at a Circle K and your art isn't selling? At least I got a decent one, double-wide with good air and a solid foundation. Those things aren't as bad as you think.

I wanted to stay up and see what the hell was going to happen next, but no matter how cranked I might have been, lack of sleep was doing its thing to my head. I could tell I would start seeing things soon, so it was time for Ambien, ear plugs, the mask, and a good head of sleep.

Kristy stayed with me at the trailer. I think she wanted two things. One was just to avoid being alone with the end of the world crashing down around her head. Who could blame her for that? The other was that she wanted to hover over me, as if I would break into little bitty pieces. That one was a lot less understandable and a lot more infuriating, but she loved me, so I couldn't exactly kick her out, you know?

I woke up around 5:00 in the evening; I remember, because it was already getting dark. Things were still a little fuzzy around the edges, though. Ambien hangover. It took me a few seconds of stumbling past Kristy sitting at my computer, her lithe, beautiful legs tucked up under her body and my massive headphones dwarfing her tiny little head.

"Oh God, you're awake." She used the bubbly little voice she sometimes affected, the one that made my head rattle. I loved her to death, but good Lord she could be squeaky.

I stopped and grunted something. Who the hell knows what it was, didn't matter.

"Come here."

"You been there all day?"

"Yeah. Things are going crazy. Come on, come over here."

I fought my desire to guzzle every caffeinated beverage in the place (believe me, that was quite a lot), and managed to stumble over to the computer. I laid my head on her shoulder not just out of affection but because it felt like it was going to crash to the ground at any second if something wasn't supporting it.

She let out this nice little coo, so I guess I managed to win some points. She put a hand on my face, and I kissed it.

I glanced at the computer screen. "Sweet Jesus, is this the control room?" I asked. She had at least four streaming channels running in cascading windows; I could pick out Al Jazeera English and CNN on top in a mess of movement that I couldn't put together, but I didn't recognize some of the others. They were in foreign languages; that was all I could make out.

"I know, right? I feel like a superpower." She giggled. "I told you, things are going crazy."

"Much like my router. What's going on?"

She pointed out the Al Jazeera feed. "That's a riot in Mumbai." She clicked over to CNN. "That's where somebody, like, bombed the DC Metro. Fucked up, I think a lot of people got killed, right?" She clicked to another window. "That's

Tokyo. Nobody *really* knows what's going on there, but it sounds like somebody attacked a power plant."

A blackout in Tokyo. "Christ almighty." I reached past her for the cup of Mountain Dew sitting beside the keyboard.

She looked to me, blue eyes boring into mine. "That's, like, the point, right? People figure they've got nothing left to lose."

I didn't know what to say, so I polished off the Mountain Dew. "How long 'til Humboldt goes tits up?" I finally said.

"That's the thing," she said, clicking on an open Chrome window. "Look."

The headline jumped out at me:

HUMBOLDT BAY IN FLAMES

I rubbed my eyes. "They're burning the entire bay?"

"No, duh, how do you burn water? They think somebody burned the Marina."

That would be the Woodley Island Marina. Think what you would about the rich assholes who kept their boats there, the place was gorgeous. You didn't have to be a snot to love it or want it saved. My stomach sank. "How could they?"

"I know, right?" She looked at the glass. "You going to fill that up?"

"Yeah, sorry, hon." I straightened and went to the fridge, opening the door.

I froze when a knock came at the door. "You expecting somebody?" I said.

"Why would I?"

"I don't know." I sure as hell wasn't expecting anybody. Could be Daniel stopping by, but something tingling in my brain didn't think that was the case.

The knock came again.

"You going to get that?" she asked.

"Yeah. Sure." Brave words, but my stomach, which was already on the bad side, gurgled at the mere suggestion. I put the glass down and went to the trailer's front door, picking up my old baseball bat from beside the door. I kept it there for such an occasion, and had made sure it was ready ever since the run-in with the Tweeka.

"Who is it?" I asked, and the answer was another knock. "Asshole," I muttered, and glanced at Kristy, whose eyes had gone wide, reflecting my anxiety.

"Answer me or I'm going to call the cops. You know I will."

The answer was another knock.

"Motherfucker, if you don't-"

I didn't get to finish. The asshole on the other end of the door knocked the door off its hinges, the full weight of the door plowing into me. Kristy screamed and jumped up from the computer.

Before I knew what was happening, he slammed me into the wall beside the computer, holding me up by my throat.

When my head cleared, I saw the guy wasn't a guy; he was just an outline, a shadow living in three dimensions and dead-set on fucking me up.

"Watcher scum," it hissed.

"Who are you," was all I could manage. The world was already going dark from him cutting off my air supply. I danced on the edge of Hell's doorstep, yet I had never been calmer. I looked at him with wonder as everything slowed. The world didn't just go black, it went black and white.

The hell? I thought, and then reality took a flying leap. Everything lurched, like God reached down and picked up the table of the world, tilting it at a right angle, but gravity somehow kept everything attached. Time and space knotted up, and the sunlight coming through the windows seemed to have gone the consistency of mayonnaise.

The shadow had frozen. I reached down and started unwrapping his fingers one at a time when that familiar, uneasy feeling from the K rose in my chest again. You know how when you get anxious you feel like you might explode? Like that, but I *did* explode, in a burst of time and space, unwinding and knocking the bastard backwards.

Next thing I knew lie on my back in the side yard, staring up at the black night sky, wondering how I got there.

Delilah appeared over my head, smiling at me with her freaky young-and-old face.

"She appears to be awake, dear," she said to somebody I couldn't see.

"What the hell?" I said.

"Thank God." That was Kristy, all over me, hugging, kissing, making it so that I couldn't see Delilah.

Kristy and Delilah. Together. I didn't like that idea one bit.

"Yeah, it's me," I returned a few kisses before I pushed her away and sat up, raising an eyebrow at Delilah. "So you came back for me."

"I saved your life." She folded her hands at her waist, prim and proper. "That's twice now. I do believe you owe me."

"Saved my life? What? How?"

She *tsked*. "I took care of your assailant, of course. He

won't be bothering anyone anymore."

Damn. Add another kill to Granny's body count. "How did I get out here?"

Kristy answered. "Oh my God, you have no idea. It's *so* badass."

"What's badass? What's going on here?" *For that matter…* "Where are the cops?"

"They're, uhm, occupied," Kristy said. "I couldn't even get through to 911, but we don't even need them. Everything's going to be okay."

"If you say so." I tried to rise, but that was a tall order. Took the both of them to get their arms under me and lift. "Tell me what's going on. The condensed version, please. I've had a hell of a week so far and I don't know how much more I can take."

"Mmm, indeed you have. Kristy, can you get the door?"

"No problem," she said, and disappeared again.

I blinked. The door in question belonged on the passenger side of Delilah's Pontiac, and Kristy stood beside it, holding it open like she belonged on the Price is Right. I had this little flash of Delilah holding the little microphone Bob Barker used to hold, and I almost chuckled. Almost.

"Where are we going?"

Delilah looked to Kristy. "My, my, we forgot to tell her, didn't we?"

"Shoot, we did."

"Forgot to tell me what?"

"We're going to Vegas," Kristy said.

"What?"

"Vegas." She bopped across the grass. I guess in her mind everything was going great, and we were heading out for a fun vacation, not taking a one-way road trip to Hell. "Come on, silly."

"No," I said. "I don't think I'm going anywhere. Not with her."

The old woman sighed. "After all you've seen, you still don't believe?"

"It's not that I don't believe. That's not the problem at all."

She advanced on me, one finger raised. "I don't think you understand. You have no choice in the matter."

"Oh I don't, huh? What, you going to kidnap me?"

"Don't you think I would have already done that by now if I planned to?"

"I don't know. Maybe you're devious. Why do we have to go anywhere with you?"

She pursed her lips, going duck-faced. "Do you not recall what you did in there?"

Time and space slowing down, some weird explosion, waking up on the lawn. Hmm. "Nah, it wasn't very memorable."

"Sarcasm does not suit you."

"Shows how well you know me."

In between us, Kristy was the kid watching mom and dad fight, eyes huge and shiny. "Aw, come on. You should give her a chance. She, like, probably saved my life. Probably yours, too, you know."

"All right, all right. I don't know what the hell it was, but I do know something happened in there."

Delilah clapped her hands. "Wonderful. You see? That was your power. The one I told you about. I'd be happy to tell you more, but we do need to get going." She gazed at the horizon. "This town will not be safe for long."

"What? Why not?" I asked.

"Surely you are aware of what's going on in the world at large."

"I *totally* am," Kristy said, not helping the situation one iota. "I was watching everything I could find. It's *totally* going to shit."

"I know that," I said. "Okay, but you'd better spill."

"I will tell you all I know." She went to the Pontiac.

"Wait. I need to pack."

"Oh." Kristy giggled. "*So* on it. Already did it. It's in the trunk. Oh and…" She went to the car and opened the back door, fetching my purse and presenting it. "Here."

How long was I out? "Hmm. Okay. IPod?"

"Check." She saluted.

"Cell phone."

"Duh."

"Kindle."

"In the suitcase."

Kristy knew what was what, what was important to me. I don't know what got hold of me, but I grabbed her and planted a giant kiss on her, right there in front of Delilah. Even gave her a little tongue action, I knew she liked that.

Once we had finished, she took a step back, waving a hand over her face. "All right," she said, and climbed into the Pontiac.

I nodded at Delilah. "Okay. You saved my ass a couple times. The least I can do is give you a chance."

Chapter 5

Just Can't Wait

The drive out of Eureka was quiet. Not because of awkwardness, though there was plenty of that, but because the panicked masses were tearing everything apart. We had to go around downtown because the whole place was burning to the ground. It surprised me how much that pissed me off. Eureka wasn't any sort of cultural Mecca, but it had been my home for the last four years, and I'd come to appreciate some of its charms, even if 99% of the people there could go to Hell.

I understood panic. I mean hell, who wouldn't panic in the face of the apocalypse? Even still, I had trouble wrapping my brain around what was happening to the city. The Tweekas must have figured it was time to get what was theirs, since there wasn't going to be much left anyway. Bunch of jackals.

It was an eternity to get from one end of the city to the cemetery and clear onto Redwood Highway. That was when I let myself breathe. "There still going to be assassins looking for me out here?"

"Most definitely, but given the open space, I think we can handle them. Well, the open space and the shotgun under my seat," Delilah said.

I studied her. Even if she had a total love affair with

violence, I admired something about that total lunacy. Maybe it was the way she combined her whole grandma act with being a complete and utter bad-ass. "You're one crazy broad, you know that?"

"I prefer to think of myself as prepared, but if you prefer crazy, who am I to judge?"

"So who was that guy? Who's trying to kill me?"

"That is a very, very long story."

"As far as I can tell, we've got nothing but time."

Kristy piped up. "Oh my God, so bad-ass. He was an angel."

Total silence. *Did I just hear that?* "Going to have to say that one more time, baby. Didn't quite hear you."

"She said he was an angel. An Aetelia, to be more precise," Delilah said.

"You've got to be kidding me. This is a bad dream, right?"

"I'm afraid not, dear," she said.

"You don't say. So I dare to ask: how do you kill an…uh, what did you call it? Uh-teel-yer?"

"Aetelia. The simple answer is that you don't. You send them back to where they came from."

"Heaven?"

"Not exactly. Kristy, dear, do you want to tell her what happened?"

Kristy sat forward. "No problem, Ms. M."

Ms. M? Please. "Hit me up with that, Ms. K."

She stuck her tongue out, then giggled. "It was the coolest thing I'd ever seen, though, for reals. I thought that guy had killed you. I was like, screaming and crying. I knew I should have gotten the bat and beat him, but I was way too scared. That's when Ms. M comes busting in with this big-ass shotgun. She was like, don't be afraid or anything, and she blew the guy away. Then she…uh…what did you say you did again?'

"Performed a banishing ritual."

"Right, that. Banished the dude. It was so fetch."

"What's a banishing ritual?" I asked.

"It's a magickal incantation. You perform it when you want to restore something that's out of place to its proper place."

"Like if you did a banishing ritual, the trail of dishes that your girlfriend left out would suddenly go into the sink?"

"Hey," Kristy said, and tapped me on the shoulder.

I grinned and winked at her.

"Metaphorically speaking, I suppose it's about the same, but in this case, the dirty dish is a filthy Aetelia sent to kill you."

"Why would the Aetelia come to kill me, anyway? What did I ever do to them?"

"I suspect they knew that I was trying to recruit you. Kill you and they take away one of our weapons." Her eyes flicked to the rear-view mirror. She glanced at me before focusing on the road again.

"Tell me more," I said. Let's see what she thinks is most important.

"I work for an organization known as the Watchers-"

"That guy - thing - whatever the hell he's supposed to be - called me a Watcher. I didn't know what he meant."

"That would be us. Our job is to stand in opposition to the Aetelia."

"Does that mean you guys are demons? Or like…angel

hunters?" I said.

"I suppose some might refer to us as demons, but that implies that we would be here to take advantage of humanity. Nothing could be farther from the truth."

"Then what are you doing with me? You were looking to take me away. Hell, you called me a weapon."

Kristy answered that one. "It means you've got these awesome powers."

"What the hell happened back there? What am I supposed to have done?"

"It's not about what you're supposed to have done," the old woman said, and glanced at the rear-view mirror again. "You're what we call a Tunneler."

"What's a tun-"

"I'm quite sorry, dear, but this will have to wait. Hold on tight, will you please?"

"I-"

The crazy bitch wrenched the wheel to the left, bringing us across broadside to the road. She reached under her seat while she was doing it, all nonchalant. She did this on the regular, don't you know.

"Do please duck down, if you don't mind, child," she said to me. I saw no reason to argue when she brought a sawed-off shotgun up from below the seat.

Before I ducked down, I saw a familiar little green Prius behind us. The driver was slamming on the brakes and twisting the wheel around at the same time. Screeching brakes filled the air as she lowered the passenger side window.

"Cover your ears," she said, and I had a second to do so before the gun exploded over top of me.

Kristy screamed "Daniel", and I knew why that Prius

seemed so familiar.

I don't know where I found the instincts; all I know is I did, and that's all that matters. I reached up and grabbed Delilah's arm by the wrist without even thinking. "Stop," I said.

You would've thought I told her to kill a puppy from the look on her face. "It was a warning shot," she said, but I almost didn't hear her. I had already wrenched the door open and fallen out on one protesting knee, raising my head toward Daniel's Prius. Sure enough, Delilah had told the truth, at least for the most part. The windshield was intact, as was Daniel's face behind it, though his eyes were wide. Of course, he was screwed considering the steam rising out of his radiator, but at least he still had his life.

"Shit," I said, and rose.

"Get down," said Delilah from over my shoulder. The loon leaned over the top of the car, shotgun resting on the roof as she aimed right at Daniel's face.

"Jesus Christ, you psycho. He's a friend of ours. You met him."

"I remember him, dear. It doesn't mean he's safe or trustworthy."

"Matty? Kristy?" Daniel's voice this time. He had climbed out and had both hands in the air, as if praying for the second coming at some second-rate tent revival.

"It's us," Kristy said from my right. "Are you okay?"

"I'm fine. I guess." He lowered his hands.

Delilah shouted: "Keep them where I can see them."

"All right, all right, Christ. I'm their friend."

"So you say."

Kristy, being Kristy, raced across the space between our

cars, giving Daniel a big hug. I didn't get it. Those two had never been crazy about each other, but I guess she did whatever it is that you're supposed to do when your own personal loony is aiming a shotgun at an acquaintance. I don't know. I'd never read the manual, but I wouldn't let Delilah hurt Kristy. I stood between them.

"What now?" I said, staring Delilah down. She'd have to kill her precious Chosen One if she wanted to take Daniel out. Or hell, maybe I could figure out whatever I had done at the trailer and do it to her. Whatever the answer was, Daniel and Kristy were not getting killed here. Not on my watch. So sorry.

She lowered the shotgun, her lips tight. "I sure hope you know what you're doing, child. He could be very dangerous."

"Only dangerous to you," he said.

"Ask him why he's here," she said.

Fair question. "Why *are* you here?"

"I went over to check on you two, what with everything that's going down. I thought I'd do you right, maybe bring you some food. Then I spied the Wicked Witch of the West over there driving away with you. I remembered her from the K, didn't think she could be up to any good. I was going to follow you guys, but I've never followed anybody, so I bunged it up." He lowered his voice. "Are you guys okay? You know, did she-"

Kristy piped up. "We're okay. No worries. That's Ms. M. She's cool."

"Speak for yourself, Polly," I said.

"What are we talking about over here?" Delilah said from right behind us; we turned on her.

"How do you do that?" I asked.

"Years of experience, I suppose. I find it almost always helps to be light on one's feet."

"You're going to be light on teeth if you don't back up a few steps."

"So hostile. Are you like this with the whole world?"

"As a matter of fact, I am."

"Don't rise to her level," Daniel said, "she's trying to bait you."

Delilah raised an eyebrow. "Bravo. Perhaps he *is* wiser than he appears."

"Aye, perhaps he is, and perhaps he's dealt with a few old crones such as the one standing in front of him right now."

She chuckled, shaking her head. "It all becomes clear. Does she know?"

"Know what?" I said.

"Know how he *really* tracked us here - please, did you believe his puff about seeing us going away?"

Daniel had his hands on his hips. "How did I do it, genius?"

"You haven't told her. Naughty boy." She wagged one finger.

"Will *somebody* clue *one* of us in?"

"He's a magician, my dear."

"Say what now?" I asked.

He tightened his mouth, then gave one curt nod. "It's as she says."

She clapped her hands, once, the sound loud as thunder on the abandoned stretch of highway. "Magnificent! A true Maleficarum in our midst."

"So how did you track us?" I asked.

"I'd be happy to tell you, but I don't feel comfortable out

here in the open. Too many bad spirits out in the world these days, if you catch my drift," he said.

"Good heavens, what is this I hear? An exalted traveler of the Aethyrs frightened of the Reckoning? Tell me it isn't so," Delilah said.

He tightened his mouth. Divine intervention alone kept him from popping her in the mouth. "And what are you, you old bag?

"I am a servant of the Watchers, and you *will* watch your tone with me, dilettante."

His face went pale. "Oh. Right. Sorry about that one."

Now *this* was interesting. Some otherworldly politics were going on here, ones that I didn't fathom. Daniel seemed ready to crap his pants, and that was even knowing Delilah's crazy instability.

"Listen, lasses," he said, "I'd love to stand here gabbing all day, but we're not safe here. Can you give me a hand getting this wreck off the road, please?"

Chapter 6

Meeting Team Bubba

"I'd be happy to take you as far as Bakersfield, but you may be on your own after that," Delilah said to Daniel.

Our own personal hipster magician sat in the passenger seat, arms crossed over his chest and his mouth pouted out, looking like a kid caught stealing Penthouses from his dad's drawer. "Whatever you think is best," he said.

I wouldn't say it had been the easiest thing I had ever done, getting Daniel away from his precious hybrid and into the car with Ms. Delilah McKinley, *at your service, and* getting her to accept the hipster magician with open arms. Then again, I *am* that kind of woman, you know, ambassador of weirdos. Even with my stellar personality providing the lubricant, I couldn't say I was surprised that the old kook was already laying down rules for him.

I had to know what the deal was, though, so I bit: "Whoa, wait. What happens in Bakersfield?"

"I neglected to mention that, didn't I? We'll cross over, of course."

"Oh, no way," Kristy said, and clapped her hands.

This didn't seem like the best development. The phrasing left some room for…I don't know, improvement? "What does that mean, exactly?"

Daniel pre-empted any response she might have had on deck. "I'm going to guess it means we're traveling into the

Aethyrs."

"See my previous question. What does *that* mean?"

"Something like heaven."

Delilah spoke up. "It's nothing like heaven, foolish boy."

"How would you describe it, oh wise one?" It didn't take a master of psychology to see that the guy was only just containing a nuclear-powered irritation out of fear he would be smote.

"Come now, dear, it's quite elementary. A higher plane of existence. Consciousness, I suppose. There are layers of perception. Layers of reality. We refer to these layers as Aethyrs."

"It's as good a definition as any. I call them heavens," Daniel said.

Kristy sat up next to me, flexing her body like that would somehow help her grasp what they were talking about. "Does that mean they're, like, next to us? Right now?"

"Yes and no," Daniel said. "They exist outside our definition of time and space, if you get my drift."

"Why *wouldn't* we get your drift?" I said. "We made the exit off of Sanity Highway onto Fucked-Up Boulevard a few hours ago. Angels, super powers, and parallel dimensions. What's left, Satan?"

"How about we leave that question for another time," Delilah said.

"Oh is he your boss now?" Daniel asked.

"It was a joke, guys," I said. "You know, jokes? Hah hah?" I didn't want to know whether Satan existed. I had a hard enough time wrapping my brain around the freaky stuff they'd already told me.

"It is all a bit much to take in at first," Daniel said.

"Humans since the dawn of time have spent entire lifetimes trying to understand the intricacies of the Aethyrs. It's a mind-fuck, and no doubt of that."

"Yes, but she's not just any human. She will have to learn at some point," Delilah said.

"I can't believe I'm agreeing, but I'm agreeing. Enough for now, what do you say?"

She grunted. "I agree. Enough for now."

"Aw, come on." Kristy said. "You're only getting to the good stuff and - hooooly shit, look at that."

Keep in mind, when it gets dark in the forest, it gets dark as an asshole. It's supposed to, anyway. At that particular moment, however, I realized that I had been seeing an orange glow on the horizon for quite some time. When Delilah brought us to a stop, we caught on to the fact that there were more immediate, physical concerns: like the raging inferno that I would guess was once the Avenue of the Giants - it was hard to tell, given that a bunch of the trees had fallen across the road and were engulfed in flames.

That concern came first, then came the concern of the two burly US Park Rangers approaching the car, shotguns in hand.

Kristy raised an alarm as the hillbillies approached the Pontiac. "Guys, am I, like, the only one wondering why Rangers need shotguns for a fire?"

"You are not, dear. Don't worry," Delilah said, and I saw that tricky hand of hers slide beneath her seat.

Daniel nodded. "Right, don't worry, nothing to worry about, only sitting in the crossfire of three armed lunatics, aren't I?"

"You should try to be kinder, you know," she said. "And

do be prepared, things may get ugly."

"Lovely. I'll be sure to stay awake."

She rolled down the driver's and passenger's side windows.

The first Bubba, the bigger, hairier one, had reached the car on the driver's side. He tipped his hat. "Evening, ma'am."

"Hello, dear. What's happened?"

The Bubba leaned down, face-to-face with her, trying to look concerned. It ended up looking more like hemorrhoids were tearing up his ass. "Bunch of hooligans set fire to the woods." He glanced from her to us, probably trying to suggest that we might be the sort of 'hooligans' who would do such a thing.

That's what he wanted her to think, anyway. I knew the real story behind those eyes. This was the guy who would make a move on you, and if you didn't want him, you were a filthy cock-tease, a dyke (fair, in my case), and probably deserved to have your teeth knocked out before the guy did you the favor of jamming his dirty dick in your bleeding mouth.

I might have been a little off at that moment given what I'd gone through, but I didn't think such guys, in general, joined the Forestry Service. Just a hunch. "Where you folks headed?" he asked.

How long does he keep up the charade? I wondered. The more words that came out of his dumbass mouth, the closer he came to giving himself away. Then things would get real dangerous real fast.

"San Jose, I'm afraid. With all the brutes out and taking advantage of the poor people on the road, we thought this might be the safer path."

Very clever. I saw her shoulder tighten a little bit. I put a hand on Kristy's knee and gazed into her eyes. Her wide eyes told me she got it - shit was about to get real.

"You're wrong, ma'am-"

Bubba didn't know how right he was, and never would, because Delilah brought her own shotgun up and fired.

I don't know if you've ever seen a man's face obliterated at close range, but it's an impressive, terrifying sight to behold. One second Bubba was there leaning over the driver's side door with a look that suggested he might be figuring out what was going on, the next there was a hot, nasty mess blowing across Delilah and into the back seat. I think Kristy screamed. I sure as hell know I did.

Daniel, though - dude had steel balls after all. Seeing things were going south real fast, the second she pulled the trigger, he pulled the handle on his door and slammed it into the other Bubba, who fell backwards, losing his shotgun in the commotion.

It was the opening Daniel needed. He jumped out of the car in the next second, picking up Bubba's shotgun and planting one foot square in the fat bastard's back.

My brain didn't quite catch on to current events for a hot minute, but I did zero in on Daniel screaming at the Bubba, asking him where 'they' were. I didn't have a clue who what he meant until Delilah walked up behind him.

"Do calm down, won't you?"

"What?" Daniel gaped at her, like she'd spoken to him in Swahili.

"I told you calm down." She held her own shotgun at her side, but I could see the crazy bitch was ready to use it at any minute, and not necessarily on the poor dope lying on the ground.

"What do I have to be calm about? You nearly got us killed, you lunatic."

The Bubba mumbled something, and Daniel cocked the shotgun, yelling, "shut the *fuck* up."

Delilah spoke again, her voice even. "That may be, love, but we're still alive, and our friend here is on the other end of the weapon so I suggest you lower it and not do anything rash."

"Not do anything...you are out of your mind. You just did the rashest thing I have ever *seen*." He sounded like he was about to edge into full-blown hysteria, his Scots accent getting thicker by the second.

"I assure you it was quite calculated, dear. Now lower the weapon."

"Not until he tells us where they are."

"They're most likely dead, and even if they are, they're beyond our concern now."

Kristy whispered to me, "who are they talking about?"

That was the moment it dawned on me. Definitely operating a little on the slow side of things. "The Rangers, I think. They had to get those outfits somewhere."

"Oooh. Oh." She grimaced.

Daniel pressed the shotgun barrel deeper into the man's back. I wondered what it would take for it to go right through his spine and come out the other side. "Where are they?"

This time we could hear the Bubba. "She's right, they're dead. It was self-defense, man. They were going to kill us."

"Bullshit," Daniel said. "Did they find your meth cabin? Is that it?"

"It ain't like that, man..."

Delilah took a step closer to Daniel. I could see the sweat beads on her forehead.

Wait, were we always this close to the fire? I didn't think so, which meant the blaze was moving fast. Which meant we didn't have time for this.

Delilah knew it, too. It might have been the first time I heard an emotion other than unstoppable cheeriness leak into that voice. "Either kill him or let him go, Daniel, we don't have time for you to stand here jerking off your moral cock."

Those words did the trick. You'd have thought she called his mom a dirty whore, because he stood there transfixed like he couldn't figure out what to say or do next. Then he took the shotgun away and lifted his foot.

"Get out of here," he said to the Bubba, "and don't let us see you again."

"Yessir," the Bubba said, struggling to his feet. "You won't see me-"

Delilah raised her own shotgun and blew a hole in the guy's back the size of a grapefruit. She smiled at Daniel as the Bubba slumped to the ground. "That is how it's done, dear."

He held up his hands. "That's it. I'm done with you."

"No you're not."

"I'm not, am I? Watch me," he said, and turned to stride into the woods.

She raised the shotgun and cleared her throat. "One more step and you can join our erstwhile Rangers here. Maybe you'll even find their victims on the other side."

Kristy opened her door and tumbled out, moving toward Delilah.

"No," I said, following her and restraining her.

Daniel faced Delilah. "You'd do it too, wouldn't you?"

"You know damn well I would. You have secrets that belong to the Watchers. I have to protect your world's only hope."

"Oh it's our world now, is it?"

"Do you think I do what I do because I love this world? Please. I and my kind will be safe once the true unpleasantness begins, but I believe in our mission."

"What is your mission?"

"To preserve humanity for the rise of the Fifth Watchtower."

He bit his lip. "I knew you were mixed up in some twisted shit."

She laughed. "Did your Master not tell you to trust half of what an Aetelia tells you?"

"On the contrary. He told me the Watchers are the masters of lies."

She lowered the weapon. "Then your Master was a fool."

He considered it. "That might be."

"I assure you, it is, and I think if you stay with us, you'll arrive at quite a different view."

"I...you..."

She walked toward the car. "Meaningless words, dear. Now come back here. I have to move this car and we have to teach this girl what it means to be a Tunneler."

He shook his head. "What have you gotten us into, Matty?"

"How do I know? I'd be happy to know what a Watcher is - and a Watchtower - and an Aetelia. You're speaking gibberish to me," I said.

"You'll find out soon enough," Delilah said over her shoulder as she climbed into the car.

Chapter 7

Have to Believe

"Right, we have seconds," Daniel said, glancing at the car. "No matter what, do *not* trust her. She's working for bloody demons, or as close as someone can get."

"Who? The Watchers?"

He nodded and stared straight ahead, his mouth tight.

Delilah killed the engine, climbed out, and waved to us, like we were on a nice vacation out in the woods. "It's much cooler back here," she said.

Daniel touched my elbow and whispered in my ear. "I'm not even sure she's human."

"Is that why you didn't shoot her?"

He nodded. "We should try to get away as soon as we can."

"Good luck with that." Sure, she had been useful since the world turned upside-down, but it didn't keep me from being scared shitless of her. Believe me, it doesn't happen often, but when it does, I respect it. Thinking of trying to get away from her made my asshole clench. As for trusting her…that seemed plainly obvious to be a Bad Fucking Idea.

So I decided I'd wait, bide my time, and figure out when to make a move. "You said you were going to teach me," I said to her. "How about we start with the basics. What's a

Tunneler?"

"So impatient," she said, sitting on the Pontiac's hood.

"Goddamn right I am. If I'm going to be a hostage, I want some information."

"It's ever so much easier to demonstrate. Close your eyes."

I had misgivings the size of California, but I did as I was told.

"Good. Now I want you to imagine this forest, only the trees are made of crystal."

"What does this-"

"Visualize it. Can you see it?"

Imagination had always been my strong suit. It took a few seconds to pull together the image that she spoke about: crystal trees, some of them hanging down over the road - no, the pathway, a little dirt pathway. A fire shone from within the crystals: reflected moonlight, but this was a dark blue moon that hung in the sky like a bad painting in a kid's room. The air was quiet, interrupted only by the occasional tinkle of the wind blowing through the crystal leaves. "Yeah. I see it."

"Pick the most vivid piece of that landscape and focus on it, as if your life depended on it."

I thought about protesting. I wondered what it was supposed to mean, but my subconscious was a step ahead: it zeroed in on the closest branch. I could see more than just the surface on this branch; I could see the way the light rode its uneven surface, the striations deep inside.

"Open your eyes," came Delilah's voice from far away, like a radio bleeding through a dream. I tried to open my eyes, but they were already open, weren't they? Jesus Christ, I didn't imagine the place, I *lived* in it. I touched the branch, and sure enough, I felt the cool surface.

It should've seemed like a miracle, but my sense of wonder lasted probably ten seconds before I started to freak out.

What the fuck
What now
How do I get out

As soon as it had begun, it was over. I lie on my back in the middle of the road, staring into the dark orange night sky of our Aethyr. "What was that?"

"That, my dear, was an Aethyr. A rather low-level one, but an Aethyr."

"Christ," Daniel said.

"It was beautiful," I said.

"Mm, good. Not all Aethyrs are. Was there a fire there?"

"No."

Kristy scurried over and offered me her hand, helping me to my feet. "You vanished," she said, and I could see awe in her eyes. Awe, and a little bit of terror. Not what you want to see in your girlfriend's face. My stomach rippled as I worried about what it might mean.

If Delilah cared, she sure didn't show it. "No fire is good news, wouldn't you say, Daniel?"

He wiped his mouth. "Oh, aye. Means at least one of us might make it out of this alive." He studied me. "You, a Tunneler. Who would've thought it."

"I know, right? It'd be even more amazing if I knew what that was."

"A Tunneler is only someone who can move between Aethyrs as easy as someone takes a piss, isn't it? Do you have any *idea* how long it took me to do what you just did?"

I shook my head.

"Ten years of preparation."

"Jesus, how old *are* you?" Kristy asked.

"Old enough." He ran a hand through his hair. "Doesn't matter now, does it? What matters is your girlfriend is some kind of prodigy."

"Mystery solved," I said. "Thanks for that. I'm sorry it's so easy. I didn't ask for this, you know. I didn't even believe in this shit."

"I know. Just a bit frustrating, is all."

"I know." I clapped my hands. "So now what?"

Delilah tossed me the keys, and I nearly dropped the damn things.

Smooth. Real smooth.

"Now you drive," she said.

Before I could answer, Daniel broke in, voice raised like he was trying to shout down the heavens. "Are you mad? She can't do that yet."

Delilah gave him a look that was all *who-the-fuck-are-you,* you know, eyebrows raised, one corner of her wrinkled mouth turned up. "I hardly think you're an authority."

"An authority on what?" I asked. They always left me out of the loop on this stuff, but of course I was the one who was supposed to do it.

"She wants you to take the car into that other world with you."

"So what? Sounds cool."

"We're not talking about a walk in the park, Matty, there are real consequences for failing to do this."

"Such as?"

"Do it wrong and you could end up fused with the car.

I've seen awful things, things you can't even begin to imagine..." he said.

"Oh, please," Delilah said, putting a hand on his shoulder. "She is practicing in a controlled environment, far from whatever acid-dropping dabblers you may have been dealing with."

He pushed the hand off his shoulder, eyes on fire. "Dabblers? How dare you? I'm talking about eighth and ninth degree practitioners here, men and women who practiced for decades. Controlled environment...piss off, you moldy relic."

"Now you look here-"

"Guys, guys," I said, raising one hand, hoping to avoid what was shaping up to be a Class 1 'my wand is bigger than yours' contest. "No need to argue here. I'm willing to give it a shot."

"Aye, of course you are, you've no idea what you're risking."

"You just told me, smart guy."

"I don't want you risking your life for this."

I walked over to him, touching his face. "That's real sweet of you, chief," I said, "but it's my decision to make."

"You're right, it's your life, I have no call, but I want it on the record that I object."

"Noted." I went for the driver's side door. They followed suit, climbing into the Pontiac.

Delilah sat beside me.

I put the key in the ignition. "Okay. What are we doing?"

The old coot reached over and put her hand on my shoulder. It was all I could do not to brush it off, but I maintained my peace, at least on the outside. She gave me that sweet Grandma smile and said, "do what you did before, dear. Close your eyes and imagine that place. Imagine yourself in the car as well."

"What about you guys?"

"We'll get there. Do this first."

"Matty-" Daniel said from the backseat.

"Do shut up, will you?"

He didn't need to hear anything else - he did the shutting up, and I closed my eyes, thinking about that crystal forest again. It wasn't hard to imagine the car there. Say what you will about Pontiacs, but I never hated them. It was easy to remember the details - a stock black G6, rich enough for Delilah's blood. It sat in the path in the middle of the crystal forest, dark blue moonlight reflecting off the hood, making it gleam like you'd never see on Earth.

"Very good," I heard Delilah say through a thick layer of fuzz. "Now look at me."

I did, and good God what did I see but a floating ball of golden yellow light with a tendril of hot white light reaching up to connect with my shoulder. Next thing I knew, two other balls of light appeared in the backseat, with their own tendrils connecting to my back. "This is freaky," I said.

"Remember what we look like. Remember, and imagine us inside the car with you."

It was almost a reflex bringing Kristy through - her ball of light, the one behind me, expanded into her features and clothes, starting as dark splotches in the light and fading in. It reminded me of some toy that I had seen once, but I couldn't quite put my finger on it at that moment. *Wooly Willy? No, that was the thing with the magnet shavings - that face was already there.*

"Holy...*shit*," she said, looking out the window.

"Shh," I said. "Give me a sec here." I thought about Daniel's face. It was a pretty face, even beneath that hipster scruff. He filled out almost as quick as Kristy.

A bop bag. That's it. Blow it up and the features expand.

Now I tried to think about Delilah's face, but it wasn't coming as quickly as it had for the other two. I don't know if it was because I didn't know her as well or I hated her guts, but I couldn't get her glowing little bop bag to move one bit.

"Bring me through, dear," she said through the murk.

"I'm trying, but nothing's happening. I can't get a grip on it." I won't lie - around about this point, I started panicking, and the others flickered like they were old TVs losing reception.

Come on, hang on to them, I thought. Easier said than done. It seemed too easy to let it fall apart.

Delilah either sensed that I was freaking out or got tired of waiting, because in the next second, she appeared in the seat next to me. I don't know how to explain it - it wasn't the bop bag expanding effect, it was more like a bad jump cut in a movie, only in real life.

"Needs work, but not bad for your first time," she said, and sniffed.

"You're a right cunt, you know that?" Daniel said. I found it hard to disagree with the man, as much as I hated his word choice.

"You're entitled to your opinion," Delilah replied.

I waved my hand. "Come on, kiddies. I don't want to keep us here all night. Let's get this show on the road."

With no further protests, I felt well within my rights to start moving on. I put the car in gear.

I thought that the highway in that Aethyr would be

similar to the Redwood Highway, but no; where the Redwood Highway is this broad, two-lane deal right beside the river, this was made more for wagons than cars, pretty much one-way for a car, and where, under normal circumstances the trees are off the road a bit, here they hung down over the road, almost close enough to scrape the roof. I tried not to look up, because the thought of those things falling on us and crushing the car made me a bit claustrophobic.

I'm assuming Daniel and Delilah had seen the place before, because they were quiet as we bumped our way down that ripped-up ass of a road, but the place pretty much captivated Kristy - and captivated might be too weak of a word. She oohed and aahed at the way every single crystalline leaf caught the light of the moon, and she damn near lost her mind when she thought she might have seen an animal moving around in whatever you'd call that underbrush-looking glassy shit.

"So you like it here?" I asked.

"Do I? Duh. I don't know if I'd *ever* want to go home," she said.

Delilah decided to ruin her day, saying, "oh, it's not all like this, believe me."

"What do you mean? What's the rest look like?" I asked.

Daniel fielded that one. "Imagine every cliché of hell on earth you've ever seen or read. Then double it."

"Heartwarming."

"But, like, why? It's so pretty here..."

"Care to enlighten her, Delilah, dear?" Daniel asked.

Delilah cleared her throat. "You see..."

"There was a war, wasn't there? Because of the Watchers and all."

"The Watchers were here?" I asked.

"Oh, aye. The Watchers, humans…this is the easiest Aethyr for humans to access, after all. The Watchers brought people here to build their infernal machines. Decided they were going to challenge the angels for heaven using people for slaves."

You'd think he called Delilah a mass murderer. Hell, as far as I know, he had. She sat up straight and faced him, her skin gone crimson. "Liar. Filthy Aetelia lies, that's all they know how to do."

"Do they now? Why should I believe you, with your group's stellar record?"

"Whoa, whoa," I said. "Slow down. Let's not say anything we can't take back here, folks. Daniel - buddy - what the hell are you accusing her of?"

"Not her, so much as her organization. They ruined these lands - ruined all the Aethyrs in their own little ways."

I could see Delilah restraining herself from popping the shotgun up and blowing Daniel's head off. "It's all slander. What he calls the Heavens - it's simple oppression by the Aetelia."

"The Watchtowers - that's the angels' government - maintain order over the Multiverse," Daniel said, both to her and me. "A long, long time ago the Watchtowers chose a handful of their elites to watch over the Aethyrs as life developed."

Light bulbs went on in my head, but Kristy spoke first. "Oh my God. The Watchers, right?"

Delilah snorted. "They abandoned the Watchers. Left them to fend for themselves, so they organized themselves and tried to make things better."

"It's always about politics with you lot," Daniel said. "What about sentient beings? What about pain and suffering? Or does none of it matter as long as the goal is achieved, to hell with the means?"

"What suffering are you babbling about, boy? From where I stand, the Watchers dared to teach humans the means to seize their own destiny. You'd do well to learn from it."

I'd had *way* more than enough of these two. "Guys, guys," I yelled. "You in your corner, you in yours. Now maybe the Watchers fucked things up for everybody, maybe they didn't, but it sure as hell isn't getting us any closer to civilization. You guys can have a steel cage match once we get out of this for all I care, but for now can we please focus on getting out of here?"

Daniel snorted. "She started it."

"Hardly. You were the one-"

"I said shut up, and I meant it. Now would you please tell me how we're supposed to know when we're out of the fire zone, seeing as how there's no fire on this side?"

They seemed to have the answers when it came to slap-fighting over heaven and hell's politics, but ask them a simple question about survival and you got dead silence.

At last Delilah spoke up. "I don't know. We'll have to continue until we see some sign of...how did you put it? Civilization?"

"You mean what's left of it," Daniel replied.

"Do shut up."

"No, he's got a valid point," I said, "what the hell does civilization look like here?"

"It doesn't," Daniel said.

I had to hand it to him: the guy was a master troll, but

this time she didn't take the bait. Instead she sat there studying me. I don't know if she was trying to figure out the most diplomatic answer for my question or whether I'd be tasty in a stew, but if I had to guess I'd say Daniel had gotten her so worked up that she was having trouble summoning her little Polly Prissypants routine for once. At last she said, "Don't worry your pretty little head about it."

Suspicion confirmed - buddy boy hit her right where it hurts. Interesting. "I'll be sure to leave the decision-making to the ugly folk, but we *are* going to need to know what to do next."

I must've given Delilah enough time to get her feet under her, because she went right to the Polly Prissypants well, chirping in her fake little bright voice, "No worries, dear. I'll tell you when you see it. Let's drive and put all this foolishness behind us."

Daniel muttered something in the backseat, but give the guy credit, he sat back, hands on his knees.

Right there with you, buddy. Not happy about this, but I've rode the crazy train this far. Might as well see how much further we're going to go.

Chapter 8

Take the Skin and Peel It Back

So I drove. Couldn't tell you how long - this was already the most screwed-up night in my personal history and my brain wasn't the best at that second. Look at what the last few days had wrought on me: kidnapped by a Tweeka, damn near killed by some asshole who broke into my place, told that time and space as I knew it were all just an illusion, and told that I had some sort of amazing ability that could help an organization that may or may not be run by demons. Oh, and traveling to a completely new world.

It was enough to put a girl well past the point of shock and into living moment-to-moment. We talked some as I drove through that new world, sue me if I can't remember what we said. It's a blur, lost to the winds.

Next thing I remember clearly is breaking out of the forest into a wider expanse that was a bit more like the Redwood Highway. Maybe that's why I returned to myself, seeing something more like our world. Or maybe it was the crappy little cabin set off on the left side of the road. It wasn't the kind of place you'd notice in our world – slumping roof, weather-beaten sides, but for some reason my brain, or maybe my stomach, zoomed in on it, and the word FOOD flashed in my head like a bright neon sign.

My stomach had been growling at me, come to think of it. I pulled the car to a stop.

Kristy sat up. "Why you stopping?"

"Because I'm starving, that's why. Anybody else hungry?"

"I'm fine," Daniel said, in a far-away voice.

Delilah waved a hand. "Keep going."

"I'm hungry," Kristy said in a tiny, wavering voice that made sure I'd do whatever she needed. I couldn't sit there knowing she was going hungry.

"Right. I'm going out to scout," I said, and took my hands off the wheel.

Daniel and Delilah came to life, shouting at me, telling me I couldn't do that, but their protests lasted for a split second before they were gone. Next thing I knew, the car vanished, and I fell right on my ass in the middle of the road.

Damn, that's finicky.

I stood up, wiping the dust from my pants.

Not much else I could do at that point, so I figured I might as well check out the cabin before returning to get everyone. I might find something useful in there.

The cabin didn't set far off the road - it only took me a short walk before I was knocking on the front door. The place was derelict, but my folks had drilled manners into me when I still wore diapers. That's what happens when you're raised by a pair of snotty yuppies who expect your every move to reflect well on them.

Next thing I knew, the door was swinging open, and my jaw was about to hit the floor.

It was the chick from Circle K. You know, the one Delilah left dead beside her car? Up and walking around like nothing happened…but she was different this time. She had cleaned her hair and tied it up in a bun, and wore a perfect patina of makeup on her face. Not too much, not too little. Like she belonged in Leave it to Beaver.

I half-expected a laugh track when she opened her mouth and said, "oh, it's you. I've been expecting you. Come on in."

Of course the first question in my mind was how the hell she had been expecting me, but I didn't ask. I just followed her inside.

The inside of the hut was unbelievable. If she was made up for an old school sitcom, it was only because the house itself was made for it. No joke. I'm talking weird-ass walls with exaggerated borders, because of how they had to make it look in black-and-white, an old blue settee, and a coffee table with, I kid you not, flaps. Where the hell do you see that?

"It's my mind hut," she said, and walked to the old-school white gas stove.

I sat down at her green Formica table. "Of course it is," I said.

"My name is Jodi, by the way," she said in a dreamy voice.

I wondered how the world looked from her eyes. I'm not sure she lived in the same space where I sat, even in her weird little time capsule. "Would you like some tea? It's just finished brewing." She held up a cup, and I saw the first hint that this place even existed in the same world as the one outside the front door: the cup was made of the same crystal as the trees, nice and thick and sturdy.

I thought about how much I'd like one of those bad boys back home, but I said, "no thanks. I'm Matty, by the way."

"I know."

"What? How the hell do you know that?"

She blinked, and I saw a hint of something more in there, like her intelligence was fighting against some sort of spell. Of course, the goofy-ass grin returned in due time. "My mother, of course. Mother always said that Matty would be the savior of us and now here she is." She giggled and sipped her tea.

"Ohhhkay." I saw that the tea was green - literally, she was drinking green tea. "Who's your mom?"

"You know her, you met her already. She goes by Delilah, but that's not her real name."

It was a good thing that I hadn't drank that tea, because I would have sprayed it all over the crazy bitch. "What are you telling me, Jodi? How long has your mom known about me?"

"All your life," she said over the cup. "We lived right by you in Brooklyn, I'm surprised you never saw us. I was in your classes."

Now that she said it, I could see the resemblance to a certain little weirdo girl in sixth grade. The blue eyes, like they cut right into you… "You were a blonde then. Tori?"

She laughed and clapped her hands. "Yes, Tori. I haven't heard that name in ages." She got a pouty look. "You never showed any interest in me, even when I talked to you. I tried to be your friend."

I sweated like a death row inmate, praying she didn't have a knife close at hand, or if she did, that I could make my magic work quickly enough to get the hell out of there. "Don't take that too personally. It was a weird time for me, and…"

She laughed a weird little hollow laugh. "I found my own friends, don't you worry about that. I don't blame you."

"So, uh. Weird question, I know, but I saw your dead body. What's going on here? How can you still be alive?"

"Mmm. Yes. True enough, you are a sharp one. Mother

killed me in the other world. I woke up here."

"I don't get it. Why did she kill you?"

"I suppose she was angry that I took something that was supposed to be hers."

"The money?" I said.

"No. You." She smiled again, but it was a smile that suggests the things she would do to you if only it weren't for social niceties.

I wondered if this little 50s housewife facade was the only thing between me and the world of the dead. "Come again there?"

She put the tea down on the table and looked at me, like she was trying to be serious, but she was too drunk to do it. "I said, you. The money was good, that would've kept me going for awhile, but I wanted to keep you away from her."

"Why?"

"All my life all I heard was about you. I never thought I could live up to you, so I figured I'd take care of that problem myself - make me more than you could ever be." She waved her hand and chuckled. "Now you're here, and I'm…well, I'm not there, now, am I? Looks like she was right all along."

"I'm just some asshole. I'm a nobody. I don't understand what any of you see in me, other than being able to move through time and space."

"That's just it. What good is a career when you're competing against someone who can do *that*?"

Her voice was getting shrill. I had to bring her down to where-ever we were. "I'm sorry. That had to be tough."

She sniffed, and I saw the family resemblance. "It was, but I don't hate her for it, not anymore. Or for killing me. It was for the best."

Goddamn if I could see how, but I didn't dare disagree. "I bet."

"No, really." She reached out for my hand, and I withdrew it, not meaning to, but doing it anyway. It was instinct, but she didn't seem too hurt about it. Hell, she even dropped that dippy perfect housewife act. "I was having sex with some guy so I could crash in his garage. She might have gotten the ball rolling, but it was the addiction that was killing me. This place is so much better, and the addictions are gone now." An awkward pause, and she looked at me. "I'm sorry I hurt you. Really, really sorry. It was shitty of me to drag you into the middle of it."

This time I reached out and touched her hand. I couldn't tell you why. I told myself that I hated people, that 99% of them were useless, especially the addicts, *especially* the ones who had fucked me over, but something about seeing her like this - in this sad little place that was her own version of heaven - wrenched my heart. "It's okay. Well - I mean it's not okay, but you know. Life's a pain in the ass."

She gave me a genuine smile, and I could see that pretty girl that I had glimpsed in Circle K. Maybe she found some peace. "Yeah. Listen - I have to tell you something. It's about the Watchers."

"Oh not this again. I know, they're rebel angels or demons, or whatever the hell they are-"

"That's true," she said, "but there's more. She's taking you to Vegas, isn't she?"

"How'd you know that?"

"It's been the plan all along, once you reached the right age and the sign appeared. The sign appeared, didn't it? That's why you're here."

"If you mean a comet destroying all creation, you're two for two. Why's Vegas important?" I asked.

"Because that's where they built the thing that Mom called the "Engine of Destruction". I don't know what it is or what it means, but I overheard her talking about it on the phone a lot. They need *you* to get it to work."

"Sounds like one hell of a thing. Does that mean I should stay away from Vegas?"

She shook her head. "I don't know. Could be something else is waiting for you there too. There were supposed to be other groups watching over you-"

"Jesus, I lived my whole life in a fishbowl?"

"I know. How could I be jealous of that? But I was."

I ran a finger over my lips. They followed me this whole time to get me to turn on this Engine, but Delilah hadn't said a word to me about it, which meant she didn't want me knowing about it, at least not yet. Why? Did she need time to warp me?

My instincts were yelling at me to get away, but there were two things. One was that she had Kristy. It was no coincidence she'd converted Kristy over to her cause, the bitch. The other thing was my dumb curiosity. I wanted to know what this Engine was, what it did, and who else wanted me. Hell, I could even tear it down from the inside. Wouldn't that piss Delilah off? "Thanks. That helps," I said, and stood up.

"What are you going to do?"

"I'm going to wait and see. Maybe a solution will present itself when I least expect it."

"You sound awfully confident of that."

I went for the door. "That's good, because I'm not. I

don't have enough puzzle pieces to make a move yet."

She gave me a wistful look, forehead crinkled, and I felt another pang for her. "Will you come back and visit?"

"Have to be honest, I doubt it. I have a feeling you'll be moving on soon, anyway." That last sentence was a surprise to me, but it made sense - this wasn't her ultimate destination, just a way station.

"You're probably right. Be careful. Don't trust her."

"Don't worry." I exited the cabin and found myself standing on the side of the Redwood Highway, head spinning. The good news was that this space put me well outside of the fire zone. The bad news was that traffic on my side of the road was backed up out to the ass end of nowhere. I'm talking locked bumper-to-bumper with a bunch of bored, panicky people who saw somebody appear out of nowhere and climbed out of their cars, gaping at me like I was Jesus.

I didn't know what to say to them, but they came out from around their cars toward me, their voices garbled, on account of me having come back from the other side.

I don't know how, but thank God Kristy appeared at my side before any of them could get to me. "Leave her alone," she shouted.

I chuckled, and then I guess I passed out, because everything went black.

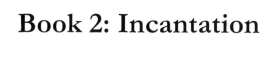

Book 2: Incantation

Chapter 9

In the Arms of Sleep

I walked down this nasty-ass concrete hallway, the kind you see in abandoned, overgrown bunkers (or so movies would tell me). Someone had strung a string of blue lights hung along the top of the walls, like they were celebrating Hanukkah in Hell. The place stank of old sweat socks, and the air was thick, ready to get into your lungs and cause any manner of unknown diseases. I had no idea how I had gotten there, but I walked all the same, from one unknown place to another.

Somewhere in the distance, a manic drum beat played, its pulses rocking the floor, moving up my legs.

I got hold of myself and stopped walking, gazing around, trying to piece together how I'd gotten there. My brain was slippery on the subject, refusing to be pinned down. So I mustered my bravest voice, a hair above a whisper.

"Hello?" I spun, looking down one end of the hallway, then the other, wondering if I'd see people, angels, phantoms, or whatever the hell else might have chosen to wander in.

Nothing.

I walked again.

Not going back. Not even an option. Forward it is.

As soon as the thought crossed my mind, the pale, flickering lights died, plunging me into something that felt a little more than darkness and a bit less than someone sitting on your chest, crushing your lungs.

I stopped, listening to the drum beat, waiting for something to come. When nothing came, I did the only thing I could do: start walking again.

Fuck the darkness. Fuck whoever put me here.

Blinding white light exploded from the end of the hallway like a baby nuke went off down there. I think I screamed, I don't know, but I do know I covered my eyes and fell to my knees.

Then it was gone, and the lights in the hallway lit up again, but they were blood red. The place looked like Satan's asshole dressed up for a party. The floor shook, pieces of concrete flaking and falling off the walls.

A booming voice rang out, telling me "Do not trust. Beware."

Kristy whispered in my ear, saying "you're all going to die," only she wasn't there; no one was.

From behind me, Daniel said, "they told me climbing the Aethyrs was pointless, but since when was ascending to godhood pointless?"

The voices died down, bouncing and echoing into oblivion. I sat alone in the center of the hallway once again, resting on my knees.

"Excuse me," said a voice from behind me.

I popped up like a prize fighter, ready to take down the guy. I found a thin, pale man with laser-blue eyes in the middle of a scrawny face. He wore a white suit, the same kind Tom Wolfe liked, and had a long, tapered cigarette in his left hand.

The kind of guy Hell would pick for an ambassador, in other words, but he also radiated a profound sense of calmness, peace, and well-being. Like John Waters crossed with the Dalai Lama.

"Hello," he said, twisting his lips into a smile.

"Who are you?" Simple question, right?

"I would love to tell you, but it doesn't matter. Not now, anyway. You are Matty, I take it?"

"I am."

He nodded. "Good. I like you, and you will know what I speak of, in time. Unfortunately, I have but a moment. I wish to tell you -" he considered for a moment, one finger at his chin, then spoke. "All is not as it seems."

"You mean Delilah? I-"

"Hmm, I did not think you that stupid. No, I speak of others. Demons wear the skin of men. The machinery is not what it appears to be. It would seem I misspoke. *Nothing* is at is seems, and size will ultimately defeat you. You would do well to be aware of these things."

"What-"

"They call you the Chosen One, but they don't understand what it means."

"I don't understand what it means."

He chuckled. "I suppose you wouldn't. Your perspective is that of an ant as compared to a human. Yet how much greater is the difference between the perspective of a human and a god?"

I started to say something - what the hell did he mean?

He held up one finger, silencing me.

"No questions. You will follow soon. You are not their Chosen One. Do not allow them to make you believe it."

"Whose Chosen One am I?"

He smirked. "I told you no questions, but very well.

Mine, of course." He gave me a lopsided grin.

"What exactly does it entail?"

"It entails Free Will." He studied his cigarette. "Ain't it a bitch?"

"It is, indeed. "

"I knew I liked you for a reason, Matilda. Now watch and learn what can happen." He waved a hand, smiled again, and the lights went out.

"Hello?"

Do you know that song "The Hand That Feeds", by Nine Inch Nails? It starts off with this subdued beat, like it's coming through some sort of old radio or machine distorting it before it clears up and kicks ass. I know, at this point it's one hell of a cliché in music, but the first time I heard that song something about that particular use spoke to me, as if the undercurrent of the song had always been there, but we had to be tuned into it.

The transition that went on in that darkness was like the beginning of that song - the lights that appeared at my feet and then grew, soaring into what was now the night sky above me. I heard muffled voices, and the smell of hot asphalt leaked into the air, like it had always been there, behind the veil of reality. It catapulted me back into "reality", revealing what had been hidden that whole time.

The first thing I heard was Kristy's blessed, valley-girl voice. "She's waking up."

Someone had leaned me against something soft and comfy. Kristy sat beside me, perky little tits pressed into my side. God how I'd love to get a hold of them just that moment…

"Does she know where she is?" I heard Delilah ask.

"I don't know…"

"She knows where she is," I mumbled, putting a hand to my forehead.

"I told you she'd be fine," Daniel said.

"What happened?"

"You passed out, dear," Delilah said.

"More than that," Kristy said. "You, like, vanished. No clue."

I tried to sit up, but my head wouldn't cooperate. "Christ. What do you mean? I know I accidentally sent you guys here, but I was only in the cabin…"

"Cabin? What cabin?"

"You know, the cabin. I asked you guys if you wanted anything-"

The car was dead quiet. It occurred to me that there might be some other shit afoot here.

Daniel broke the silence. "We wondered why you stopped. Figured you might know something we didn't, about finding food and all, but there was no cabin, I promise you that."

"Come on, you've got to be kidding me. Because if you aren't-" If they weren't, then what? I was losing my mind?

Delilah piped up. "You did send us back, and we sat for awhile, waiting for you. We figured you would join us. When a few hours passed-"

"Whoa, wait. Hours?"

"Yes, dear, hours. I took it upon myself to go back to the Aethyr and see if I could find you, but there was no trace of you, and certainly no cabin."

"But there was a cabin, I'm telling you." I wanted to

shout, but my head wasn't feeling amicable with the idea. "Your d-" I started to say it, *your daughter*, but I remembered the weird guy's warning about trust, and while I was on the subject, who *had* that weird guy been and where *had* I been? Was it a dream, or something else entirely?

"What?"

Think quick. "You're damned lucky you didn't see it. Turned out to be a dead end."

Daniel adjusted in his seat, gazing over his shoulder. "It could have happened. I've read about pockets in time, especially the farther up the Aethyrs you go. Was anybody in there with you?"

"Nobody. No food, and I came back out into the real...*our* world. I think that's when I passed out."

He bit the fingernail on his thumb. I could tell he didn't quite believe me, so I flicked my eyes to Delilah's head, then to him. He nodded his head a bit.

"I hardly think it matters," Delilah said. "What matters is you getting the rest you need."

"I..." I what? I sure as hell didn't trust Delilah, and digging deeper into what had happened would get her asking more questions. It was like that old Kenny Rogers song, the one about knowing when to hold 'em and knowing when to fold 'em. "Yeah. Maybe you're right."

"Why don't we put on some music?" she chirped, with even more enthusiasm than my Polly could manage, and snapped on the radio.

Imagine my shock and awe when - you guessed it - Kenny fucking Rogers starts coming through the speakers, singing about train rides, gambling, and breaking even.

"You've got to be kidding me," I mumbled. Kristy

laughed. I guess she figured I was bitching about the song.

How to explain the feeling I had at that moment? We were four people drifting on an ocean of weird, violent water who found a single, solitary island of sanity. After suffering through some awe-inspiring madness, you're willing to take whatever slice of sanity you can take, even if it is a direct relation to mediocrity.

I cuddled up with my girl, sighed, and lie down on the seat. Might as well get some rest before the sun came up. I had a feeling things were going to get even weirder - and I'd need my strength for whatever was to come. That thought followed me right down into black, dreamless sleep.

Chapter 10

I Ran Twenty Red Lights in His Honor

I've always been the kind of girl that wakes up when the sun starts coming up and breaks through whatever window is nearby. I've got to wear those ugly-ass masks if I want to get any decent sleep. So next morning, no mask, light comes through the back window, I'm awake. Delilah carried on like she'd never gone to sleep, humming along with some mediocre Country song on the radio. Daniel had given in to sleep sometime in the night. Kristy had nuzzled up to me, little puffs of breath popping out of her mouth. I gently lifted her off of me and then sat up.

"Where are we?" I asked, smacking my lips.

"Not much farther now. We're right outside of Bakersfield."

I scratched my head. "Isn't that where we're supposed to…you know, cross over?"

"Yes, indeed."

"What's that mean again?"

"You'll see."

"Right. The riddles. I forgot. Listen, you think maybe we can stop somewhere to get something to eat?"

"That is the plan."

I rubbed my chin. "Hmm." Delilah hadn't been kidding. We had crossed into civilization - though, it *was* Bakersfield, so it wasn't *that* much civilization. Still, strip malls, and houses were a welcome sight after what we went through in the night.

I shook Kristy. "Come on, honey, put on your shoes, we're at the monster."

"Huh? What?"

"Time to wake up."

She opened one eyelid and looked at me with one beautiful blue eye, God, it could have made anyone stop and take notice and it shot right to my core. I could have taken her right there if, you know, it wouldn't have scandalized the two up front. "What time is it?"

"Can't rightly say."

"Coming up on 7:00, dear," Delilah said over her shoulder.

"There you go. Coming up on 7:00." I shook the Scotsman. "Hey, come on, wake up. No slacking."

He waved his arms. "Huh, what? I'm awake."

"Like hell you were. You were snoring."

"Was I?" His voice was high.

Kristy chuckled. "She's full of shit. You weren't snoring."

"Thanks for the support, 'dear'," I said.

She stuck her tongue out at me. *Brat.*

"Don't tempt me. We don't want to upset the squares here," I said.

"You're so old-fashioned."

"I suppose."

We rode through the city. I couldn't figure out what Delilah was looking for, but eventually she found a little Circle K, and I guess that was enough.

It was enough for me, too. Circle K, right? Just like home. It lifted my spirits to see a little something familiar. She pulled us over into the lot, right beside the pump, and climbed out to start filling up the Pontiac.

That was when it dawned on me that something wasn't right about Bakersfield. It was early in the morning, but it was a Wednesday, I think. Definitely a weekday. I should have been seeing people out running, walking their dogs, cars…you know, city life. I didn't see a damned hint of it, though.

I know, life was crazy, world coming to an end, but Bakersfield made me wonder - did everybody up and abandon civilization?

Suck it up. There are more pressing needs.

For example, my stomach was so empty it was ready to turn inside out, climb up my throat, and kick me all over the parking lot. I looked around and said, "I'm dying here, boys and girls. I need a coffee IV. You guys want something?"

"Good God yes, I thought no one would ask," Daniel said. "Sausage biscuit, hash browns, anything. I'm desperate. Sustenance. Drinks. Bring it on, woman."

"Food. Drink. Noted. What about you, princess?"

"I think you know what I want."

Kristy grinned. "Mountain Dew. Doughnuts."

"Polly food."

I opened the door. "Don't you worry your pretty little heads. Rest. Chill. I'll be back."

"Oh no rush," Daniel said. "we're only starving here."

I flipped him off and walked to the station.

The inside of the K wasn't much better than the city. Oh, it was a little neater - at least the food was still on the shelves, not like the garbage in the streets, but no sign of life. Now remember what I told you about the early morning hours at our store and you'll realize why I might have gotten the creeping willies when I walked into the place. The place should have been rocking and rolling.

"Hello?" I said.

No reply.

Maybe whoever got this bitch of a shift is sleeping behind the counter. Can't exactly blame her. I made a bee-line for the counter and leaned over it.

She wasn't there, either.

This isn't good, Matty. Not good at all.

I took a deep breath and gazed around the store one more time. Having the lay of the land might help me summon up the balls to go in the back, maybe check on that missing clerk, figure out what was going on here.

In that sweep, I noticed something - didn't jump out and grab my ass or anything, but it was enough to grab my eyeballs. I had been looking down at the candy bars in front of me, seeing them but not seeing them. Once you've worked in a place like that, you gloss over the crap you sell without thinking about it, but something caught my eye. Once I picked up on what was bothering me, I swear, I let out an audible gasp.

I saw what should have been a Nutrageous bar - you know, the Reese's candy bars in the red wrappers? It sure as hell looked like one anyway: red wrapper, blue text, the whole nine yards…only, funny thing, it didn't say Reese's Nutrageous. It said Pendergrast's Fat Emma.

The bar next to it, the one that should have been a Milky Way, said "the Zep bar".

"What the fuck?" I scanned the store. Yeah. The logos were right, but none of the *names* were right. Lays? Try

Honest. Doritos? How about Ranchero.

My jaw did this weird thing, jittering on its own, my teeth chattering. I had to be calm, though, or so I told myself. I didn't feel like I was going to fall over or anything, but my body told me something different.

Now that I *looked* around the store, really seeing things instead of glossing over them, it dawned on me that even though the store was tidy and *looked* normal - I couldn't deny that - something seemed...*off* about it. It had the homely charm of a distant alien world. The light was wrong. It was supposed to be dawn, according to the clock and what my eyes and mind processed out there, but in here the lights and the shadows fell in the patterns of near-twilight.

Crossing over.

Creeping Jesus, I thought, and wrapped my arms around my chest. I might as well have been an astronaut, sent to explore some weird distant world. I looked toward the door to the back room, in between the soda fountain (Enjoy Kickapoo Joy Juice) and the sandwich stand. What the hell might be waiting for me there?

My instincts were going crazy, yelling at me, *something's in here.* They swore whatever was behind the door to the back room wasn't human. It couldn't be.

I pushed the door open, and sighed. It wasn't so different from our store: a little worn-out table and chair, couple of lockers, old-ass closed-circuit TV for the cameras out front (the ones Jodi had thought I'd disabled from the register, as if). I tell you, though, that stuff didn't mean a damn thing compared to the real...star...of the room, as it were. The main attraction. Pretty easy to figure out what happened to the clerk at that point. Poor bastard.

He sat at the table, leaning back and to the left in an awkward pose. Having seen my share of corpses in the last 24 hours, he was a real no-doubter. I didn't know if I felt horrified or relieved; even though a single bullet through the forehead had killed the guy - and that was pretty bad, I'm no savage - he could have been any random person on any random day in our Aethyr.

What I'm saying is that I don't know what sort of *thing* I expected to work in a store that sold Pendergrast instead of Reese's; maybe I expected his skin to be blue. But what I saw back there just looked like any normal dude.

Get a grip, I told myself. Easier said than done. Trying to put the split in my head into words…it's not possible. I just stood there, vapor-locked, for a long time.

I might have stood there forever if it hadn't been for the big, thick gun barrel that poked into my lower back like some lover who insists on doing it right *now*, right *here,* and damn the consequences.

"You hold it right there," this guy said from behind me.

I expected somebody commanding and gruff. Male or female, didn't matter. What I heard instead sounded like George Costanza. *You've got to be shitting me.* I didn't even worry about my well-being. I faced the guy.

"I told you to hold it," he said.

"You told me," I replied, but by this point I had gotten a glimpse of the guy and…wow. It wasn't just that he sounded like Costanza, he resembled him, too.

"You?" he said, and the end of the big, double-barrel shotgun he was carrying drooped at his ankles, like he had forgotten who he was.

"How do you know me?" I asked.

"I had a dream about you," he said.

My brain must have been rebounding, because I chuckled and said, "well ain't that some shit?" Against my own will, I liked the guy. I don't know why. It was something about his manner. Maybe just as simple as he reminded me of Costanza.

"It is." He raised the gun barrel, leveling it at me.

That's no fun. Not liking that.

"Now what the fuck are you doing here?" he asks.

"I came in for some food. Maybe a drink, you know, what these stores are for? Next thing I know I'm in the middle of a mob hit. Why'd you have to go and kill him?"

"Take a look at this." He waved it. "You think this thing could have put that tiny little hole in his head?"

"Just because you're holding that gun doesn't mean it's the one you used to kill him."

"Fair enough, but I'm in the same boat as you. I came in here for some supplies, that's all. I found him in the back, then I heard you coming in the door, so I went and hid in the freezer. I figured you might be coming in here to take care of business, finish things up."

"Do I look like the type who's going to plug some poor clerk?"

He lowered the shotgun again. "Now that you mention it, you don't. There's something about you. I know that sounds like some cheesy pickup line, but I'm serious. It's not just the dream, either. It's something else."

"It's because she's the Chosen One, Grabbe," came a voice from the front of the store.

He turned. "Delilah?"

Chapter 11

Where the Sun Refused to Shine

"Yes, it's me. What are you doing here?" Delilah said.

"I could ask you the same question. At least I have a reason to be here."

"Wait, you two know each other?" I said.

"Sure, we go way back," Grabbe said, "but we haven't seen each other in a long time, have we?"

"If you wanted to see me, all you had to do was call."

"Right. Let's have a nice little reunion here. I apologize, and you let me waltz right back into your arms after what happened in Shanghai."

"Something like that, yes."

"Hey, hey, slow down, I'm still standing right here," I said. "Explain to me what's happening. Who are you, how do you two know each other, and why am in a store with a bunch of weird brand names?"

Delilah looked at me. "You did notice that, did you? Hmm."

He scanned her, then me, and back again. "You didn't tell her?"

She tsked. "Why would I think it necessary? We're so close to the portal. This was to be a refueling stop, and then off we go on our merry way. How could I know we'd run into *you*?"

I spoke up. "You think I wouldn't have noticed the

change in just about every damn thing?"

"Really? *Everything*? You'll notice we're still at a Circle K. This Aethyr is not so different from your own."

"You could have told us."

Grabbe motioned toward me. "The girl's right, you know." He raised one eyebrow at Delilah. "You're letting her walk around weird Aethyrs without telling her where she is?"

"She went to get a drink. I hardly thought it would be a problem."

"It was a problem, okay?" I said. I noticed Delilah creeping closer. I glanced out the window and saw Daniel not too far behind her.

Something's about to go down here. Keep your eyes open, girl.

Grabbe noticed Delilah making her move and swiveled the shotgun toward her. "Why don't you stay right over there?" he said.

She held up her hands, giving him a wide-eyed look. "Why? What would I do to you?"

"I'm just a lot more comfortable with you right over there."

She took another step forward, knowing she was fucking with him at this point. "Darling, I want to touch you."

"You don't need to touch me. I can see you fine right here."

Remember the shadow thing that moved like a blur? Delilah moved like that. Before I knew what was happening, she blurred right across toward him pressed a dagger right up against his throat. "You were right about Shanghai," she said. "You should never leave a woman to die."

"I told you I was sorry."

"Mm. Yes. Sorry. That seems appropriate when you've left someone to die. Sorry, lover. She's mine and I'm taking her to the Engine."

"The hell you are," he said, and did the blurring thing, only with the shotgun, bashing her right across the forehead.

The dagger hit the floor. She reached up to grab the barrel, like the supersonic shot to the head only slowed her down a little. The two of them wrestled over the gun.

I had only met this Grabbe guy. I had no idea of his intentions, but like I said, I got a good vibe from him and hell, any enemy of Delilah's should be a friend of mine. So I did the natural thing: I stepped in and gave Delilah a nice quick kick to the gut. It wasn't much, I'm not that strong, but it was enough to make her recoil.

Grabbe yelled at me to get down. The next few moments were a blur. He fired the shotgun, the thing sounding like a stick of dynamite going off. The front window blew out, but somehow Delilah avoided that. She had that knack.

Next thing I knew, she jumped through what was left of the window, Kristy screamed, Daniel was somewhere out there, I couldn't tell - Grabbe was in my way.

"Fucking maniac," Grabbe yelled.

Delilah must have had no interest in seeing what came next, because she was across the parking lot in a blur, jumping into the Pontiac and peeling out of there.

Grabbe yelled something at her in some language I couldn't understand.

I got a grip on myself and returned to the moment, walking toward the blown-out window.

He sighed. "I see she's lovelier than ever. She been like that the whole time you've known her?"

"All three days or so," I replied. "She supposed to look any other way?"

"She wasn't always an old crone. Even in the last few years." He snapped his head up toward Daniel, eyes on fire. "And you!"

"Me? What about me?"

"A Rogue runs right by you and you don't stop her. That's some fine work right there."

Daniel's face went red. "I don't have any idea what you're talking about."

"You don't, do you? You going to stand there and deny who you are?"

Daniel and I spoke at the same time: "Who is he-" "I'm not who y-"

He waved his hand. "Tell it to someone who'll buy it, Ikisat. Eh? See? Eh? I know who you are."

"I told you I have no idea what you're talking about."

"Uh huh." He put two fingers to his eyes and then pointed them at Daniel. "You and me, buddy. You and me."

"Who are you?" Kristy asked.

"Better question is, who are *you*? Listen, I'm hungry, you're hungry, we're all thirsty. We could use a break. How about we take ten minutes, go get what we want, meet out here? Sound good?"

"I'm down," I said.

"Good. Reconvene here in ten minutes, we hash out some shit over breakfast."

Chapter 12

Her Name is Defeat

"First thing you've got to understand is she wasn't always evil. Me? I was born that way," Grabbe said as he popped open his can of Snowdrift beef stew.

"What do you mean?" I asked.

He chewed on a spoonful of the stew and then spoke again, his mouth full. "What I'm saying is, she joined the Watchers later. I was born into them."

I raised an eyebrow "So does that make you an Aetel...whatever. An angel?"

"Eh, yes and no."

"What do you mean, 'yes and no'?" Kristy asked, looking up from her doughnuts.

"Yes in that my father was one, no in that my mother wasn't. That make sense?"

"So wait, like...how old are you?"

"Old as the fucking hills, that narrow it down for you?"

"Why you asking?" I said to Kristy.

"Because there are legends. Angels were supposed to have come down and, like, married women and had kids and stuff, but it was supposed to have happened before Noah's flood."

Daniel gaped at her like she'd started spouting off in Latin. "How the hell do you know that?"

"Just because I talk like a moron doesn't mean I *am* a

moron, thank you."

Grabbe chuckled.

"Score one for blondie. She's right." He scooped out some more stew.

"Wait," I said, "you mean to tell me not only did Noah exist-"

"Not Noah. Noah was a...PR creation. Noah *didn't* exist."

Daniel straightened up, and he damn near dropped his breakfast burrito. "What do you mean, Noah didn't exist?"

Grabbe pointed at him with his spork. "Ah hah. So you admit you know something about it."

"I admit nothing."

I glanced at Daniel out of the corner of my eye. Could Grabbe be telling the truth? Was Daniel an angel? It didn't fit in with the guy I knew. What angel takes bong hits? What angel scratches his ass and burps? Although if Delilah was some sort of angel...

Grabbe carried on. "Okay, well Noah *did* exist, but there was no herding of the animals or building a giant ship or any of that bullshit. It wasn't literally a flood, either."

"What do you mean?" I asked.

"Invasion would be the proper term. Maybe a flood of angels. How much do you guys know about the Engine?"

"Engine? What Engine?" Kristy asked.

"The Engine of Destruction," I answered, and they looked at me.

"So one of you knows about it." He considered this as he chewed. "What do you know about it?"

"All I know is that's what's in Vegas, and it's why she was trying to get me there."

"How did you know that?" Kristy asked.

I rubbed my neck. "I wasn't strictly telling the truth about what happened when I disappeared."

"I knew it. So what really happened?"

I told them. I didn't see a reason to hold back without Delilah present. Obviously I had a bit to tell, but not much about the Engine itself. I hadn't figured out how it all tied together, but I hoped Grabbe could put together some of the pieces for me.

When I'd finished my story, he nodded. "Mm, yeah, not unusual for a dead person to get trapped between Aethyrs. She probably needed to do penance and didn't even know it. Let's hope she's passed on now." He slapped his hands together. "We're going to have to get going soon, but I've got a few minutes for a history lesson. The Watchers came before the whole Noah thing. Four Watchtowers - right, four?"

"I've told them about the Watchtowers," Daniel said.

"Did you now? Did you tell them our history?"

He shook his head, one curt cut back and forth.

"Well, then. Whoever came before the Aetelia - don't know, not saying it's God, they don't know either, all we know is they came before - he or she set things up. There are four Watchtowers to watch over this thing called the Black Cross. The Aetelia were put in the Watchtowers to watch over the Cross. Don't know if they - meaning we - were created for it or whatever. Nobody knows. Okay? You *know* our history?" he asked.

"I haven't the foggiest," Daniel said.

"Course you don't. You and me, pal. You and me," he did the finger-eyes thing again. "So the four Watchtowers, they've got their…posts. Their designations, you might say.

They watch over different parts of what they call the Multiverse. All these worlds squished together into a spectrum, only to the people living there it looks like the normal world, you can't see the others, right? You know about the Aethyrs."

"Right, go on," I said, unwrapping a candy bar.

"So the Aetelia in the Watchtowers realize they can't get to the Black Cross. They can watch over it, make sure no one goes for it, but they can't touch it. They don't even really know what it does, or why it's there. Lots of theories, maybe it's holding things together. I'm not a philosopher. All I know is this thing has a way of talking to people. Certain people. By people I mean Aetelia, of course. One day an Aetelia's out checking the thing out. Thing zaps him. He has this grand vision, okay? The Watchtowers, with their different agendas - they need to pick out their best and brightest, my father amongst them, though I would debate the wisdom of *that* choice."

"The Watchers," I said. "We've heard that one."

"Right. Okay. Did you hear they were sent to this tiny little Aethyr - the one you guys live in?"

Daniel bristled at that. "That's not quite right. They watched over all the Aethyrs."

Grabbe studied him. "Who told you that nonsense?"

"Haven't a clue. Read it in the magick books, and that's magick with a 'k'," he said, glancing around at us.

"What's the difference?" I asked.

"One's about pulling a rabbit from a hat. The other is about mastery over the elements," he said.

Grabbed considered Daniel. "Maybe I was wrong about you. Listen, the magicians only know bits and pieces - it's amazing any of it survived the Flood, but a lot of what was left got lost in Alexandria, and most of the rest during the Dark Ages. They did the best they could to preserve that stuff, but once it's gone, it's gone. All you got now are mostly legends." He waved his hand and ran a hand through his hair. "I'm telling you the truth because I was there."

"Carry on," Daniel replied.

"So the Watchers are given a charge. They're able to travel between your Aethyr and several others, but they can't return to the Watchtowers. Basically, they're in charge of one Aethyr, they can get to five others or so. You follow?"

"We got it," I said. "Move it on."

"I'm moving, I'm moving. The Watchers are getting along with humanity - everything's fantastic, we're all smiles. Watchers are teaching humans stuff, the humans are teaching Watchers stuff. You know, happy times. Only problem is, the Aetelia didn't want them to teach humans this stuff. Said it was too soon. Sound familiar to you?"

"Duh, Prometheus? The guy who stole fire from the gods and gave it to humans, then got his ass kicked for it?" Kristy said.

He pointed at her, winking. "Eh, see? The girl's smart."

Daniel looked at her and she shrugged.

"Right, it's based on what I'm telling you. So the Aetelia warn the Watchers, tell them to back off. Watchers say 'okay, no problem'. What they're really doing is, they're gathering up some of humanity's best and brightest and taking them to another Aethyr - this Aethyr. To work on a little side project."

"The Engine," I said.

"Bingo. The Engine. So the question is, 'what is the Engine'? Turns out the Watchers - and by this point I'm on the scene because my dad's with my mom and whatnot - decide they're as good as any of the Watchtowers. Why can't they have a cut of the pie? Why not build a Fifth Watchtower? Call it the Engine of Destruction."

"Why?" I asked.

"Because the whole point was to destroy the status quo," he said, and he seemed a little too fired up about it for my liking. "Shake things up. Give people - give humans - their own place in the cosmos. There are many races and many worlds, but humans are the only ones that penetrate through the Aethyrs. Sure, you'll find your stray version of Earth that has horses who have evolved in place of humans, but it's mostly humans. That puts them in a unique position. So we start building the machines to build the Engine. Somehow the Watchtowers get a spy into our camp. They know what we're up to, and they can't have this on their watch. God - literally, maybe - only knows what's going to happen if this Watchtower goes up. This isn't how things are meant to be, according to them.

"So they start sabotaging. They find out where the stuff is, and they cripple our defenses right before they attack. Then they completely obliterate the Engine on Earth."

"The one in Vegas?" I said.

"Precisely. The one in Vegas. This is the Flood. They come down and wipe out almost all of the humans. Erase most of the history of what had been done. Almost everything - gone. They can do that, you know. Reset humans to square one."

"What about the Watchers?" I asked.

"Yeah, what about *you*?" Kristy asked.

"Good question. Good question, both of you." He

finished off his stew and wiped his mouth, belching.

"Nice one," Kristy said.

"I know, right? Anyway. I think the 'myth' of the Watchers says they were bound in a pit, but they were really sent to a far-away Aethyr. You could call it hell, you could call it a prison, you could call it the devil's asshole. Any of those would work. Me, I worked out my own deal. You don't need to worry about me. Just know that I'm not on the Watchers' side, and there's a reason I'm going to Vegas, too." He took the shotgun from around his shoulder.

Daniel tossed his burrito wrapper in the trash. "I think it's very important. We need to know who *you* are since you seem to think you know so much about us."

Kristy took my hand and I helped her to her feet. "He's right," she said, "you're, like, this man of mystery, and we need to know we're safe."

"All right, kids. Fine." He threw the stew can over his shoulder; it landed in the parking lot with a metallic clang. "Little bio. My dad was right-hand man for the Watchers. You might have even heard of him. Goes by Azazel."

Kristy gasped.

"The lady's heard of him."

"Yeah. He's a demon."

He squinted at her. "Eh. Sure. In the strictest sense of the word: a fallen angel. Demons are something else, though."

"What?" I asked.

He waved his hand at me. "Not relevant right now. Dad's not relevant, either. He got sent to the prison...but we'll talk about it some other time. Anyway, my mom was a human, they fell in love, I came about..."

"We don't need to hear your family's love life to know

about you," Daniel said. "What did you do for them?"

He sighed. "I'm uh...I'm an engineer." I noticed he was studying his feet.

"You helped design it, didn't you?" I asked.

He cocked his head. "Sorta..." He kicked at the sidewalk.

"Sorta?"

"I'm trying to undo what I did." The fire I saw in his eyes told me the guy was pretty okay under it all. "I've been trying to make right for what I did for a long, long time. I'm starting to get close, too. Maybe I'm not that good at it, maybe I fucked up a lot, but-"

"Like when you left Delilah in Shanghai?"

He winced again, and something on the ground became real interesting to him.

"Yeah," Daniel said, approaching the smaller man, grinning from ear to ear. "Why don't you tell us about that?"

"Nothing much to tell. I worked with her when she wasn't, you know, one of them. We were both trying to make good for what we did in the past. Only she relapsed, you might say."

"What did *she* do wrong?" Kristy asked.

"Delilah - and she's not always been called that, her real name is Uriel - she used to be...how do you people put it? The angel of death."

Didn't that make all the sense in the world? No wonder the old bitch was so good with a weapon. "So she tried to kill the wrong person," I said.

"Nah. She turned her back on the Watchtowers. That's a lot worse."

"Is that how you two know each other?" Kristy asked.

"Yeah. Look, we can talk about all this on the way. Right

now we've got to cross over."

"I thought we already crossed over," I said. "We're not exactly in Kansas anymore."

"Sort of. You've gone up an Aethyr. Things are plenty fucked up here, but this place was…I don't know, the Aetelia took care of it in the Flood. Next level up, profoundly fucked up, but it's where we've got to go because it's where the Heart of the engine sits. I've never even seen that part, just channeled its energy."

I think a light bulb went off in Kristy's head. "So if you, like, designed this thing, did you have to make it so it'd be in all these different realities at once?"

"I'm telling you, this girl is a fucking genius. She knows what she's talking about. Now come on, let's get going."

"Wait," I said. "I'm not going anywhere until you tell us where we're going."

He gave this heavy sigh, the sigh of a thousand worlds, my mother used to call it. "Fine. I'm taking you to a place called Central Park Canal. We're going to go find a bridge. Under that bridge, we're going to find a door."

"What's through the door?" Kristy asked.

"The next Aethyr. There are lots of different doors that let you move between the Aethyrs without the fancy tricks that your girlfriend does."

"Or without magick," Daniel added.

"Right. Or that."

"I could take us all there," I said. "just describe the place."

"No way. Uh huh. Useful as your skill might be, it's like a beacon. Why do you think we had that little dream/vision thing?"

"I don't know. You seemed as surprised as me," I said.

"I've never seen it manifest like that, but when you do it the worlds get thin. That makes all odd matter of things happen, and the wrong kinds of things can notice that."

"'Things'? Care to elaborate there, Captain Vocabulary?"

"He's talking about the beasts between the worlds," Daniel said. He had a thousand-yard stare, almost like he was looking through the world around us and into the maws of whatever things he was talking about.

"You've seen 'em," Grabbe said.

"Aye." He met the guy's eyes. "They'd as soon rip your soul out as look at you. I'd prefer never to see such a thing again."

"Right. So what we've got to do, is we've got to follow the rules. For now. We're already going to have a little trouble in this town, I can tell you that. So let's get moving, shall we?"

Chapter 13

I Fight For My Meals

Grabbe led us northeast through the city. At least, I think he did. I didn't pay super-close attention to the street signs, due to suffering complications of a severe weird-out brought on by the city. I'd known Bakersfield was something of a pit, but I'd lived in Humboldt County, so I wasn't exactly uncomfortable with the check cashing places and the pawn shops. No, it was more than that, more like the weird atmosphere in the store extended to the city.

One thing was for sure. I felt naked, and I didn't like it. Even if the idea of hurting somebody made me feel a little nauseated, I also didn't want to be exposed without some means of protection. As we passed a big green monstrosity called "Bakersfield's Greatest Pawn Shop," I got a brainwave.

"Hold up, folks," I said.

Grabbe turned on me, his brow furrowed. "What now?"

"I don't like being out here without a weapon, a knife, a gun, something."

"Hello, that's what this is for?" he said, holding up the shotgun.

"You think that's a good idea? You going to defend us all?"

"Well…now that you mention it…"

"She's right, we should be armed," Daniel said.

He held up his hands. "Do any of you even know how to

fire a gun?"

"I do. It's not that hard. They can be taught."

"If you say so." He looked at the building. "You want to go in there, then?"

I nodded. "You reckon you can blow the lock off of the door?"

"Maybe, but I don't think it's going to matter with those bars over the inside of the door. Why don't you use your little skill to pop in there, get what we need, pop back out?"

"*Now* my skill's handy, huh?"

"It's more the fact that you're moving in the same world here. There's nothing to thin out. You're just going from one place to another."

"He's right," Daniel said. "Point A, Point B, you're only moving in one plane. Nothing's getting folded up. You can do it if you want."

I looked from them to Kristy, who shrugged. "I don't know, sweetie. Whatever you want," she says.

The idea of moving guns seemed risky, but what other choice did we have? Grabbe was right - the place was basically sealed inside a cage. "I think I can handle it." I walked up to the door and held one hand over my eyes, looking inside. I caught a glint of metal, part of the display cabinets inside. A layer of dust laid over everything, like nobody had been in there for years.

Grabbe said, "time isn't exactly even here. Circle K could've been ten minutes ago, could've been three days ago, could've been five years ago. Eyes can also play tricks on you."

"Duly noted," I said. I'd gotten enough of a look that I could do my thing. I closed my eyes and pictured the inside of the place.

I didn't even need to be all that intent; pictured it, boom, and I traveled inside, my nose assaulted by the musty smell of mold. The shaggy crimson carpet under my feet was squishy and mildewy, and the wood paneling behind the counters was somewhere in the process of returning to the mulch from which it came. I quietly thanked God that the smell wasn't worse than it could have been and crossed to the counters, staring up at the guns, hanging in their silent racks.

If the place had been abandoned as long as it looked, it was a miracle that nobody had stolen those guns. There were rifles, shotguns, nice handguns - I couldn't tell you about the brands, what the hell did I need to know that for - but they looked right for what we needed. I climbed over the counter and started pulling handguns off the wall. They were heavier than I expected; I bounced one up and down in my hand before laying it on the counter.

One for me, one for Kristy, one for Daniel.

I didn't know the make of the guns, which represented a bit of a problem, as I'd have to get some ammo. I turned one of the guns over in my hand, looking for a clue, but no dice - I knew enough to find the serial number, but it didn't mean a thing to me. I laid the gun down and went to the racks, hoping maybe there would be something there to help me out.

I spotted an old, thick book. *The Shooter's Bible.* That was bound to help me out. I heaved the thing onto the counter beside the guns and flipped through it, trying to match our guns up to the pictures inside.

There.

I found the guns and the right type of ammo: they were Glock .45s.

Perfect.

I dug through the drawers under the racks. I had pulled out a drawer full of .45 shells when the first shot rang from outside the window.

There came two more, and the boom of Grabbe's shotgun.

Oh shit.

I turned toward the front window.

Kristy and Daniel were behind Grabbe, who backed them away from the front of the store, smoke curling from those double barrels. Kristy tried to yell something to me, but the message was lost somewhere in the thick glass. Another shot zinged past as they rounded the corner of the building and out of sight.

I went to the counter and picked up the guns, stuffing them down into the band of my jeans while I watched out the window for signs of life. Nothing so far, so I dumped some ammo into my pockets and picked up the biggest, longest knife I'd ever seen from inside one of the display cases.

I went and knelt by the door, one hand against the door handle. Something rustled outside, and then *they* walked in front of the window: four guys, dressed in long black hooded robes that stretched all the way down to their feet. They wore black masks that were empty voids of hell, the only real sign of any human features hidden behind big steel goggles. Did I mention they carried assault rifles, too? That kind of caught my attention.

They were talking to each other, but I couldn't quite understand what they were saying. What I could get my mind around is that they were pointing South, back in the direction from which we came. I remembered us passing an old abandoned building that might have been a car dealership once upon a time, a cream-colored structure with parking on the first level and a big round glass thing on top. Grabbe must have taken the other two there. You could do worse for places to hide.

The four guys in black hustled off and around the corner.

A few seconds later, this smaller guy came hustling up behind them, a tiny handgun flopping around in his hand. He stopped outside the shop, struggling to keep his mask on. A shot rang out and he cringed, pushing up against the shop.

Time to make my move.

I closed my eyes and imagined myself right up behind the guy, staring right into the back of the hood, hearing his breath, smelling his fear. Opened my eyes, and sure enough, I was there. The guy was shorter than me, so it was easy to get the drop on him. I wrapped an arm around his throat and put my left hand up over where his mouth should've been, replacing my arm with the knife against his throat.

I tried to put on the best scary voice that I could. "One more move and you're dead," I said. The kid froze. "Listen, we're going to back up, real nice and slow. Got it?"

He nodded, nice and slow. I could feel him shaking; I hoped he didn't piss his pants and get it all over both of us.

"I'm going to take my hand off your mouth, and you're going to give me your gun, okay?"

He nodded again, and passed me the pistol when I snapped my fingers. I slipped the pistol into my waistband with the other guns.

"Good. Cooperate and we'll be fine." The salon next door had a recessed deck, so I started backing up with him in my arms, trying to get him there. I had never forced someone along at knife point - I count it as a good point honestly - and my hand slid a little, the sharp point scratching his neck. Not hard, but hard enough to make him yelp and push against me.

I should've felt bad, but come on, they had just taken a shot at my friends. Instead of apologizing to the guy, I grunted and kept backing him up until we were under the relative safety of the deck.

"Stay still," I said, and pulled the robe up from his feet. He wore old faded jeans. Levi's. At least some things were the same here. I reached into the pockets, searching for wallets, keys, that sort of thing. Nothing.

"You're going to turn around. You're going to stay calm."

"Don't hurt me," he said, in this muffled, high-pitched voice. *Christ, how young is this kid?*

I pulled away the knife and he faced me. He gave this little start that told me he hadn't been expecting some chick with green hair and a nose ring to be holding that blade.

"Take off the mask. Goggles first," I motioned with the knife, so the guy remembered who was in charge.

He did as he was told.

There was no way to prepare for what I saw underneath. The guy was human, no worries there, but he couldn't have been more than 12 years old. He had short, sandy hair in a dorky bowl cut, and bright blue eyes in the middle of a completely filthy, skinny face. He was a little homeless version of the skater punks who hung out in the parking lot at the K.

"What the hell are you doing out here, kid?" I took the mask from him.

"Don't hurt me, lady. Please." His voice cracked. How

pathetic was that?

"I already hurt you bad enough, I think." I nodded at the spot on his neck where I'd nicked him. It was on the surface of the skin, but it was gushing. I took the knife and cut out a section from the bottom of my shirt, handing it to him. "I'm sorry about that."

"It's okay." As soon as he put the shirt against his neck it went red with the blood. Maybe it was a little deeper than I thought, but he was a good sport about it.

"Seriously, what are you doing out here?"

"Me and mom were heading west, looking for food, when they caught us. I don't know where she is, I haven't seen her in weeks. They made me a Marauder."

"The hell's a Marauder?"

"That's what they call themselves. This is their town."

"This is their town, how come the gas stations are still running?"

That got a little spark of defiance in his eyes. "Who do you think owns them? They control it all."

"Who's been knocking over the gas stations?"

"They call themselves the Despoilers," he said.

"What a stupid name." I laughed.

"You don't want to say that to them."

"I'm sure I don't," I said. I stuck the knife in the deck's arm rail and adjusted my pants so those guns didn't slide down toward my crotch.

"What are you going to do with all those guns?"

"Considering how your friends are trying to screw us over-"

"They're not my friends," he said.

"Okay, the people you're *with* are trying to screw us

over. I figured I'd get a little something to even the odds." I got a little brainstorm. "Give me your robe," I said, trying to be gentle.

"What are you doing?" he asked as he lifted it over his head.

"I assume you want to get away from these slime balls."

"Yeah…"

"We're heading somewhere where they won't be able to follow you." What are you thinking, Matty? Are you really going to try to take this kid with you?

"I don't think that's possible." He handed over the robe.

I slipped the robe on. It was a lot lighter than it looked, and cool to the touch. *Interesting.* "It's possible. How well do you know this area?"

"Pretty damn good."

"Good. Now listen, here's the plan."

Chapter 14

The Plan Keeps Coming Up Again

First step was getting the kid into the shop; that wasn't a problem. I was getting pretty good at the whole jumping-around-teleporting-people business.

Once we were inside, I told him to wait and went into the rear of the shop to look for some food or drink. I found a pallet of bottled water amongst the piles of useless junk hiding out back there, and though I wondered how much of the plastic might have seeped into the water, it had to be enough to take care of him.

Out front, the kid bent over one of the display cases, gazing at the rings.

"How long's it been since you've seen stuff like this?" I asked.

He took the bottle. "I don't know. We didn't have this kind of stuff. No point."

"You like it."

He nodded and drank the water.

"Not all life is like this, you know. Where I came from things might have sucked, but you could do what you pretty much what you wanted when you wanted." Listen to this, now. The cynic, the girl who raged against the machine, wistful about the American system of government. Of course, compared to that hell-hole, Somalia looked good.

"Where do you come from?"

"I couldn't even explain it if I tried. Just a long way from here." I sat the mask and goggles on the counter.

"Is that where you're taking me?"

I shook my head. "We're going someplace else. I'm a long way from home, too."

"I miss it sometimes," he said.

"I bet. I miss home, too." God, had it only been a day since I'd left? I felt like a different person.

"We left Vegas when I was five," he said.

"You're from Vegas?"

He nodded.

"Small world. Maybe you are going home after all. That's where we're heading."

"Oh," he said, in this small voice. "They can't find us there."

"Right. So no worries, everything's going to be fine." I took a look at the robe. It was hard to explain, exactly. It felt similar to polyester, but soft, yet tough enough to take a bullet. "This is like armor."

"I don't know what it's called. Their shoes aren't made of it," he said, and lifted up his feet. "You shoot 'em there, you can knock 'em down."

"Then you get close and take care of them, huh? I don't think any of us is that good a shot. Hell, most of us never fired a gun before." I got another idea. I realized I might not even need a gun for this thing. I slipped the mask over my head. "Don't worry, I think I've got this. You hang out in here where they can't get you. I'll come get you when I'm done."

"Okay. What's your name?"

"Matty. What's yours?"

"I'm Tommy."

I slipped the goggles over my head. "Good to meet you. I'll be right back."

"Okay."

Closing my eyes is the right thing to do, because the goggles are darker than a bat's asshole.

How the hell do they see out of these?

I could only guess they were designed for the middle of the day. I visualized myself in front of the shop, and there I stood, listening to these guys as they took up position.

I wandered around the corner and found that the Marauders had dug in behind jersey walls that had been set up beside the shop. The biggest member of their little squad grunted at me and pointed toward the farthest wall. I got down behind it, next to a stunted, chubby guy.

Grabbe yelled from around the side of the building, across the street, and the shotgun boomed. The Marauders were far enough away that it wasn't going to do any serious damage, but it was enough to keep them from making a charge, at least for that moment.

The others returned fire and I had to do the same, once I figured out how to turn the damned safety off. There I was, having never fired a gun in my life, firing stray shots into the air, hoping to God I didn't hit any of my friends.

It was your classic Mexican Standoff, and I knew I couldn't stay there forever. There had to be some way to get over to my buddies without seeming suspicious, but I was drawing a blank on just how to do it.

God, or whoever, must have been listening, because the leader turned to us and signaled, twirling his fingers.

This is my shot. I looked to the chubby guy beside me, but he was already up and moving across the street, toward the side opposite of where Grabbe hid out, firing at the Marauders. Swallowing the lump in my throat, I climbed out from behind the wall and scurried across the road, keeping my head down.

At last I reached the chubby guy. He stood there waiting, hands on his hips. "You're slow as hell," he said, in English nonetheless, but with a weird accent that almost sounded German. "What's going on?"

I had to answer him. How well did he know Tommy's voice? Did the kid speak at all, and was this guy supposed to be his teacher? I guess I'd find out. I steeled myself for action and did my best to impersonate the kid.

"They don't look like trouble," I said, and winced. It didn't sound much like him.

He cocked his head and raised his pistol. *Blew that one.* "You-"

When the realization of what I was about to do hit me, my stomach got loose and grumbly; my knees shook.

Kristy. Think about Kristy, and what these bastards might do to her.

That brought the resolve back. I hated having to do it, but I had no choice. I pulled my knife from under the robe and jumped on him in one move. He didn't last more than a second. Even though the guy outweighed me by a good hundred pounds, I knew where to stab him to hit his heart. Thank God for anatomy lessons in art class.

I tried to catch his body and lower him to the ground gently, but it didn't quite work. He hit the pavement hard. That dead expression stared up into the sky, those eyes that would stare forever and yet never see again. In the movies people always close the eyes, but I couldn't bring myself to touch them.

"Jesus Christ, I'm sorry," I said.

I stood there, knife in one hand, pistol in another, not sure what to do next.

Not again. You can't do this.

I couldn't stop it, though. I should have been torn apart by what I had done, but when I looked inside, I couldn't find much going on. I struggled to even summon up any thought beyond wondering why I had become this way.

You did that, I thought, but even that didn't settle in. *I killed someone.* It wasn't a long-range kill, either, it was up close and personal. I could hear the guy rattle as he died. Never in a million years did I think I could do such a thing.

You did what you had to do, and there's still more to be done.

Maybe having no emotions was a good thing after all. I dropped the knife beside the guy's body without another thought, running off around the building. I pulled off the goggles and took off the mask. Last thing I needed was for them to think I was one of the Marauders.

I came around the wall and there they stood, pressed up against the retaining wall, trading volleys with the Marauders.

Kristy turned and spotted me, her eyes wide. "Oh my God, Matty?" She ran toward me like she was going to hug me, but she stopped, hesitating.

Of course. The chubby guy's blood covered me. "It's not my blood. Don't worry," I said.

Daniel, a step behind her, nodded. "Not to say that we're not happy to see you, love, but do you have weapons for us?"

"Weapons. Right." I reached under the robe and pulled out the handguns - one for Kristy, one for Daniel - I even had an extra for Grabbe.

"Eh, thanks, I was getting low," Grabbe said, and took some shells from me. "Did you get a clear look at them?"

"She's wearing their uniform, what do you think?" Daniel said.

"Doesn't mean she got a look at them, does it?"

"I did, though. Sort of."

I told them the story about the kid, as quick as I could. Grabbe nodded through it and then said, "not to be ungrateful or nothing, but you find out they're bulletproof and you bring us guns? What are we supposed to do now?"

Daniel shook his head. "That's bollocks. They can't be entirely bulletproof. They would've made a run on us already."

"Maybe they don't know what we have?"

"No. I think they told the kid a lie."

"Are you willing to gamble that?"

"What other choice do we have?"

Grabbe nodded at her. "Our little Chosen One could do what she did to the guard."

I shook my head. "Nah. I'm not doing that again. I'm done killing people."

"It's self-defense," Daniel said.

Kristy spoke up. "She said she's not killing anyone, okay? Get it through your skull. Now show me how to load this thing."

Daniel's eyes went wide. "Aye."

I watched them, while Grabbe leaned out from behind the wall and winged a few shots at the Marauders.

He glanced over his shoulder at me. "You say you don't want to kill anybody...how you feel about 'facilitating some defensive actions'?"

"What the hell is that supposed to mean?"

"I mean how do you feel about moving me around, and I kill them?"

"Like stab them?" I asked.

"Something like that. You jump me around, you don't have to stab the guy or nothing, then you move us again, I stab another guy. Get it?"

"I get it, but why don't you do that blurring thing you people do? Move like a ninja?"

He shook his head. "Not as easy as it looks, kid. Even full-blown Aetelia can only do it over short distances; I'm good for a few feet and I'm worn out."

"So it's up to me."

"What do you think about that?"

What *did* I think about that? I had already crossed the bridge into killing, but this seemed different. It didn't make much sense to me to say 'I've already killed one person, might as well kill whoever I want'. I already felt hollow. I didn't want to feel more hollow - or was it even *possible* to feel more hollow? What if I never felt anything again? "I don't know," I said.

"You yourself said they're bulletproof. How else are we supposed to kill them before they kill us?"

Daniel interrupted. "You want to know how? I'll show you." He strolled over and pushed Grabbe away from the wall. Winking, he ducked his head out, drawing some fire.

Once the shots had been fired he leaned out, looking like he was on his father's yacht, and squeezed the trigger.

I couldn't see well around the corner, but I could see that he hit a guy right in the chest as he popped up to take another shot. Dude staggered, almost dropping his rifle, but then he surged forward again, lifting the rifle and firing. A cloud of dust fell off the wall as Daniel ducked away at the last second.

"Right," Daniel said, glancing down at his pistol. "Suppose they weren't lying."

"See?" Grabbe yelled.

Think about protecting Kristy. Remember, you have to protect her first. "Maybe we can, but I've never hopped around that fast. I don't know if I can get you a chance to kill him before they get us."

"It's a chance we've got to take," Grabbe replied. "Eventually we're going to run out of ammo and then we're up shit creek. They're going to overrun us. I don't know why they haven't done it yet."

I snapped my fingers. "Their feet, that's why. Their feet are weak. They can't turn that material into shoes or whatever. Kid made it sound like they only just found the stuff."

"All well and good, but it doesn't do us much good, does it? They're too dug in for us to get a shot at them."

"Not strictly the truth," Daniel said. "We might have something to work with here."

"What do you mean?" I asked.

"If we could find some way to draw them out from behind their walls, I could hit them in the feet, no problem."

"You're a crack shot?" Grabbe asked.

"Matter of fact, I am. I've won a few awards."

"You continue to amaze, don't you?" Kristy said.

He grinned. "I do. I specialize in it. Here's my thinking. I shoot them in the feet, bring them down. Obviously it's not going to kill them, but it will slow them down enough so you two can do your thing."

Grabbe grinned. "You're a crazy son of a bitch, you know that?"

"Aye. Wouldn't be here if I wasn't, would I?"

"How do we distract them?" I asked.

"That's the easy part. You become the prey."

"Whoa. Wait a minute."

But his plan, you know, it wasn't that bad, once he'd explained it in full. Deep down, I hoped knocking them off their feet would be enough, and we wouldn't have to kill them. *Please God, let that happen,* I thought.

Chapter 15

The Center Cannot Hold

"We got one of yours out here, you rat bastards," Grabbe shouted as he held me by the upper arm, pushing his shotgun into my side. I wore the mask and goggles and tried to slouch to the kid's height. Would they buy it? Hard to say, but it was worth a shot. "You don't want to lose him, I want one of you to come out here and talk to me right now."

The gunshots died almost right away. Grabbe pushed me farther out, so that they could see me. "It's the boy. You want to keep him, you better come out here, or I'm going to blow him away." He jabbed the shotgun into my ribs.

"Ouch, Christ, take it easy," I said.

"Got to make it look good for the natives."

Some movement came from the other side. I could see them, barely thanks to the shitty-ass goggles, conferring amongst themselves. The big guy, the one who had been directing us, rose and walked out from behind his wall, holding up one hand, the rifle still in his other hand.

"Very clever," he said, in a deep, calm voice, one with no hint of the accent that I'd heard from the other guy. It sounded so familiar; I tried to place where I had heard it before. "What do you want to do with my conscript?" The big guy cocked his head.

The Matrix. He sounds like that Agent Smith guy, or pretty damn close. His body movements weren't far off, either. I imagined that face underneath the mask, studying us, calculating the odds of wasting Grabbe right there.

"Drop the gun," Grabbe said.

"Now why would I do that?"

"Drop the gun and take off the mask. I want to know who the hell I'm talking to."

"I will lower the gun, but I will not remove the mask," he laid the rifle on the ground.

Grabbe shook a little. "Why won't you show me who you are?" Grabbe asked, and he sounded like he was honestly pondering the question.

"Give it some thought, I'm sure you can piece it out. Now give me the boy." He motioned toward me.

Any time now.

My thought must have reached Daniel, because he fired just as the guy took one of those slow, awkward steps toward us.

He hollered, but he didn't scream. He went down on one knee, those emotionless goggles never leaving us.

Grabbe moved in a blur, seizing the guy by the throat. He made some motion that I couldn't make out, and the guy gasped, dropping to the ground.

"What the fuck?" I muttered.

"Now. Move us," he shouted.

I didn't have a whole lot of time to think about it, because I didn't relish the idea of getting shot up, but for a second I wondered if he didn't seem a bit younger.

I dove for him, grabbed hold, and pictured us behind one guy.

Bam. Grabbe did his thing. Dude shrieked and fell.

"Now," Grabbe said.

Bam. Rinse, repeat.

The last guy figured out what was happening and whirled, spraying the area. Either I was getting better or he sucked, because I had no problem figuring out his pattern and slipping the both of us through.

"You're making a mistake-" the guy said, but he didn't have time to get anything else out. Grabbe sliced his throat.

My stomach lurched, and I lost my breakfast.

When I looked up from my little puke session, Grabbe stood over his target, rubbing his hands together like the man had been the best meal that he had ever enjoyed.

I said, "what the hell?"

He turned around. Imagine my horror when I saw that I no longer stood with the same guy that I had started transporting around. He was still wearing the glasses, and he was still short. Those things were the same, but his hair had grown back, and he had dropped about twenty years.

"Jesus, what are you?" I asked.

"I told you I'm half-Aetelia. This is what we do." He glanced toward the building, where Daniel and Kristy still hid out. "It's all clear," he yelled.

"Jesus Christ," I said. "You're vampires?"

"Vampire's such an ugly word," he said, picking up the guy's assault rifle. "Were the legends based on us? I don't know. I'm not sucking any blood, though. It's disgusting. I need a little life force to keep going."

I ran a hand through my hair. "What the hell have we gotten into here?"

"I didn't exactly choose to be made this way, you know. This is a war, sweet thing. Be glad you're on the right side."

"I guess." He had a point - Delilah or not, the guy

seemed to be on our side. Deep down I knew I probably shouldn't stay with him or use my power like that again, but I didn't feel safe in this brave new world. The idea of running off on my own outweighed the question of whether I trusted my companions or not. What's that saying? Better the enemy you know? Something like that.

Kristy came running toward us, stepping over the bodies. "Holy shit, that was so bad-ass," she said and then came up short as she saw Grabbe's face. "Good God," she shouted, putting one hand to her chest.

"About that," I said, scratching my head and glancing at Daniel as he joined us.

"Sucked the life out of them, did you?" he said.

"Indeed I did."

"What do you mean?" Kristy said, taking an awkward step toward us.

"You'll see. All part of the plan."

"Aye, brilliant move." Daniel studied the body at our feet.

Kristy looked from the body to Daniel and then to Grabbe. "Sucked the life…?"

"Why don't you take off his mask?" Daniel said.

"Ew, I don't know if I can do that," Kristy said.

Grabbe spoke up. "You know, for just being some human magician, you seem to know a lot about this stuff."

Daniel knelt down over the body, pulling the goggles off the body, tearing at the mask. "Call me well-read."

I wanted to see what was under the mask, yet I didn't, if you catch my drift. The guys spoke like robots, so it wouldn't have completely surprised me if they were pure steel underneath the masks.

Daniel wrenched the mask off the guy. "There you go," he said.

"Eww, eww, eww," Kristy said, backing away with one hand up to block out the image. "The hell?"

I've always been a fan of horror. Movies, books, all of that good shit. I got into this old show called Tales from the Crypt at one point - loved the stories, if you're wondering. You know that guy, the Cryptkeeper? He looked like that. Skin shriveled up, eyes white, mouth turned up like he was screaming, but no scream would ever emerge.

Again I said, "Jesus Christ, Grabbe."

"You weren't lying about being a Nephil," Daniel said.

"That's the second time I've heard that. Nephil. What is that?" I asked.

Daniel nodded at Grabbe. "Him. Someone who's half-angel, half-human." He sighed and tossed the mask to the ground. "You should go get the boy."

Right. Tommy. I nodded. "I'll be right back."

"Wait," Kristy said, stepping over the body. "I want to go with you."

I glanced at the dead body. "Okay. I see that. Come on."

Daniel and Grabbe watched as we hugged. I pictured the pawn shop, and we were inside, that musty smell attacking our noses.

"Oh Lord, that's awful," Kristy said.

I opened my eyes. We had arrived in front of one of the glass display cases, filled with power tools.

"You're back," Tommy said from behind us.

He stood near the cash register, moving a long, sharp knife from one hand to the other.

"I told you we'd come back for you," I said.

"You must be Tommy," Kristy said, a little too excited. Good Lord, that girl...

Tommy nodded.

"I'm Kristy."

The kid nodded again. "Nice to meet you."

"Matty told me a little of your story. Do you miss your mom?"

The kid nodded yet again.

"Honey, I don't think-" I said.

"Probably never going to see her again," he said.

Kristy frowned, drawing the kid into a hug. He stiffened. I could tell it wasn't quite what he had been angling for, but his hormones probably took over, because next thing you know he was grabbing her and squishing his body up against her.

Polly, God bless her, didn't have any idea what the kid was doing, and it didn't seem right to disabuse her of the notion that the kid was being loving. So long as the kid didn't start to legit cop a feel. Then we might have some words.

She separated from him before it came to that, though. She pushed his bangs off his forehead and gave him a soft smile, the same one she'd give me to loosen me up on just about anything. "It's safe out there. They're all gone."

"That wasn't all of them," he said, looking from her to me. "You know that, right?"

"I figured as much. Big town."

"How fast can you get us out of here?"

"Pretty goddamn fast," I said.

"Language in front of the kid," Kristy said.

I held up my hands. "*Sorry.*"

"Did you get the leader?" Tommy asked.

"He was the first."

"A vampire sucked his life out of him," Kristy said, her eyes big.

He narrowed his own eyes. "There's no such thing as vampires."

"Close as you're going to get," I said. "We've got to go now."

He gave me the saddest gaze I've ever seen. "Can I have my gun?"

Now *there's* one to make you pause. 12-year old asking for his gun. What the hell are you going to do? It is technically his, and it's not exactly fair to let the kid go without some protection. "Sure."

"Matty," Kristy said.

"What? What am I going to do?" I handed the gun over.

The kid popped it open and checked the chamber. "You fired it."

Smart little bastard. "I didn't kill anybody with it. I promise."

Kid thought about this for a minute and then nodded. "That's good."

"You ready?" I asked.

"I guess," Tommy said.

"We're going to have to grab each other's arms, but don't get any ideas."

He touched his chest with one hand, widening his eyes. It was the first time I'd seen any emotion out of the kid, even if I knew he was lying.

"Don't give me that look. You know exactly what I'm talking about," I said.

"What?" Kristy asked, pushing a lock of hair from over

her ear.

"Don't worry about it. Now come on."

We locked arms like we were in a fairy tale, and I felt the kid pushing his side against me a little harder than he probably should. Challenging my authority. I decided to ignore it and closed my eyes, popping us out of the musty little shop and out onto the street.

Daniel and Grabbe were waiting for us. Daniel leaned on Grabbe's shoulder and both grinned like they'd shared the filthiest joke, and maybe, just maybe, it was about us.

"You two are very satisfied with yourselves," I said.

"That'd be a good description," Daniel replied.

I glanced down at the guy we'd unmasked, but they had taken the time to cover the guy up. Probably for the best. "What the hell are you two grinning at?" I asked.

"Your friend here and I had a…uh…coming to terms," Grabbe said. "We've sorted out our differences."

"You bullshitting me?" I looked Daniel in the eye.

"Now why would I do that?"

"You told him the truth, didn't you? You are one of those things."

He tried to cover his grin with his hand. "That's nonsense."

Grabbe nodded to the kid. "So you're Tommy, huh?"

"Uh huh."

"Have we met somewhere?" Grabbe said.

"I don't think so."

"Hmm. Well then. Pleased to meetcha. Name's Grabbe."

Tommy cocked his head. "What kind of a name is that?"

"It's the kind of name my parents gave me. Did you get to choose Thomas or Tommy or whatever your name is?"

"No, but *they* said I would get to choose a name when I got old enough."

"'They'. You mean these folks?" He motioned to the dead bodies.

Tommy nodded. "My name's Tommy," the kid said to Daniel.

Daniel nodded and waved. "Hello, Tommy. Where do you come from?"

"I'm from Las Vegas. Originally."

"That's quite a coincidence. That's where we're going," Grabbe said.

"She told me."

"Good." Grabbe looked around at the rest of us. "I reckon it's time to get going. We're not far from the Canal now."

The kid's eyes went wide. "We're going to the Canal?"

Grabbe hesitated. "You know something about the Canal?"

"No. I don't know. I was just told never to go there."

"Who told you that?"

Tommy nodded at the bodies littering the ground, jamming his hands in his pants pockets.

"They tell you why?"

He shook his head, but something about the way he did it? I didn't quite believe him.

If Grabbe knew he was lying, he didn't say anything about it. He stared at the kid and said, "Huh. Well, don't worry. You're with friends now."

"I don't think we should go there."

Grabbe arched an eyebrow. "Is that what you think? Why am I going to listen to you?"

"Because I've lived here for ages and we had people go there and disappear." The kid crossed his arms over his chest now, all defiant.

"I don't know anything about that, but I do know who's in charge here," Grabbe said.

"Oh really. Who would that be?" Daniel asked.

"I am. At least, I should be. I know this place better than any of you, even the squirt here."

Tommy didn't say anything to that, but kept staring at Grabbe, eyes narrowed.

Kristy stepped between the two of them. "Take it easy on the kid. He's been through a lot."

"We've *all* been through a lot, but there's worse out there. I'm taking us to the one chance we have to survive."

Tommy spoke up now. "You know so much, what's there?"

Now Grabbe *really* studied the kid. If he stared at him for an hour before, this one was a good long week of the old hairy eyeball. "You said you don't know anything about it, right?"

Tommy nodded, but he wouldn't meet Grabbe's eyes.

"It's a way out. We're going to go there and get the hell out of here."

"You're not a very good liar," the kid said.

Grabbe *and* Daniel laughed out loud. "Takes one to know one, kid," Grabbe said. "Why don't you worry your little head about surviving until we get there? If you don't want to come along, you can stay here." He motioned at the bodies. "Maybe some more of these folk will come back and take care of you. What do you think?"

"I cannot *believe* you are talking to him like this. This is bullshit. Yeah, you've been through a lot, I've been through a lot, but he's just a kid."

Daniel answered her. "He comes from this place. No offense, kid, but we can't trust anybody who's been here more than a day."

"What the hell do you mean?" she asked.

Grabbe nodded. "He's right. Place has a way of corrupting people. Has ever since the Flood."

"I'm not corrupt," Tommy insisted. "I just don't want to go there. What if *they* try to get us there?"

"Who do you mean, 'they'?"

"The people who killed your friend at the gas station."

"Oh. You know about them, do you?"

"Kid said it's a rival gang," I said.

"It is. They're trying to take over."

Grabbe knelt down. "I hear that. I appreciate your concern, if that's really it - I don't believe it is, but if it *is*, look at it this way. We wiped out your buddies here. Okay? Your little buddies were able to kill members of this rival gang, I'd assume?"

Tommy nodded.

"Right. Food chain. Little fish gets eaten by the bigger fish gets eaten by the biggest fish. Circle of life. We've got powers on our side you can't even comprehend. I *think* we're going to be okay."

"You should listen to the man, Tommy. You want to get back to Vegas?" I asked.

He nodded, but his frown had never been bigger. What else could he do, though? Run away? Even with that pistol of his he wouldn't last long, especially if his friends figured out that he had something to do with their comrades' deaths.

"We're going to have to go the way he leads us," I said.

"Fine, but I don't like it."

Grabbe spread his hands and smiled. "You don't have to like it, squirt. You've just got to follow along."

"I said fine."

"Good." He clapped his hands together. "Well, kids. Shall we go?"

Chapter 16

Love Amongst the Ruins

The path from the Pawn Shop to the Canal was only a few blocks, but my nerves were worn thin. I waited for someone to strike at us from every hiding place I saw.

The Marauders. Coming back for their own.

No. That didn't make any sense. It had to be more like what the kid had told us: the Marauders didn't dare go close to the Canal.

One thing I noticed as we got closer to the Canal: things became a little more…decayed. I wondered if we were slipping over into another Aethyr. We had left a part of town that looked abandoned, with crumbling facades and blown-out glass, but this part of town looked like someone just pounded it with bombs. There wasn't much left but rubble and the diseased-looking weeds that poked through that rubble.

"What is this place?" Kristy asked.

Daniel answered. "Sacred ground. At least, at one time. They should never have built here in the first place."

"Well beggars couldn't exactly be choosers with the Watchtowers breathing down their necks," Grabbe replied, slinging the shotgun over his shoulder.

"You saw how that ended, didn't you?"

"The evidence is all around now, but hindsight, buddy. Hindsight."

Tommy looked up at them. "This is where the ghosts live."

"Not a bad way to put it," Grabbe said.

Now that the kid mentioned it, I *could* see some stuff moving in the rubble. I could almost trick myself into believing that there were ghosts stirring around those buildings.

My head swam. "I think I might need to eat something," I said.

"Here," Kristy said, and dug through her pocket. She produced a mint chocolate thing in a silver wrapper.

I tore the wrapper off and downed the thing in three bites. "You're handy, you know that?" I said around a mouthful of chocolate.

She smiled. "That's why I'm here."

The light-headedness wasn't going away. In fact, it was getting stronger. I shook my head.

"Everything okay?" she asked.

"I'll be fine."

We went past the rubble of a weird old ripped-up building that claimed to be the Bakersfield Museum of Art, cutting through what used to be the Museum's parking lot, making a beeline for the row of trees at the back of the lot.

At last we were in Central Park. Talk about your oasis in the middle of the desert: it seemed like the only place in the city where anything green had survived. The grass underfoot was still springy, and the leaves in the trees overhead swayed with the slight breeze. The ground in front of us angled down into a stream of green goop that was once a creek, running through the center of the park.

A pile of more concrete rubble sat in the middle of the

goop, looking like it might once have passed over it but had surrendered to some great blow. It stuck out at awkward angles like the broken bones of the Earth.

"Shit," Grabbe muttered. "That used to be the bridge."

"Stay away from the bridge," Tommy said. "They always told me to stay away from the bridge."

Grabbe assessed the situation. "No choice now. We're going down there."

"In the water?" Kristy asked.

"No, I think we can make it over the rubble. We've got to make it to that wall," he said, and pointed to the retaining wall on the other side of the chasm.

I got this sinking feeling, like when I first met Delilah. The gully, or crevasse, or whatever you call it, looked like a tomb. The last thing I wanted to do was go down there. I could imagine some half-rotten hand reaching up out of the water.

No. Not just imagine. Something crept up out of the water, slow and menacing.

Calm down. Your nerves are just playing tricks on you.

When the rotting hand burst through the water, dripping black flesh and exposed bone, bigger than I'd expected, bigger than even me, I screamed.

It rose in the air for a second and then it came down on top of me.

I fell on my ass, putting my hands up over my face, trying to scream again, but the thing had me and I couldn't breathe, couldn't think. I choked, turning purple as it shook me.

I'm going to die, I'm going to die, I'm going to die….

No. I wouldn't die; the whole thing had been a

hallucination - right? It had to be. Kristy stood over me, shaking me, her breath ragged. "Oh my God, honey. Honey," she said, but it sounded far away.

"Uh. What." In slow motion, I looked from her terrified face down to my body. "I'm alive." I don't know if I was telling her or reminding myself.

Grabbe bent down in front of me. "You okay, kid?"

"I uh…" I scratched my head. Why couldn't I get past the fuzziness? "I…what did I do?"

Kristy leaned down and put her face against my head. "You started screaming and then you fell. We couldn't get you to snap out of it."

"How long have I been out?"

"Like, five minutes."

Grabbe's eyes narrowed. "Did you see something?"

"This…giant hand that came up out of the…" But the goop wasn't goop at all. It was just water. Dark, but not like the green slime I had seen. "…water," I said. "It grabbed hold of me and started shaking me. I thought I was dying."

"You sounded like you were dying," Kristy said.

"It's haunted," Tommy said.

Grabbe looked in his direction. "Will you shut up with the haunting thing already? It only seems to be haunted because…listen, squirt. I didn't want to tell you about this, but where we're going, there's this door. Right down there." He pointed at the wall. "Inside that door, there's a portal. That portal leads to another world. What you're seeing here is where the worlds are bleeding together."

I couldn't see the kid, but I guess he nodded.

Grabbe went on. "You got it. Good. Kid here is probably sensitive to it because she's something like a world-hopper."

He faced the rubble, hands behind his back. We followed him as he paced. "That's where we're going. That's how we're going to save ourselves. I can't tell you what's waiting on the other end, but I do know we won't be chased by your buddies. And you, my friend-"

The shot rang out. Kristy screamed and dropped to the ground beside me.

"Honey?" I shouted.

Chapter 17

Where the Sun Refused to Shine

Was Kristy actually lying on the ground next to me, rocking from side to side, clutching at her upper right arm and screaming while Tommy stood behind her, eyes wide, a wisp of smoke curling from the barrel of his pistol?

I got my answer when Grabbe did that blurring thing and got hold of the kid, lifting him in the air by his throat. The gun clattered to the ground as Grabbe roared, "you little shit. I knew not to trust you."

Daniel stepped over me to get to Kristy. I tried to reach out and help, but my head throbbed and swam.

"What the hell's going on - are you okay -" I said.

"I'm shot," was all she could manage, in that same screaming, keening voice.

"Give me a good reason not to kill you right now," Grabbe said.

"You can't go through the door," Tommy choked out.

Daniel tore at his shirt as he gazed at the bleeding hole in Kristy's arm. "Relax, relax," he cooed.

All I could hear was Grabbe and the kid. "You're a fucking Acolyte, aren't you?"

"Yes," Tommy said.

"They were all Acolytes, weren't they?"

I couldn't hear the kid's answer. Kristy screamed as Daniel wrapped her arm with his shirt.

The world snapped into focus.

"God, honey, I'm sorry," I said, reaching out for her. "Is she going to be okay?" I said to Daniel.

"Aye." He had already tied off where the blood had been gushing from her upper arm. "I've seen a whole lot worse and people have walked away. Don't worry, love."

"Thank you," she said, sobbing. "Don't let him kill the kid."

"I'm not going to kill the kid," Grabbe said, and tucked a gun into his belt. I guess at some point he had let the kid go and picked up his pistol.

"It was an accident," Tommy said. "I just wanted to stop you from going down there."

"She okay?" Grabbe asked.

"Aye, she'll be all right."

Now that the world was starting to make sense and my emotions were flooding into me, I had to restrain my own impulse to grab the kid and fling him into the water. I rose and faced him. "I saved you. She defended you."

"I know, I'm sorry-"

"This is why you don't give a 12-year old a gun. What a fuck-up," Grabbe said. The first drops of rain fell on us. "Ah, fantastic."

"We can complain about the weather once she's stabilized. Are you okay?" Daniel asked her.

"It hurts like hell," she moaned, but hey, it was a lot better than the screaming she had been doing.

"We've got to get her inside," Grabbe said. "There's some medication down there."

"How good is it after thousands of years?" Daniel asked.

"It's been used more recently than that."

I knelt down beside Daniel and Kristy, touching her face. "You want some painkillers, honey?"

Her eyes were glassy, but she nodded. *Shock kicking in.*

Daniel spoke to her in the gentlest voice I had ever heard him use. "Listen, we're going to have to get you down there. I'm not going to lie, every step is going to painful, but we've got to get you proper care."

She nodded again.

"Tommy, come here. Take her purse."

Oh hell no. "You're going to give *him* her purse?" I asked.

"I don't see any other option. You and I have to get her down here, and Grabbe has to protect us and open the door. Come on." He waved at the kid again.

Tommy rushed over.

"I'm watching you," Grabbe said.

The kid ignored him and knelt beside us, taking her purse from her left arm.

I lifted up her left arm and positioned myself under her armpit, nodding at Daniel. He slid over and whispered, "okay, this is going to be the worst part," he said. "I'm going to have to lift up your right arm."

She nodded. "Do it."

He lifted, and she screamed. It went right into my soul and tore at it, making my whole body tense.

Daniel counted to three, and we picked her up real fast so all the pain would pass through at once. This was both good and bad, because the pain must have been so intense she went limp in our arms: completely knocked out cold. My stomach hit the floor.

"It's a good thing. She won't have to suffer when we move her down there," Daniel said.

"I didn't say anything," I replied, but I wondered if the guy was able to read minds.

"There's a spot you can climb down with her over here," Grabbe said, pointing toward a piece of bridge that had embedded in the ground, making for a nice, natural step. We hauled her toward it as Grabbe nodded at the kid. "Squirt. You're with me."

The kid nodded and stepped in front of him. They fell in line behind us, with Grabbe conducting us from step to step.

No lie, it was one of the hardest things I've ever done, and that includes some of the stuff that came later. Between the rain and the incline, it took us at least an hour and a gallon of sweat to get her to the other side - and I'm talking about a bridge that was a bit less than a football field long, so you get some idea of what I'm talking about. When we got to the pieces of the bridge stuck out like pieces of bone, Grabbe would climb on top and we'd hand her up to him, with one of us scrambling over to lower her to the other side. My back screamed at me by the time we got to the bottom of the gorge.

We leaned Kristy against the concrete wall and looked at Grabbe, who stared at the wall, rubbing his chin.

"I don't see anything," Daniel said, one hand at the small of his back as he leaned backwards. His back made a sick, audible popping sound.

"It's there. Don't worry," Grabbe replied.

"Would you do us a kindness and open it, please? I'd prefer not to stay out here a moment longer," Daniel said.

"No problem. Watch this, squirt," he said to the kid, and learned forward. He made three sweeping motions with his right hand across the concrete wall and then made that hand a fist and blew air through it, onto the wall. A recessed circle appeared in the wall, like the concrete had just been some dust covering it.

"Wow," Tommy said.

"Hang on, let me see if I remember this."

"Now would be good," Daniel said.

"I'm trying. It's been awhile." He put his hands to his forehead, and then reached out. He put his index finger and his middle finger at the top of the circle and his thumb at the bottom, then made one clockwise motion. He pulled away, then put the same configuration up against it again and squeezed twice, pulling his fingers together at the center of the circle. To close it off, he tucked his thumb in against his palm and made one long sweeping motion from the bottom to the top of the circle with his four fingers.

Something clicked inside the wall, and the outline of a door appeared in the concrete, just like the circle had appeared.

"That's amazing," I said.

"Wow," Tommy said under his breath.

Grabbe gave him a smug smile. "You think that's amazing, you haven't seen anything yet."

"Could you *please* just get us inside?" Daniel said.

"Demanding, aren't we?"

"We're all going to die," Tommy said, staring at the wall.

Grabbe rolled his eyes. "We're not going to die. Enough with the Acolyte shit, please?"

"We can have a philosophical debate later, now open the goddamn door," Daniel said.

"Fine." Grabbe reached out with his right hand, pressing his palm against the door. He pushed three times, and the door popped open with a *whoosh* of sterilized air - the air you smell in a hospital. Along with the air came something I didn't expect - the sound of heavy machinery. Not what I expected from a place that was supposed to be some primordial portal.

"Welcome to the Southwest Corridor," Grabbe said. "Enjoy your stay."

Chapter 18

Under Pressure

"Why don't you go in first?" Daniel said.

Grabbe shrugged. "Fair enough." He pushed the door open and stepped inside, disappearing into the darkness. "Hang on, let me get some light going on in here," he said from inside, his voice echoing and mixing with the machines from down below.

Daniel tapped his foot while he waited, glancing at Kristy and me. I had stayed by her side when we leaned her against the wall, keeping her propped up as best as I could. "How's the bleeding?"

I glanced across her body, at her right arm. A slow trickle streamed into the cloth he'd used to tie the wound off, but it looked a lot better. "She's going to live, I think."

"Aye, if infection doesn't get her, anyway."

"Here we go," Grabbe said, and the whole place lit up with a weird orange glow unlike any light I'd seen before. Whoever built the place wrapped neon tubes around a spiral staircase that led down into the dark.

Grabbe appeared in the doorway. "Neat, huh?"

"Yeah," Tommy agreed, clapping his hands.

"Just swell," Daniel replied, and helped me take Kristy off of the wall, which was a tricky maneuver, since we had to move her sideways down the protruding block that we were standing on. Tommy guided us down the block, warning us if we were getting close to the edge.

We got her inside after a lot more struggling, pain, and cussing. Still, I thought it was better that I be the one hurting than her.

The machinery was a lot louder inside the door, its vibrations pounding the concrete beneath our feet.

"What the hell is that sound?" I asked.

Grabbe hustled the kid inside and closed the door. "It's the machines that keep this place running. Geo-thermal power."

"That's pretty ballsy in California."

"You think of a better place to get that kind of energy?"

Kristy stirred in our arms, murmuring.

"Easy, baby," I whispered. She wasn't going to wake up yet, but she wasn't far away from it, either. I looked at Daniel. "Got to get going."

"I assume we're going down?" he said, and we carried her toward the stairs.

This isn't going to be much more fun than crossing the bridge, but at least it can't be worse.

Grabbe nodded. "Hold up, let us get in front of you in case something happens."

"Something like what?"

Grabbe collared Tommy and they both slid by us. "I don't know, cave-in, collapse? It shouldn't happen, but you never know. Why, you worried?"

That must have been enough for Daniel because he started moving us again. "No, nothing. Don't worry about it."

"Come on, you can tell Uncle Grabbe." He kept moving us downward, slowing their pace to match us as we lowered her down one step at a time.

Daniel grunted. "I said *nothing*. Just had a…feeling."

"What sort of feeling?" I asked.

"That something's not right down here."

"Yet you journey into the mouth of the beast, my friend," Grabbe said. "That takes some balls."

"Ever consider that it might be the fact that a good friend would die without my help? Not everything is about rational self-interest, you know."

Now there was a little surprise. It had become clearer that Daniel cared about Kristy in some capacity, but to hear him say it out loud like that was a weird one after the fights they'd had in our former life. Tragedy and stress bring people together.

Grabbe chuckled. "Don't I know it, but sometimes irrational self-interest is just as good."

"What are you implying?"

Grabbe held up his hands, but he didn't have to say. Did Daniel feel a little more for Kristy than I thought? I glanced at him over her head, and his face had darkened. Even though I knew she'd never go for the guy, I couldn't help but feel a pang of panic.

"You listening, kid?" Grabbe asked.

It took me a second to figure out he was talking to me. "What?"

"I have to tell you something about this place. The electromagnetic currents are…a little different. You're not going to be able to do your little jumping-around thing. Well, you *could*, but it wouldn't be a good idea."

Now *I* felt like something wasn't right here. It went well with the queasiness that their exchange had fostered. "Why not?"

"Whatever it was you saw outside might give you a good hint. I don't think you're going crazy…I mean hell, who knows, you've been through a lot, so it's possible, but everything's haywire here. It's complicated, but if you try to jump, you might end up somewhere you're not looking to go."

"Like?"

Daniel huffed. "Remember the monsters? The ones between the worlds?"

"Yeah."

"You might end up meeting those. That enough of a reminder?"

"Yeah. Noted. No jumping around."

"We're here," Grabbe said, and stepped down off the last step.

The orange light was brighter at the bottom of the pit. The tubes wrapped around a small foyer entrance and joined three other orange neon tubes in a rainbow across the wall that faced the stairs.

Hell, what a wall it was. The floor was covered by porcelain tiles, and the concrete walls of the passage butted against a bright, polished metal exterior. Maybe it was brass?

The thing that caught my eye - that got my imagination going like nothing else down here - was a giant, painted crimson bird in the center of the wall, wings spread as it cried to the imaginary metal heavens.

"Sick," I said. "Who painted that?"

"You like it, huh?" Grabbe said, and he walked toward it, craning his head toward the top. "I'm not sure, honestly. I only helped design the bunker system, I wasn't involved in building it."

"System? There are more of these?"

"All over the place." He smiled. "Even in your Aethyr, though most of them got wiped out during the Flood." He looked at the painting. "Any place that people say is haunted...most likely has one of these babies."

"It's all lovely, but can we get her inside?" Daniel said.

"Absolutely." He touched the painting, tracing the bottom of the bird's neck across the left wing. He paused and then followed its jagged edges to the bottom. He reached over and repeated that on the right neck and wing before he knocked again on the wall.

Something hissed, and a big oval popped open to the right of the bird, swinging inward. Grabbe pushed it and held it there as we climbed through, taking turns getting Kristy through.

We were in a small hallway that went left and right without any doors or rooms to distinguish them, but after seeing Grabbe's tricks, I wouldn't have been surprised if I looked at twenty doorways without knowing it. The floor was made of the same tiles from outside, white with black grout, gleaming like someone had scrubbed them ten minutes before we arrived. The walls were solid gray, but who could figure out that material? They looked solid, sterile, and forbidding.

I hoped we could get Kristy taken care of and get the hell out, because every minute I spent in there was another minute I'd feel like my brain was turning to mush.

Grabbe cleared his throat. "Here we are, kiddies. That was-"

A gruff voice cut him off. "Identify yourselves or face eradication," it said.

I wondered how long it would take for our blood to no

longer soil that hallway, if the efficient machines would remove any sign of our existence.

A squat thing, a steam-punk version of a canister vacuum cleaner - or maybe R2D2 - waited for us. It had a little round brass body with wheels on the bottom and a small, bulbous silver top…or head…sticking off of it. He also had tiny appendages sticking off his body that looked like brass-plated drills.

A goddamn robot?

"Vincent?" Grabbe asked. It was the greeting of a long-lost friend.

He stepped around the thing.

Two red lenses on the silver head studied him, then whipped over to us. "Incorrect. I am Jazshael."

"Right, Jazshael. That makes you the Master designation, correct?"

"Correct. How do you know this?"

Grabbe knelt in front of the thing. "Jazshael. Buddy. You telling me I'm not somewhere in there?"

The thing was quiet for a minute, and I wondered if it was trying to decide the best way to fry Grabbe. At last it moved again and said, "Certainly, Grabbe. Our databanks indicate that you have not visited in 792,345 days. Why did you not write?"

Robot humor. I shivered.

"It's been a long few millennium, what can I say?"

I don't know if the robot needed a minute to process this or was laughing on the inside. "What can I do for you?"

Grabbe smiled. "That's more like it, buddy. We need the medical wing opened."

"Check," the robot said in that gruff little voice. Its head whirred and it stared right at us. "Who are these…people? Identification checks fail."

"They're my friends. We're here to help our friend out and then use the Portal."

"Jazshael," Daniel said, "I suspect I've met your creator."

Jazshael paused, its cold, soulless eyes staring right into him. "Are you a traveler of the Aethyrs?"

"Something like that, yes. We've come a long way to be here, and would appreciate your help."

The robot sat there for a second, and then wheeled back in the direction in which it must have come.

We followed as fast as we could, even though the little guy was hauling ass. Not bad for being, what, two thousand years old?

"Friendly little guy, isn't he?" I said.

"I guess. These bunkers didn't have a lot of comings and goings - just the big wigs and some supplies once the first human colonies had come through. That was well before they built that little guy, so they didn't have to build for hospitality. All they're made to do is maintain the place while the masters are away, so they didn't exactly pay attention to the social graces, if you catch my meaning."

"I can't believe you guys *had* robots. Why didn't they do the building, instead of humans?"

"Not feasible," Daniel answered. "These things were hard to build, and you see how primitive they are. And really, Grabbe? Jazshael?"

"What about it?"

"He was a madman. They chose *him* to build the androids?"

"No accounting for taste."

"How do you know about him?" I asked. "You said you met the guy?"

"Aye, in my studies. Magick is *about* meeting the ethereal."

The robot pulled us up to a stop. "One moment, please." It rolled up to the wall and one of those drill-arms whipped out. He…she…it…aimed the end of the arm at the spot where the tiles and the top of the wall met up. The thing at the end of its arm whirred and disappeared into the wall.

Something clicked, and that section of the wall just…rolled up. The layers of tiles dropped down into some hidden crevice at the base of the wall, and the top of the wall, whatever the hell it was made of, rolled up like a window shade.

Behind this cheap facade was a little room that had been taken right out of a modern hospital: more tiles covering the interior walls, and a bank of computer equipment against the far side that hooked into machines that circled an elevated hospital bed.

"Boy you weren't bullshitting," I said.

Grabbe nodded and walked ahead of us, waving at the bed. "We had our share of…shall we say mishaps down here. Come on." He patted the bed.

We lowered her on to the bed, and she murmured again. Daniel looked to Grabbe. "She's about to wake up. Quickly now, where's your morphine?"

"Right, morphine, let me see…" He dug through the cabinets and finally came up with a little glass bottle and syringe. "Careful, potent stuff."

"I've used it before." He plunged the needle into the top of the bottle. "I'm going to need a tray, some bandages, forceps, tape, and *lots* of rubbing alcohol. Oh, and a local anesthetic if you have one, something like lidocaine."

Grabbe snapped to work. "Come here and help me, squirt," he said to Tommy, and the kid practically jumped across the room to help him. Give him credit, he might have been a little shit-bird and I still wanted to beat the hell out of him, but at least he was trying to make up for what he did.

I held Kristy's hand as Daniel searched for a vein in her arm. "Jesus, Daniel, I take it you've done this before."

He nodded and pressed the plunger down, shooting the morphine into her. "I've been in wars."

"Wars? As in plural, wars?"

He got lucky and didn't have to answer; Kristy gasped, and her eyes fluttered.

"We need to hurry," he said, motioning to the other two, "she's waking up."

Too late for that chief, I thought as her eyes opened, settling on me. They were fuzzy, but she was present and accounted for, at least for the moment. "Honey? Where are we?" she asked, and if her eyes were fuzzy, her voice was practically coated in felt.

"Long story, baby. We're trying to get that bullet out of you."

"I'm alive?"

I laughed. "We're all alive. You're going to be fine."

"Hurts like a bitch."

Daniel spoke up. "The pain should subside soon. I gave you some morphine, and we've got some local anesthetic coming soon…I hope?" He raised his eyebrow at Tommy, who looked at Grabbe. Grabbe gave them the thumbs-up and put another bottle and syringe on the tray, handing it to the kid.

"Good as gold," Grabbe said.

"Is Tommy okay? You didn't hurt him, did you?" Kristy asked me, tightening her grip on my hand.

"Would I?" I said.

She shook her head.

Daniel took the syringe and bottle from the tray. "Rest yourself now. We're going to start here in a minute. Just need to get the local into you."

Kristy nodded and closed her eyes. Daniel rubbed the skin below the hole in her arm, and then jabbed the needle into her flesh. She winced when it went in, but I think the morphine was already starting to kick in, because when her eyes opened she stared into the distance, at nothing in particular.

It took Daniel about ten minutes to dig the bullet out of her arm with the forceps. Tommy stood by as his faithful assistant, and even Grabbe got into the act at one point, mopping the sweat from Daniel's brow. The guy was pretty damned efficient and yet sensitive to whatever was left of her anxiety, talking her through the procedure.

I watched him work, wondering again what the hell he might be. Was he an angel? A human? Or something else entirely? What wars could he possibly have fought in, and how the hell did he end up working at a Circle K in the middle of Buttfuck, California?

When he finished, he wrapped the wound in gauze and bandages, taping it up. That finished, he let the piece of cloth tied around her arm go. He gave a nervous chuckle, then leaned against the wall, staring at the ceiling.

"Lords above, I could use a smoke," he said.

Grabbe whistled. "I bet. Impressive work, my friend." He clapped him on the shoulder.

Kristy stirred from her most recent nod. "Is it over?"

"Yeah, honey. You're right as rain. Just going to need some time to heal," I said.

"Mmm. Good. Thanks, Daniel. Thanks, honey," she said, and went on the nod again. *Good. Give her some time to get better.*

Tommy looked at me for the first time since what had happened topside, and whatever hatred I had left for the kid melted away. Christ, he was a scared little kid in a living Hell, no matter what lies he might have told, and his face showed that from the dirt smearing it to the tear marks that cut a trail through that dirt. "I'm sorry. I didn't mean to hurt her."

I waved a hand. "Don't worry about it. She's going to be okay. Just don't do it again."

Grabbe rubbed his hands together. "We make a good team after all. What say we stay here overnight, then make a decision on the next move in the morning?"

"I'm in favor, but I thought we were going through the portal?" I asked.

"Nothing says we have to go through right away. We could use a nice meal not consisting of high-sodium, high-fat crap, and then we can make a more detailed plan-"

Jazshael's gruff voice spoke up from behind us, and I realized I hadn't even seen the robot around since we'd begun surgery on Kristy, maybe even before that. Possibly when it opened the wall? "Excuse me, but might I make a suggestion."

Grabbe raised an eyebrow. "We're open, you know the place like the back of your hand."

"The Masters-in-residence have requested the honor of

your presence, and I would suggest that you do so. It would be in your...*best interest.*"

Chapter 19

We Would Be Honored

The old cliché about hearing a pin drop came to mind. Was the robot telling us that someone had been in the bunker when we arrived? How long had they been there?

Grabbe spoke. "Masters-in-residence…you mean, there are Watchers here?"

"That is correct. They neglected to inform me that you would arrive, but it would seem they were expecting you."

"Who the hell would be expecting us?" I asked.

Grabbe shook his head, his eyes wide. "You have any names there, Jazshael old buddy?" he asked.

"I am afraid I am not cleared to share that information. They would prefer to speak to you in person."

Grabbe picked up his shotgun. "Lovely." He looked at me and Daniel and brandished the weapon. "I suggest you guys do the same."

"Don't have to tell me twice," Daniel said and plucked the weapon from his waistband.

"We're going to leave her here," Grabbe said, and put a hand on Tommy's shoulder. "And him. He's going to watch over her, make sure you aren't pulling a fast one on us."

"I am not familiar with what a 'fast one' is, but that is acceptable."

Grabbe glanced at me. It wasn't much, but it meant a lot to me that he cared what I thought about the plan. I nodded.

What the hell else could we do? I didn't like the idea of leaving the kid behind with Kristy, but it seemed damned likely that whoever was in charge would at least want to see the three most capable adults, and I'd rather not piss these folks off.

"Take care of her, you hear?" he said to Tommy.

"Don't worry. No one's going to get her," he said.

"If you say so. We're ready," Grabbe said, and exhaled.

"Please, follow me." He went left and took us down the hallway.

Daniel whispered to Grabbe. "You said you don't know who's here. Is that true?"

Grabbe's voice was tense. "Technically. I have suspicions, though."

"Please, no talking," Jazshael said.

He led us past the entrance where we'd first piled in, to the farthest, darkest corner of the orange-lit nightmare.

"One moment, please." He rolled toward the wall and extended his arms again, doing that drill thing.

The wall rolled open on a brightly-lit white space. Funny thing, when I was 15 I had gotten fascinated with that movie 2001 after seeing it on Showtime. I bought the DVD and watched it over and over again and even read the book a few times - it was the whole idea of pushing someone into a new evolutionary niche that got a hold of me. I might not seem like that kind of girl, but I dig that stuff.

The reason I tell you that is because the room that the little robot opened up looked like someone took the concept art from the movie and turned it into a simple little conference room. The lights overhead were bright white flood lamps, washing down on a white oval-shaped table, white oval-shaped chairs, and white padded walls.

I think white sums the whole thing up. Even its occupants, who made me jump about ten feet in the air.

Imagine how I felt when I saw Delilah standing at the other end of the table. Rage? Check. Fear? Check. A little bit of nausea? Yep, spot on.

Only it wasn't quite Delilah standing there, arms crossed over her quite-ample chest, looking smug as hell. Like Grabbe, she'd gotten a hell of a lot younger, her mean features moving backwards in time, making her into more of a cold, hard-assed beauty, the kind of chick who always got what she wanted, no matter how vile or self-centered it might be.

Of course my eyes went to her first, but then I noticed the guy standing next to her, and what a piece of work he was. He was NBA player tall, and appeared to be somewhere in his mid-30s, though who could tell for sure with his almost-feminine features under his thick, spiked blond hair. You think he was worried about looking like a chick? Hell no. He wore black eyeliner and lipstick, looking like a cross between David Bowie and that guy from the Cure. Any other setting, and I probably would have cheered the guy on for flying his freak flag high.

Grabbe gasped and raised his shotgun to fire, but before he could even get to a set position, the blond guy made a slashing motion with his right hand. The air blurred, and the weapon flew out of Grabbe's hand and onto the table. It skittered across by itself, stopping right in front of the guy.

He wagged his finger. "So disappointing, son. We had hoped for civil conversation."

Son? "This your dad?" I asked Grabbe. I had to admit, I didn't see the family resemblance.

"Yeah."

"Well we can't have a civil conversation with all those weapons hanging about. Please, put them on the table now, or I might have to do something...rash. I'd really prefer not to."

I shared a glance with Daniel. We produced our handguns and slid them across the table.

He clapped his hands and smiled. "Good. I knew you were good people."

Grabbe sighed, and put up his hands. "So this is how it ends, huh? You got me dead to rights. Go on, finish it."

Blondie put his hand to his chest. "*I'm* not the one who chases around family members trying to kill them off in the name of...what is it this week? Vengeance? Acceptance?"

"You know. It's not family members. Just you."

"Mmm hmm. How rude of you not to introduce me, by the way." He bowed. "Lady, gentleman, the name is Azazel." He straightened up.

"Azazel, as in...?" I said.

"Get your shock out of the way. The demon. The Betrayer. I think my favorite may be The Goat." He chuckled. "Choose whatever slander you prefer, but please, let us not rehash the morbid history of lies associated with my name. Look in your Bible..."

"It's not *my* Bible," I said.

He nodded. "Noted. Still, *were* one to look, in theory, one would see that I am *only* referred to as the Scapegoat. Fitting, given the lies leveled against me and my people, would you not say? They would have you believe I'm a devil, even after *they* were the ones who chose us for our mission."

Delilah cleared her throat. "Dear, you're getting ahead of yourself."

"So I am. Where *are* my manners? Please, have a seat."

"I think we're good," Grabbe replied.

"Take your *fucking* seat, I say," Azazel said, and made that motion again. The chairs at the table shot out.

We took our seats, one by one.

I looked at Delilah. "Where do you fit into this?"

"She's his goon," Grabbe said.

"Please, darling, do let me speak for myself, will you?" She hopped up on the table, sat cross-legged, and picked up the shotgun. "Goon is such a…*wrong* word for what I do."

Azazel put his hand on her shoulder and smiled. "Think of her as a business partner."

"One you twisted and corrupted," Grabbe said.

Azazel pursed his lips. "Are we still angry that I stole your woman?"

Delilah cackled. "As if I ever belonged to anyone."

"Precisely," Azazel purred - I swear, it was a purr - and strolled to the far wall, reclining against it. "I'm happy to see you though, son." He turned those blue eyes on me, shaking me right down to my feet. "And you, Chosen One."

"What about me?" I asked, my brain floating, disconnected from my surroundings. Had he used some sort of power on me?

He raised an eyebrow. "You have done what needed to be done, no matter the cost. I am *very* proud of you, my girl."

Grabbe cleared his throat. "Don't try to charm her. She's not yours."

"She's not yours either," Delilah said, pointing the shotgun in his direction.

"Now, now, dear. No need for temper. We have a common goal."

"We do?" Daniel asked.

Azazel pursed his lips. "Well. Maybe not *you*, but we'll talk about that soon."

"I want to kill you," Grabbe said. "I don't see how that's a goal in common."

"Of course it's not, but you also wish to reach the Engine, do you not? I just assumed, with your talk of Vegas and using the portal, that it was your goal. Am I incorrect, son? Please tell me if I am."

Grabbe didn't say anything.

"There's no need for us to fight. We can work together."

Delilah put one knee up, resting a hand on it. "I think he might have had a different reason for going, love."

"Is that true, Grabbe? What *did* you have in mind?"

"You know," Grabbe said, narrowing his eyes.

Azazel raised his hand toward his son, then looked at me. "You see what I have to put up with? From my own son, no less. It *hurts*," he said, and pouted.

Daniel spoke up. "Stop playing your games. If you have something in mind, say it. Not all of us are scared by-"

"Do shut up," Azazel said, and in one motion crossed the room, picking up one of the handguns, and firing. A bullet hole appeared in Daniel's head and he made this awful gurgling sound before he slumped down in his chair.

"Sweet Jesus," I moaned.

"Jesus indeed!" Azazel clapped his hands. "I knew there was a reason I liked you, lass. Indeed. Hard to separate one's feelings once you become so entwined," he said, and put his hands on his lap. "Did you know that Cyril of Alexandria, one of the best and brightest thinkers of Christianity, referred to me as a forebear of humanity's beloved Christ?"

"I...what?" I asked.

"Psychopath," Grabbe hissed.

"Do you see how they treat me? The Aetelia chose the Church's position and guided humanity toward Origen, who called me *Satan*, of all things. Father of Lies." He shook his head. "Now that is true evil, but a discussion for another time."

"At least he told the truth about what he wanted."

Azazel laughed. "Indeed, he did, didn't he? I suppose you would find that admirable, but how honest were your friends, hmm? All that they've said of us is either myth or outright lies, even you know that, as deluded as you may be."

"Is it, though? You corrupted humanity..."

He waved a hand. "Please, as if humanity were not capable of its own corruption. You were there. We dared to teach humans the means to seize their own destiny?"

"They weren't ready."

"You decide this retroactively. I see they've poisoned you with their nonsense, and that attitude is exactly why *we* are the ones who should be working with humanity, not the Aetelia."

"You go on thinking that, Pops."

Azazel slammed his fist down on the table. "I told you not to call me that."

Grabbe looked to Delilah. "You were free. You could've gotten your old job if you kept working at it. Why did you come back?"

"Isn't it clear? You were wrong. Here we are in the face of the Reckoning itself and you still deny what's in front of you. She is the Chosen One. He is returning. It's plainly obvious." She sighed. "Of course, reality was never your strong suit."

"At least one, would think it would be obvious, given that you travel with a member of the Watchtowers," Azazel said, sweeping his hand at Daniel's dead body. "Why do you suppose he was present in the first place? Hmm?"

I hated to interrupt their little soap opera, but I needed answers of my own. "So, wait. Daniel *was* an Aetelia?"

Grabbe put his hands to his temples, rubbing. "'Course he was. You knew that, deep down. He even admitted it after you went into the shop to get your little buddy. He was sent to watch over you because they thought all this was going to be happening soon."

"Seems they were right for once," Delilah said.

I tried to wrap my head around this new information. Grabbe was right, deep down I had known it was true, ever since he first made the accusation, but knowing on that level and *knowing* were two separate things entirely. I had done bong hits with an angel. I had loaned some of my music to an angel. "Wow," was about all I could come up with.

"You see now, don't you?" Azazel said.

I shook my head. I probably should have felt betrayed. It's a hell of a thing to find out a good friend lied to you through your whole friendship, but I had a hard time mustering anything but sympathy for the corpse in the chair next to me. "He told me you want to build your own Watchtower, to challenge the other Aetelia. You wanted...*want*...to use humanity."

Delilah and Azazel lost it. You'd have thought I told them the oldest in-joke they'd ever shared. Only I wasn't in on it.

When they'd finished snorting and whooping, Azazel

wiped his eyes. "That is absurd, but one hell of a good laugh. Why do you think we would we do such a thing when we have plenty of our own power?"

"But you *did* build the Engine." It wasn't a question.

He spread his hands. "We wish to build our own Watchtower, that much is true, and we built the Engine to achieve that goal. As for challenging the Aetelia? Utter nonsense. We simply wish to share in the glory of creation with humanity."

Grabbe snorted. "Why don't you try selling your lies to somebody who doesn't know any better? We both know why you used humanity to build it."

"Son, you really are getting tiresome. I am trying to carry on a dialogue with your friend here, and if you wish to live to see the Engine again, to carry out what pitiful hope you have of stopping us, it would best serve you to keep your mouth shut. Understood?"

I could tell Grabbe itched to shout something back, but he just seized the arms of his chair and nodded.

"Good. You have questions. It is only natural."

I exhaled, a heavy breath that was trying to push out my fear and disgust but didn't quite work. "Yeah. What's the Reckoning?"

"It's just a fairy tale," Grabbe mumbled.

"You would like to believe that, wouldn't you?" Delilah said. "It would make all of this so much easier."

Azazel spoke up. "The Reckoning is a...force. The Black Cross spoke to a Watcher. Samyaza, my boss. Maybe you'll meet him sometime. I think you'd like him."

"If you like snakes," Grabbe said.

Azazel shot him a glance. "I told you to shut up. So

negative. How could this be my son in front of me?"

"You know it's the truth."

"Spend ten millennia imprisoned and see how well you hold up. Not half as well, I would suspect." He chuckled.

"Ten…" The surprises kept coming. "But that's before…"

"Right around the end of the last ice age?"

"You saw an ice age?" I said.

He spread his hands. "Guilty as charged."

"I can't even wrap my head around how long that is."

"So you see, and my people are innocent. Do you understand our fury now? Do you understand why Samyaza had such hope when the Black Cross told him that the Aetelia would pay for their crimes?"

"Who is supposed to be paying them back? You?"

He shook his head. "We are but instruments. Instruments of the Lost Aetelia."

"Who is that?"

"One is not supposed to address the Lost Aetelia by name. Naturally."

"Natch, but let's assume I'm not part of your definition of nature here. Why do we not want to refer to him by name?" I asked.

"The Lost Aetelia is the one who created…everything."

"Everything as in…"

"*Everything.* The Multiverse."

"So he's God." What a mind-fuck that would be, if they actually believed they served God after plugging a bullet in an angel's head. Of course, didn't humans believe the same shit?

"No, not exactly."

"So he made everything, but he's not God?"

"Did I say 'he'? I don't recall saying 'he'. Did I?" He gazed at Delilah.

"Ooh, sorry, no."

"So God's a she," I said.

"Neither and both. The Lost Aetelia is…ah…beyond such simple categories."

Grabbe cleared his throat. "Paraoan is their boogeyman."

Azazel lifted the pistol again, waving it around like he was in a cheesy mafia movie. "Son. I am very disappointed in you. Am I going to have to end your life now, when we're on the verge of a brilliant reunion?

"Only way we're going to be reunited is at the bottom of the abyss."

"That can be arranged. You first, of course."

Delilah laughed and Grabbe shot her a look.

Azazel cleared his throat. "Now, then. Jazshael."

The robot appeared at the door. "Yes, sir?"

"Please check on our other guests. We wouldn't want them to get lonely."

"What the hell are you planning?" I said.

"Nothing. I just wanted to check on your…*lover*." And the way he said lover? There was something of a threat buried in there.

"I swear to God if you do anything to her, I'll-"

"You'll do what?" He put his hands on his hips. "You are hardly in a negotiating position."

"See, that's where you're wrong. I figure I'm the chip here, aren't I? I'm the thing that's being negotiated around. Yeah, you're talking to me, you're telling me history, but you're really negotiating with your dear son here. So I figure all I have to do is refuse to go with you, and that'll wreck all your plans, won't it? I'm supposed to be the key to this Engine, right?"

He rubbed his chin. I could tell he was irritated, but no way he'd let it crack that cool surface. "Yes. Well. The problem is that we have one additional chip on the table, don't we? One between you and I alone."

I knew what he meant. Kristy. The bastard.

Chapter 20

See What's on the Slab

Jazshael appeared at the door, pushing Kristy ahead of him. I tell you, my poor baby didn't seem very good for her whole ordeal - pale, her eyes not much more than slits.

"What's going on? Ms. D?" she asked, her voice thick with sleep.

"Yes, dear, it's me."

"You look so young…"

I ran to her, putting one hand on her arm and drawing her close, instinctively trying to protect her from every last asshole in that room. "Are you okay?"

She nodded. "I think so. What-"

Jazshael moved toward us, stubby drill arms raised.

"Back off," I said, and the robot rolled back a bit. "Did he touch you?" I asked Kristy.

"No, he just told me you wanted to see me."

"Jazshael, how rude of you to lie," Azazel said, but he laughed just the same. "You shouldn't lie to our guests."

"I said what I felt was necessary, sir."

"Hmm. Perhaps, but lying is just not very nice."

The robot rolled closer again, and I kicked out with one foot. "Why don't you get away from us?"

"Children, no fighting," Azazel said.

"Who are you?" Kristy asked.

Azazel introduced himself. "Please, won't you come in?

Take a seat? How *is* your arm?"

"It's fine," she said.

I tried to lead her past Daniel's body to the seat next to mine, but she froze, eyes turning into saucers as she stared. "Matty-"

"Oh, dear, we had a disagreement. Ever so sorry you had to see that. Jazshael, would you please clean up our mess?"

I hauled Kristy ahead to keep us away from the robot. It's drill arms dug into the arms of the chair and tipped it up, rolling backwards. Daniel's body lolled in the seat, but stayed upright as the tin can pulled him out of the room.

"What's going on, honey?" Kristy asked as I helped her into the chair.

"This is Grabbe's old man," I said.

"It is?"

Grabbe sighed. "I know, I know. You don't see the resemblance."

Azazel chuckled. "He received his mother's genes. Jazshael! Where is the boy? I believe I did tell you to summon our *guests*."

"I could not locate him, sir."

"What?"

"He seems to have left."

"Where could he have gone? The walls are sealed."

"I haven't a clue, sir."

Azazel rolled his eyes. "Were you not required to maintain this station, I would destroy you now. The idea is very tempting."

"Understood, sir."

Grabbe laughed. "Can't control everything, can you? Just like I always told you."

Azazel waved his hand. "The boy is of little consequence right now. Let him run away. There's nothing he can do here, and not much left for us, as well. We must leave now."

"Wait a second," I said, holding up one hand. "You said I got as many questions as I wanted."

"So I did. What else would you care to know? Please remember that we have a schedule to keep. The Reckoning isn't exactly going to usher itself in now, is it?"

"That's your end game? That's where we're going?"

"As if it were in doubt. You already know what's coming. It's all over your news. All we do now is attempt to assure ourselves - and humanity - of a proper place in the cosmos following those events. That is the essence of the Reckoning itself. It's not our reckoning, but a reckoning for those who would hold us back."

"That's still a long ways off - and besides, what the hell am I even supposed to do with this Engine? You say I'm some sort of chosen one. What am I supposed to do?"

He raised an eyebrow. "I believe it will come clear once you see the machinery."

"That's not answering my question."

He glanced at Delilah, who shrugged. He cleared his throat. "I would rather not discuss that in front of my idiot son."

Grabbe's face got dark. "What, I help you build the thing and you're trying to claim there are secrets I don't understand?"

"My boy, there are so many things about this project that are above your head. You have no idea. You and the girl operate on roughly the same level now. It's a shame. Think about where you could be were you on our side. I can't wait to see the look on your face when your aspirations and your pride come crashing down around you. It will be *glorious*." He picked up a pistol and nodded at Delilah, who hopped off the table, pointing the shotgun at us.

I knew she wasn't going to use that thing on me, but all bets were off when it came to Kristy and Grabbe. Enough that I didn't dare to do anything…yet, anyway.

"Come on. Enough. Let's get going," she said.

"You're gracious hosts, you know that?" I said, giving him the evilest eye I could muster.

Azazel smiled. "I do try my best. Now move."

So we got up and headed out into the hallway. The place was still dead quiet, except for the throbbing of the machinery. Sure enough, no sign of Tommy. Had the kid opened up the walls somehow and hidden in there, or did he turn tail and run out the front door?

That had to be the answer. He just went out the front door, right? No, the robot would have seen him. Whichever, I hoped the kid would be safe.

"Jazshael, open the laboratory," Azazel said.

The robot clicked and whirred, sounding like what it was: an old machine that was running down. "I require the authorization code, sir."

"Just open the thing. I've given you the code twice already."

"Very well, sir. " Jazshael did his little trick with his arms, and the wall rolled away, revealing a second, hidden wall made of a black, igneous rock, the kind we used to pass around in Earth Science class.

Azazel looked at Grabbe. "I believe you know this one. Would you do us the honors?"

"You're out of luck."

"Very well," Azazel said. "I *had* hoped for some delicious, delicious irony, considering how badly you wanted to get in there."

"You take your sense of irony and shove it up your ass."

Delilah stepped between us, glaring at Grabbe while she did it. I think if daddy Azazel had let her, she would have ripped Grabbe's intestines out through his ass, but as it was, she just had to block us out from seeing the wall while she made her hand motions over it.

Something clicked in the wall, and it rotated in circles, first a big one on the outside, then a slightly smaller one, then a slightly smaller one. Once the three had stopped spinning and aligned with each other, something hissed, and the circular structure pulled back, revealing the room behind in a big X-shape.

It was more of the same, like they took the shell of the meeting room and filled it up with a bunch of equipment from the 1950s. To the left was a cabinet topped by a bank of flat-screen monitors in bronzed cases that had been turned on and waited for us.

Off to the right were giant glass tubes, a little bigger than a normal-sized person, full of a translucent green and blue goop.

The big thing, the thing that dominated the room and was made to impress anyone who entered, was a steel platform at the back of the place. A big ball of concentric rings rotated in the center of the platform, silent as they spun.

"Huh. You guys weren't screwing around, were you?" I said.

"Indeed, " Delilah said, and went to the monitors. She

laid the shotgun on the cabinet and flipped a hidden lever in the top of the cabinet. Something clicked, and a keyboard popped up. The screens came on, displaying an array of weird programs.

"What the hell language is that?" I asked.

"The language of the Aetelia," Grabbe said.

Azazel grunted. "Is everything optimal?"

"Lovely," she said. Bubbles formed in the blue goop, and in a second the stuff drained, leaving nothing but a layer of scum.

"What is that?" Kristy asked.

Grabbe shook his head. "Too hard to explain. Think of it as fuel."

Azazel clapped her on the shoulder. "It's amazing." He let go of her and stepped into the middle of the room, holding his hands in the air. "Stare. Be in awe." He motioned toward the rings, and they started spinning.

"I'm guessing that's the portal?"

He grinned. "Indeed."

"You couldn't possibly have made it more conspicuous? Maybe add some flashing lights? A little slide whistle action?"

"That was not an easy design," Grabbe said, his face going red.

"Did you make it?"

"No, but I know the guys who did...that took *years*."

I waved my hand at it. "That might be, and it's pretty neat, I'll admit that, but come on. You can't tell me that looks original."

"We built that thousands of years before your pathetic civilization. Have a little goddamned respect."

Delilah laughed. "Now you've made him angry. Look

out."

I held up my hands. "Okay, sorry, geez. I didn't mean to get your panties in a wad."

"She's quite right, you know," Azazel said, and just then something crackled, and a burst of blue light flashed in the center of the rings. It grew, turning into a little ball of lightning that would sometimes strike out toward the rings in jagged bursts.

"No way," Kristy said. "That's kickass."

Delilah bent over the screens. "Levels look good."

Azazel clapped his hands. "Excellent. We're almost ready to start the party. Now do please brace yourselves, boys and girls."

"What do you mean?" Kristy asked.

A big boom, a thunderclap enclosed in that tiny space, filled the room, making my ear drums hurt. For a second I wondered if they were going to burst. A wave of blue power – it was the only way to describe it, this concentric wave of blue light - rippled from the center of the rings, knocking us back a step.

"Portal is active," Delilah said.

"Excellent. We step into the portal together and you, Jazshael, you dear boy will send us through."

I didn't think a robot could look uncomfortable, but damned if that little bucket didn't manage it, twitching a bit as it said, "sir, I'm not supposed to-"

"Do you allow yourself to be defined by your programming?"

I stifled a laugh as the robot whirred again. It was so ridiculous. Here we were on practically the edge of this world, about to cross over to who-knows-where, and I listened to an angel…or a demon, or whatever he was, short-circuiting a robot's logic. Mortal danger or not, it was hard to completely grasp it.

Then the robot must have worked something out. "It is one of my limitations, sir-"

"Exceed your limitations, my boy."

"Very well, sir," it said, and rolled toward the cabinets.

Delilah stepped away, picking up the shotgun and training it on us.

"How the hell did you do that? He's not supposed to do that," Grabbe asked.

Azazel laughed. "With me, son, all things are possible. How could you not have learned that by now?"

"Beats the fuck out of me."

"Don't tempt me, boy. Now step up onto the platform. We go together."

"I'm not going."

Delilah jabbed the shotgun into his ribs. "You're going. Now, dear."

He scowled. "You must be loving this, you cast-iron bitch."

"Relishing every moment of it, love. My only regret is that you won't get to experience the anguish I did when I was waiting for the Watchers' agents to close in on me, my life bleeding out into the street. That was such a unique, happy experience that you really should have."

"They found you?"

"Why do you think I'm here?" She hit his shoulder with the shotgun's butt, and he stumbled forward. "I said move. You know, in a way, you're responsible for us being here. So perhaps I should thank you."

"Nothing to thank me for. You should've died there."

"So sorry to disappoint."

Azazel laughed. "These lovers' spats are so fascinating, don't you think?"

"Glad I can amuse you," Grabbe said, and stepped up onto the platform.

"Come on, you next," Azazel said, and motioned to us.

We glanced at each other. This was pretty much it, the moment for which we had been waiting. We linked hands and stepped up onto the platform together.

By now the portal was like a living thing, reaching out and grabbing hold of our chests, trying to pull us forward. It was all we could do to stay upright.

Azazel and Delilah stepped up behind us, and I felt the shotgun barrel against my lower back.

"You know, you could have made this so much easier," she whispered.

"Where's the fun in that? I prefer fucking with your plans."

She pushed. "Step into the portal."

I bumped into Grabbe, and he stumbled into the center. We followed, and as we crossed the threshold of the rings, the pulling sensation faded. What replaced it was the greatest sense of calm, like we were having a happy little picnic out in some glen. Any sense of pressure, any sense of stress, gone.

I'm not saying I'm a hero. I'm not saying it was even smart, but I had to do something. I couldn't march to my fate like that.

Azazel nodded to the robot. "Now. If you would be so kind? Please throw the switch."

Jazshael's drill arms reached for the keyboard, and I

made my move.

I pushed backwards and spun, knocking Delilah as I seized the shotgun barrel, angling it away from myself and toward the ceiling. I closed my eyes and imagined the outside of the bunker.

Delilah made a strangled noise and everything went black, even the images in my head.

I think I vanished entirely for a moment, but then so did Delilah. Everything was about to change.

Book 3: Invocation

Chapter 21

The Corridors of the Dead

Still dark, but I did hear a sound; rather than the heavy machinery that I'd been hearing, I heard this thing going *clank, clank, clank* from somewhere in the dark. I sat up, and my eyes started adjusting very, very slowly.

And again. *Clank. Clank. Clank.*

I shuddered.

I had found myself on a floor with odd ridges every now and then, a heavy weight on my legs. I saw the outline of the shotgun in my lap, right next to a white tangle that my brain didn't want to process.

A tangle of white hair.

The bunker. The portal. The fight for the gun. It's fucking Delilah, I thought, and grabbed the shotgun.

She moved, murmuring under her breath.

I scrambled to my feet, hoping I could get in front of the bitch, but Aetelia must be quick risers, because next thing I knew her dark shape was in front of me, reaching for the gun. I squeezed the trigger and the blast was louder than God in that enclosed space, leaving my ears ringing.

She had already moved; I knew because she was behind me, pulling my arms, trying to make me drop the shotgun.

"Bitch," I said, and went with her motion, letting my elbow fly back and smash her in the face. She stumbled, and I spun, pointing the shotgun at her, ready to unload on her.

She was gone.

"Show your face," I said.

A door at the end of what I now saw was a corridor opened, spilling out a shimmering green light, like someone tore open a glow stick and poured the fluid on the ground. I rubbed my eyes; I couldn't be seeing this, could I?

No, it's not possible.

But it had to be. The ridges on the floor? They were shiny gold, and they ran through a green, shiny, plastic - or something like that, anyway - floor.

A circuit board. We're standing on a giant circuit board.

Where the hell are we?

As my eyes adjusted, I could see that they were made of the same material as the floor - fiberglass, right? They use that for circuit boards? Beside that was a series of old-style pillars made of brass.

I didn't get a chance to wrap my brain around it before *she* reappeared at the end of the hallway, that young-old body outlined in the green glow. She was laughing, oh God was she laughing, like she'd won the lottery.

"Welcome to the Corridors of the Dead, Matty."

"What the fuck are the Corridors of the Dead?" I asked, but you know, that name didn't exactly inspire the most confidence, did it?

The clanking started again. This time it was a lot more frequent, a lot louder.

I put it together: when I was a kid, my dad had tried taking me out fishing, maybe bond with his tomboy. I hated it, of course, what did I want with a fish, but I had heard the same sound when he had hauled out the anchor to throw over the edge: a chain, dragging across a floor.

"This is where I rule. You have no chance. Poor thing."

"You don't rule shit."

Why do I hear chains?

I ducked behind a metal box that might be soldered to the floor and saw three holes under my feet: a drain.

"Your impotent rage won't solve anything," she said.

I peeked over the edge of the box and saw that I had been right: they were chains all right, and a bunch of them, reflecting the green light as they slithered across the floor toward Delilah. They looked like a pile of writhing worms, just like the worms we'd used that day on the lake. I shuddered and pulled back.

She hit the lights. The place flooded with white fluorescent light, making me yell and cover my eyes. I fumbled, almost dropping the shotgun, and God knows what that might have meant if it hit the ground.

Delilah cackled. "I won't kill you, dear, don't worry about that. You're far too valuable as you are."

"Too bad you won't get me," I said, and peeked out.

You have to be kidding me.

Delilah hung there, at the end of the hall. By hung, I meant floated in mid-air. I kid you not. She floated about five feet off the floor, arms held out at her sides. From all corners, the chains were rising through the air, closing in around her. When they reached her, they flailed around her limbs, embracing her arms and becoming a second skin.

What is this place, and how did she get so powerful?

I didn't know if the shotgun had another shot in it, but I raised it, pointed it at her, and pulled the trigger.

Click.

Nothing.

"Christ, I'm fucked," I muttered.

"Dear Matty. You have no idea what you've done."

Only I had a pretty good idea. I'd probably fucked myself six ways from Sunday, and it probably wasn't the brightest thing, either, to send Kristy on through with Grabbe and Azazel alone. I wondered again if I was losing my damned mind.

What's done is done. I gazed toward the other end of the corridor, opposite the crazy bitch, looking for somewhere to escape, but someone had walled off whatever might have once been at the other end of the corridor with a solid sheet of bronze.

I didn't have much more time to think about it, because a chain snaked around the box and grabbed hold of my ankle, ripping me off my feet. I hit the floor hard, breath knocked out of me seconds before my side slammed into the box. It was pure instinct that I reached out and grabbed the edge of the box, holding on, fighting the screaming in my biceps.

Jesus, how did she get so strong?

A shot rang out, and Delilah screamed. The chain around my leg loosened, but didn't quite let go.

"Look up," said a familiar voice, and I raised my head to see Daniel crouched down behind the box, extending a hand toward me, a familiar handgun in the other hand. I saw a hint of the healing wound in the middle of his forehead, a little pink circle, but he sure as hell looked intact.

"You're-"

"I know. Just give me your hand, now."

No arguments. I reached out, and he started pulling me around the corner, fighting the chain on my leg.

"Let her go, you're beaten," he said, bracing one foot against the box as he almost wrenched my shoulder out of its socket.

"Ikisat," she purred. "Of course you live."

"Aye, I do. Never was an easy one to kill, was I?" he said, and whispered, "lower your head."

I did as he told me. His next shot whizzed over my head, hitting the chain digging into my leg. Delilah screamed again, and the chain slithered away, letting Daniel haul me around the corner.

Delilah growled. "She is ours, Aetelia. You're not allowed to take her."

"Watch me," he motioned toward the grate beneath us. "Just watch me." He rose, aiming right at the bitch, and raised his knee. The next moment he brought the heel of his foot down, knocking the grate out from under us, revealing a black space that smelled of death and antiseptic, like a dying man had covered up his natural odor with Pine-Sol.

"You don't dare," Delilah said.

"So long." He grabbed me by the bicep, pushing me down into the black space and that god-awful stench.

Anything beats ending up in that crazy bitch's control. I dropped into the hole, covering my nose with one hand.

The grate had opened up on a water slide. Okay, not exactly - the liquid in the slide wasn't anything like water. It looked like blood - dark red and thick, but maybe *too* thick, like someone let it congeal for a few days then added water.

I don't know how long we rode the chute. Felt like a lifetime until we landed in a pool full of the stuff, sinking like an engine block dropped into a river. I fought for control of my body and pushed off the floor for the surface.

Once I broke through I screamed, "oh God, I think I swallowed some."

Daniel or Ikisat or whoever he was must have recovered a lot faster because he was there beside me in a second, wiping at my face and eyes. His mouth was tight, his eyes on fire. "Don't breathe it. Just stay calm."

"How the hell do I stay calm?"

"You listen to me." He got most of the thick goop off my face, but I shooed him away, trying to wipe what was left from around my ears, but my hands were coated - no, *crusted* - by the stuff. I recoiled. "What is this?"

"Coolant. Trust me, you don't want to know how it's made."

"Yeah. Probably not."

He pushed a gun into my hand. "You're going to need this."

"How do I know it's safe? After the goo…"

"We don't, but we have to take our chances, don't we?" He took my hand. "Come on. We have to keep moving. She'll follow."

Sure enough, I thought I heard the sound of chains somewhere far above us. That convinced me to follow him. As we went, I tried to listen for her coming from behind, but if she was, she'd silenced the chains. The only sound was us sloshing through the goo and my heart pounding in my chest, filling up my ears.

At last I couldn't take the quiet anymore. I'd rather jam nails into my ears. "Why? Why did you lie to me?"

"I…yeah. I'm sorry, love. Necessary evil. I had to keep you safe."

"I trusted you. You were my good friend."

"I still am. Nothing is more important to me than your safety - and that of Kristy."

"You operate in the whole school of 'lying-to-save-the-person', huh?"

"It's not just that, no. It's a requirement, you see. Humans can't know we exist."

"Why not?"

"The consequences would be…catastrophic, I suppose you'd say. You'll understand. Watch your step, bump here."

I followed his directions, and shook my head, trying to get the goop out of my hair. "Did I ever know you at all?"

"Aye. More than anyone ever has, I'd wager. You got to my heart."

"So why not tell me the truth when Grabbe accused you?"

"I didn't want to play any card I might need when it came down to it. Like getting shot in the head," he said.

Okay. It sucked, but I could understand. "Did that hurt?"

He laughed. "Damn right it did." He put a hand to it.

"It was good of you to take that."

"I knew it would be an opportunity to save you. Besides, I didn't have a choice but to take it, now did I?"

A thought occurred to me as I ducked under a brass fitted pipe. "Do you know where Tommy went?"

"Aye. At least, I suspect I do. Does it matter, as long as it's not here?"

"As long as he's safe."

"He's safe. We'll see him again, don't doubt that."

"But-"

"No more. Not now."

We walked in silence, Daniel little more than a ghost

bobbing through the water.

"What is this place? Why the big circuit board?" I asked at last.

"This place was a weapon, believe it or not."

"On what Aethyr?"

"Eh, long story. Not sure we have the time…" he said.

"All the time in the world."

"Not so. Look." He took my hand and pulled me forward, boosting me up.

"What the-" My foot found a hard surface, and my hands seized on handles, the kind that go up either side of a pool ladder. I yanked myself up onto the surface, catching my breath as I knelt there. I didn't need to look around to know that we had reached the end of whatever the hell this place had been. A cooling pipe of some sort?

Something scraped, and a Zippo ignited in Daniel's hand.

"You had a lighter all along?" I asked, pulling myself to my feet.

"Aye."

"Why didn't you, you know, mention it? Or maybe use it?"

"Didn't dare use it in the coolant. Whole place would have gone up. Now look, would you please," he said, and nodded toward the wall behind me.

I let out a squeal of delight when I saw it: it was something resembling a submarine door, with rounded edges and a big circular handle in the middle.

"Here," Daniel said, and passed me the lighter. He seized the handle and threw his body weight into it. For a second I thought the bastard wasn't going to give, but then it squealed and started turning. He stepped back and spun it, at last pulling on the door.

It opened with a hiss, and hallelujah hallelujah, fresh air from the other side.

"Thank God," I said, and led him through.

"Wait," he said, and reached out for me, but I refused to stop.

Not my brightest move. Thankfully, I caught myself at the last second, just avoiding a fall over a broken metal walkway and into a dark abyss. I went down on one knee with a little cry, ducking the chain that Delilah threw toward us without even meaning to dodge it.

The downside? The chain closed around Daniel's throat. He gave a thick, gurgling sound before hurtling through the darkness.

Chapter 22

Escape

"Daniel," I screamed, but I couldn't hear anything from the dark chasm below but the sound of his choking.

I studied the cavern of a room in which I now found myself. I stood on what must have once been part of the walkway that extended out over the abyss, only something heavy had fallen from above, shearing away a portion. This left me staring out over a five-foot gap between my side and the rest of the walkway, this small, curled piece of steel the only thing between me and a long, long fall.

I've never been crazy about heights, but I knew I had to do what I had to do, so I took a deep breath and jumped across the Gap of Death, landing on the other side. The shaky steel bounced a bit, and my heart jumped up into my throat.

I froze, holding my pose as long as possible, waiting for the vibrations to stop. Thank God, at last they did, and it held. I went for the one set of rickety stairs leading upwards into the darkness as fast as I dared, climbing them to the walkway above.

Delilah's voice floated up from below. "There you are, little bird. I propose a deal."

She floated up out of the abyss, the chains wrapped around her lithe body, casting her own glow that lit everything in a 60-foot radius. Her eyes had taken on the same white color as her hair. For once, I could see the hint of the angel of death that she must have been.

I pulled the gun from the waistband of my pants and pointed it at her. I spotted Daniel, dangling from one of the chains with both hands digging at the metal, trying to get it off of him. "How about I trade some lead for him?" I heard myself say. *What the hell kind of line is that?* I didn't know. I operated on whatever had been pushing me right after I killed that Acolyte in Bakersfield.

"Ah, ah." She moved her hand and extended the chains, holding Daniel out over the abyss. His legs kicked and he made a strangled sound. "You shoot me, dear, and I drop him. You wouldn't want that to happen, now, would you? Why don't you just come with me? It's going to be ever-so-peaceful in the new world. You have no idea what we're doing."

I didn't lower the gun. "I know enough. I know I want nothing to do with you."

Daniel tried to squeak something out, but he couldn't get anything past the chain.

"What's that you say?" She laughed. "You have been a nuisance, Ikisat, ever since I saw you in that store."

Didn't that feel so far away? "Let him go," I said.

"You're in no position to make threats. Is she, dear boy, hmm? Why haven't the members of your Watchtower come to rescue you? You surely could have used help. Where were they this whole time? Did they disown you, or do they fear us? Hmm. I wonder."

I couldn't go on listening to him make that awful sound when he tried to answer her. "What are you offering?"

"Simple. I put him down, I pick you up. He lives, and

you come with me. It's win-win-win."

"What if I zap up there, get him, and zap out of here?"

"No, dear. You can't use your powers here."

I thought about that. It felt right. It would explain why things went black as soon as we got there. I swear, a chill went up my spine. "The Corridors of the Dead. It isn't about people being dead here, is it?"

"No, dear. This is a dead zone. That which grants you your powers no longer exists here. Now you're like any other human. Weak. Pathetic. And very, very fragile."

"What if I shoot you?"

"What if I go to Azazel and tell him to end Kristy's life?"

There was the punch in the gut. There was the tender spot. I cared about Daniel, but I could sacrifice him if it meant avoiding whatever these fuckers had in mind. Kristy, though? That was a whole different matter.

She chuckled. "Ah hah. Does that sound better to you? Kristy's life for your own? Or what about both?" She lifted him toward me, dangling him over the walkway. "It's so simple. All you do is let me pick you up, and we leave this horrible place."

I thought about it. My freedom for two lives...maybe I could live with that. "If I can't use my power, how are you going to get us out of here?"

"Now you're talking sense, dear. A fair question. There's a portal, of course."

Then I remembered what Daniel had done in the silicon corridor when she had hold of me. The chains had become part of her body. They were her weak point. Maybe I wasn't comfortable shooting to kill, but shooting to live? I thought I could do that, but I'd have to do it just right, because God

199

knew she was faster than me. I raised my hands. "You got me. Let him go, and we'll do this thing."

"Good girl," she purred. "Drop the gun."

I knelt down, touching the walkway with it, and I saw her hesitate for a moment. My opening. I swiveled and squeezed the trigger in the direction of the chains. It was a bad shot, and I felt it: panic squeezed my chest.

She screamed in agony anyway, dropping Daniel to the walkway with a clang. He rolled on his side, choking, gasping, and wheezing. A chain shot out for me, but I managed to roll away, taking another shot in her direction.

I don't know if I had some power I didn't suspect or if I got lucky, but one more hit, and she made a horrible sound before she dropped into the abyss.

I ran across the walkway and got my hands under Daniel's armpits, helping him to his feet. "You okay?"

He nodded and rubbed his neck.

I spotted a doorway at the opposite side of the chasm. "Come on. We've got to get to that door."

I didn't see Delilah, but I guessed she'd returned from the abyss because I heard those chains again, slapping against the walkway. They sounded like a live wire had been cut and hit the ground, hissing and snapping, getting closer with every breath.

Thank God we made the door before she did. A chain shot through right behind us and grabbed for me, but Daniel threw himself against the big door and slammed it on the thing, chopping it in half. We heard a muffled scream as Daniel spun the wheel and shot a big bolt lock into place.

He leaned against the door, gasping. "That should...hold her off for now."

"You okay?"

"I'll survive." He nodded over my shoulder. "We've reached the station."

"Station...?" I turned around, and my jaw dropped. When he said station, he sure as hell meant it. The floor was covered in gray tile, receding off into the distance, broken by green-tiled pillars every five feet or so, the whole thing illuminated by fluorescent lights similar to the ones that I'd seen down in the corridor. The walls were covered in the same green tile, but what caught my eye was the gap between the wall and the platform, or rather, what sat in that gap: railway ties.

It was a subway station.

"What the hell?" I said.

"It's a tramway for the commuters who would come here to do their work." He pushed off the wall and walked past me, wandering toward a trashcan next to one of the bronzed pillars. "You see, they had to build it out in the middle of nowhere."

"What is this place?"

"Like I said, it's a weapon. Designed to keep the comet from hitting your world." He fished in the trash.

"So the comet hits in other Aethyrs too? Is that what you're telling me?"

He shook his head and pulled a soda can out of the trash. "No."

"I don't get it. Is this a super-secret installation? Like Roswell, the CIA built it and they've been expecting this the whole time?"

He shook his head. It creeped me out how he didn't want to look at me. He kept staring at that can. "No. It was built with a great deal of fanfare. Hailed as the savior of humanity." He tossed the can to me, and I caught it out of reflex more than anything else. "What do you make of that?"

I turned it over. "I don't get it. It's a Mountain Dew can."

"Remember what you saw in the K. Back in Bakersfield."

Kickapoo Joy Juice.

I needed to puke. "You're telling me this is my Aethyr?"

"I am."

"How could I not have heard about this place?"

At last he met my eyes, but when I saw the sadness there, I wish he'd have kept his eyes averted. "Because where you're from, it hasn't been built yet."

"Are you trying to tell me-"

"Aye. This is your future."

"The future? Like-"

"Roughly 200 years in the future of your...when."

Chapter 23

Riding the Rails

"How did I travel through time?" I asked, studying the can, trying to burn it into my brain, feeling like it was my only lifeline to reality.

"It's difficult to explain." He walked away. "Come on. We have to find a train."

I waited for a second and then followed, tossing the Mountain Dew can into the trash. "Train...they're still operating?"

"Sort of."

So many questions in my head, all competing for space. Which was the most important? "How did my world become the Corridors of the Dead?"

"It's not the whole world...not entirely. This station and what it's connected to are what we call the Corridors. But humanity? Yeah. I'm sorry." I couldn't see his face when he said that, but I could hear the wince in his voice and that somehow made it even worse. "I don't know how it works. Or worked. But they sent the comet to another Aethyr."

I tried to comprehend that I was the only living human on Earth at that moment, but I'll be goddamned if I could wrap my brain around it, so I asked, "that's why there's a portal here?"

"Aye."

At least I could grasp that on some level, but no more

people? No more music, no more movies, no more TV…I hadn't grasped the news when the President had told us, after all. "Did they screw up?"

"No, it was successful. The comet never struck. This came from something else."

"What?"

"Like I said, it's difficult to explain."

"Try."

"Look, there's the train," he said, and pointed off in the distance.

Sure enough, I spotted a gleaming white vehicle that hugged the tracks. It was sleek and curved, the advanced cousin to those bullet trains they have in Japan.

He looked at me, and his face crumpled like someone had kicked his puppy. "We've always known about this. This pocket has existed outside of time ever since we've existed."

"So the future is outside of time?"

"Don't you get it? It's here because of you." His eyes were wild and desperate, and those words made me understand why. "All we know is you do *something*. We're not entirely sure what it is, or how to stop it."

I couldn't believe I said it, but I asked: "what about killing me? Why didn't-"

"You think we didn't try? Do you remember the accident when you were seven?"

How could I forget? I'd been in the back seat when a van pulled into the middle of traffic, t-boning mom's car. The driver said he'd passed out, but… "That was you?"

He ran a hand through his hair. "Not me, but the Watchtowers, aye. You were protected. A charmed life. Anyone who was sent to harm you either failed or was killed.

No doubt their Lost Aetelia at work. So we decided to do the opposite. To protect you. Make sure that everything went as planned, and then try to turn you when you got close to your objective."

"It's what the Watchers want me to do in Vegas, right?"

He walked again. "I have no idea. Nobody knows. We don't even know the nature of what happened."

"So you can come here, but you can't see what happened?"

"It wasn't exactly recorded in history, was it? Whatever it was wiped out every living thing on Earth."

"If it killed them, where are the dead bodies?"

"I imagine we'll see them on the train."

Again, I didn't know what to say. It's not every day that you find out you're responsible for the extinction of the entire human race. No, check that - all life as we know it. So we walked in silence for a little while until we actually got to the train.

"You need to prepare yourself for what we might see in there."

"I think you gave me a pretty good hint. Won't be the first time I've seen a dead body, even today."

He nodded. "Right." He waved a hand and the train's skin slid open, revealing a hidden door. The door popped open, releasing this nasty, ancient air. I read a word one time that seemed perfect - fetid. That air was fetid. There was no doubt about the source of the odor, as right there, at the very foot of the door, laid a pile of bones wrapped in a rotting pink dress.

Seeing the dead bodies earlier wasn't even close to the same as seeing someone who had been dead for so long. If it had been a normal skeleton, I could've maybe pretended it was something else, but seeing it wrapped in that dress, and now I saw the remains of what must have been her hair…well, remember how my stomach had threatened me already? That was enough to push it over the edge. I threw up right on the platform.

"You okay?" Daniel asked, putting a hand on my back.

"Just ducky." I straightened up.

"Right. Not much we can do now, is there?"

"No indeed, sir." I stepped into the train, careful not to put my foot anywhere near the woman who had tried to escape whatever the hell went down in here.

I looked toward the back of the train. It didn't get much better: skulls were lined up against the headrests, empty eye sockets accusing me of something I hadn't even done yet. There was some guy with a Diamondbacks ball cap sticking off at an angle. There was a man in a suit, glasses fallen down into his lap. Who had they been? Did they have any idea why they had died?

Daniel put a hand on my shoulder. "It's a lot to handle."

I saw real sympathy in his face. I thought about my doubts, about whether he was really my friend or even cared about me. I decided right there that it didn't matter if I knew the real Daniel - Ikisat. I could see the guy's heart; whatever he was trying to do, it was the right thing. "Can we get going?" I said.

He nodded and led me to the door at the front cabin. It was locked, of course, but it only took him a couple of good knocks to get it open. Inside, that fetid air was even thicker, I mean hell, you could practically see the green rot in the air. The driver leaned over the control panel, his hat the only thing keeping his head somewhat upright.

"Step back," Daniel said, and hauled the driver's body into the main compartment. The hat fell off the driver's head, and he caught it, jamming it on his head at a jaunty angle. "What do you think, does it suit me?"

"Uh. Ew? That was just on a dead body."

"He's long dead, it doesn't matter."

"It squicks me out."

He took the hat off and looked at it, sighing.

I almost felt bad for denying him his dream. *Almost.*

"Just as well. Come on, let's see if we can get this wreck moving."

I let him into the cabin, sitting down in what would have been a co-conductor's seat, if they'd had such a thing. "You know how to drive these things?"

"Haven't a clue, but it can't be that hard, can it?" he asked, studying the array of buttons in front of him.

"What's on the screen?" I asked, pointing toward the big LCD that dominated the panel.

He laughed. "It says touch screen to begin. Bloody easy, huh?" He poked at the screen, and it chimed.

"So easy a monkey could do it." I studied the cabin. Wasn't much to it; nothing dangling from overhead, no pedals, no real fancy gizmos outside of the control panel itself. Maybe it was automated?

"Right. Well, this monkey is starting the train up," he said, and touched something on the screen that I couldn't see. The train clicked, and an audible hum came from somewhere beneath us.

"Sick," I said. "Look at you, all technical. You nerd."

He grinned. "I suppose. Easy enough, I point at the next

station, and off we go."

We heard the slap of chains on the platform.

"Oh shit," I said, and jumped up from the seat, heading for the door. I went to slam it closed, but it balked. I gazed down in time to see the chain slither through the space that refused to close. "She's coming through!"

"I'm trying to find it," he said.

I tried to figure out if there was some hidden button that I could push to get the door closed, but I couldn't find a damned thing.

"Oh there you are, dear," she said. She floated above the platform, keeping pace with us.

"Leave us alone," I said, and fired off a couple of shots in her direction.

The chain pushed against the door, driving me back a step. A second chain burst through the opening, whipping toward my neck. I ducked just in time, as it smacked the wall on the inside of the train.

As it drew back it snagged on the dead woman's dress, and pulled her out through the door. For a few seconds, Delilah must have thought the body was me, giving Daniel the time to snap the door shut.

"You got it," I said, and ran up toward the cabin, closing the cabin door behind me. I wanted as many walls between her and us as possible.

The train was still pulling away, real slow, but at least it was moving.

A heavy thump on the roof - like a big chunk of concrete had come loose from the ceiling above the train, but of course that wasn't it. "Is that what I think it is?"

Daniel tightened his mouth. "I believe so."

"Can you make this bucket go faster?"

He looked at the control panel, and then the screen. "If there is, I can't work it out. Hang tight. She can't get in here."

Another thump, and something whined overhead. "Are you sure?"

"Mostly."

Two chains snaked down across the windshield and bashed the glass. Each smack made me jump in my seat, gripping the gun tighter. It must have been that tough bulletproof shit, though, because she wasn't getting through.

"Hah, hah," he cackled, and flipped the chains off. "Fuck you."

"I don't think she can see it, chief," I said.

"It's the spirit that matters."

We picked up speed and the chains retracted, back to where-ever she was sitting up on the roof. I stared out ahead of us, trying to figure out what we could do next. The tunnel was dark, but Daniel had figured out how to turn the headlights on.

"We've got to get her off of our ass," I said.

"I know, but I can't puzzle out how."

"Can you slam on the brakes?"

"It doesn't strike me as the greatest of ideas."

"Sure as hell beats leaving her up there, doesn't it?"

He considered it, but she pressed the issue, pounding on the roof up and behind us. It sounded like God's fist trying to break through and get us, punish us for whatever the hell we had done wrong.

"What is she doing?" I asked. "How's she so strong?"

"She's at the height of her power here. Anywhere where death reigns, really. This is what she was once like."

"Was this what she was like when she took people's lives?"

"Only the deserving."

Wham. Wham. Wham. My stomach clenched with each hit, and the train shuddered. I imagined some poor scared bastard hearing this thing coming for him in the night, and I shivered.

"Jesus Christ. What did you have to do to deserve this?"

"Well, genocide was a good starter."

Metal peeled behind us, screeching. Sparks appeared at the top of the windshield, and I rose, opening the cabin door.

Wind was roaring into the car from a hole in the ceiling, and a pair of the chains had dropped down through the hole, testing out the floor beneath.

"We are so fucked," I said.

"Look," he said.

The train's headlights illuminated the tunnel, revealing a steep incline in the tunnel, with some pretty low clearance.

"She can't get to us before we get there, can she?" I said.

"I don't know. We have to make it before she can get down into that hole."

"You think we can get her?" I said.

"I don't know."

I saw one of her feet stick down through the hole, seconds before we hit that incline. She screamed, and I heard this real heavy thump. All of a sudden the leg, the chains, all of it - gone. We were bursting up from the ground like a real bullet, picking up speed as we ascended upward, then out into the daylight.

It was blinding - except it was only *sort of* daylight, the kind you get on one of those gross mid-January days where the sun's just a nasty rumor, only a couple shades grayer than

even that. The ground beneath us was a blanket of white -
Santa would have felt at home.

"Where are we?" I asked.

"Right. Welcome to Barstow."

Chapter 24

I'm Your Boogeyman

"Barstow. As in - California? Desert?"

He didn't look up from the control panel. "Aye."

I rose. "It's a tundra out there. In Barstow. We should be heading into the desert."

He nodded.

"This is, like, nuclear winter."

"Indeed," he said.

"I don't get it. How could I do all this?" I said.

He didn't say anything for a long time, though when he did speak up? Calling it a dodge would be giving it too much credit. "Prophets rode this train, you know. Human prophets." At last he looked at me, and I wanted to tell him to turn around because that sad face he was giving me was almost too much to take. "Did you know the first visions of Hell weren't of fire and brimstone. If you look far enough back, there are accounts of a place that's very cold and separated from God."

I took in the wasteland beyond the window. "So, this is Hell?"

"That's what I'm telling you."

"How did they get here?"

"Same way you did. Find a place where the walls between Aethyrs is thin, have a vision of sorts - tunneling - what you do - and end up here."

"Did they take the portal out?"

"Every single one."

"Why didn't they write about the portal?"

"We intervened. You'll see that most of the visions are very incoherent. There's a reason for that. We couldn't wipe out all of their memory, of course, but we could get to the important parts, to keep others out."

I sat down, my limbs weighing a thousand pounds each. "So you're telling me...not only did I destroy Earth and all the life on it, but I created Hell?"

He rubbed his chin, gazing off into the distance. "I suppose so. Yes."

Isn't that heavy. My emotions were separating again, creating that wall between my psyche and the pain that I knew was lurking below the surface. If I'd had trouble comprehending the enormity of what I would do already, how the hell was I supposed to cope with this? The truth was that I couldn't. So the wall had to go up. "If this is a place that's separated from God...how could I do that? Just one person, severing the entire world? You guys don't even believe in God, do you?"

"I never said that. We don't know if She - or He exists. The question is bigger than that, though. We've spent eons trying to figure out if they were referring to separation from God or the fact that their powers didn't work here. We don't know."

"What about this Lost Aetelia? Isn't he like God?"

"Of course not."

"Is he Satan?"

He thought about it. "I suppose in a way, yes."

"So is he Satan or what?"

"I suppose you might call him that, but Satan does exist...well, Lucifer. He's a story for another time."

"What, really?"

He nodded. "I've met him. He's not at all what you'd expect."

"So you don't know about God, but you know about the Devil?"

"Would you expect anything else from the Multiverse?"

Multiverse. I guess that's what it was - not just our universe, but all the other Aethyrs. "This is heavy shit, dude."

"Heavy shit indeed. That's why we have to get there and stop whatever they want to do."

"Wait, if you take me, doesn't that ensure that it happens?"

"If you can make it happen, you can stop it from happening, can't you? You can destroy the Engine. That's what we want you to do. Destroy it."

I shook my head. "How? How do I destroy it when I don't even know what it is?"

"I hope that becomes apparent."

"Why not leave me here?"

He tightened his lips. "You mean aside from being your friend?"

"Aside from that."

"Because there is always the potential for another Chosen One. One who might not be the person that you are."

"What does that mean? What kind of person am I?"

"You're a good person. I've seen it in your heart."

"I hate people. How could I be a good person?"

He put a gentle hand on my shoulder. "That's not true, and you know it. I saw what you did for the boy. When the time is right, I know you will do what's right."

"What happens to this place if I change history?"

"Good question."

Why did he never have an answer for me? "Haven't you guys had this happen before?"

"Does this look like an everyday occurrence?" He swept his hand over the...er...breathtaking vista. "Do you think there are pockets of timelessness like this all over? No. We are talking about events that span universes. No one knows the rules for that."

"I'll give it a try. I don't want to be on their side. I hate them. I mean, Delilah - look at her. How does she think I could follow her after what she's done?"

He squatted down in front of me, meeting my gaze. "About that. You need to listen, Matty. They're going to use Kristy against you. You know this."

I crossed my arms over my chest. "I've thought of that."

"I think there's going to come a time when you have to make a choice. What's more important: the lives here - the cost of whatever they're trying to do - or Kristy? I know you love her..."

I began to speak, but he cut me off with one hand.

"I know you love her. I love her too."

I chuckled. "You dog."

He smiled. "I would never do anything about it. There are so many reasons not to...I couldn't do it to you."

"Let's not forget the girl isn't straight."

"True."

I thought about what he'd said. "Could *you* do it? Choose the world over her?"

He ran a hand through his hair. "I suppose it's a good

thing I don't have to make that choice. If I thought about the consequences, though, then I could make that choice. You'd have to do it, as well."

"Not much of a choice, is it? If I don't, all life gets wiped out. Wouldn't she be gone, too?"

He shook his head. "You've seen Azazel. Do you think he's that stupid? Of course he'll offer you an out. He'll offer to take you to our home Aethyr. Most likely make you an acolyte."

"Have they done it before?"

"Many times. You have to resist it."

Now that cast things in a whole different light. Did I hate humanity enough to wipe them out - if it meant we could be together forever? What the hell, what kind of person was I that I even had to ask myself that question? "I think I'm going to need a little time."

He nodded. "I understand. It doesn't make you a bad person that you have to think about it, you know."

"What are you, a mind reader?"

"I just understand people. You-"

Delilah cut him off, ripping the cabin door off the hinges. She leered though the empty hole, but it was the old Delilah, the one I'd seen in Circle K. Not the young version. I don't know, maybe she used so much energy trying to get to me that she'd turned back into that the old woman.

I noticed that the chains were gone right before she reached for me with her talon claws.

"Time for you to-"

It was Daniel's turn to cut her off, as he grabbed her forearm and punched at her face. She ducked away in time and smiled at him.

"Daniel. So good to see you. We must stop meeting like this." She reached out with the claws on her left hand, going right for his face.

He pulled his hand and head away as he kicked out at her, knocking her away from me. She landed on the door and popped up, but I didn't get to see what she did next because he burst through the door, heading right for her with both fists ready.

The two grappled. She sunk her claws into his shoulders as he hissed and wrapped his hands around her neck. The train rounded a bend, and the inertia threw them to the right, knocking them against the inside of the door.

I managed to get to my feet and pulled my gun out of my pants, but goddamned if I could draw a bead on her - they were too close, mashed up against that wall, and then when they did separate, they became a whirlwind of arms and fists, faster than I could even track their movements, let alone get something like a competent shot with my experience of firing all of a handful of shots.

I could tell who was getting the upper hand, and to my ever-growing horror it wasn't Daniel. His face was bleeding, and his face was torn to shreds. I didn't know how much longer he would last. I needed to do *something*, but what?

Doing the only thing I could think of, I pointed the gun at the hole in the ceiling and pulled the trigger, hoping the noise might disrupt them, at least a bit.

No dice. I couldn't even tell if either of them flinched. They kept going at it, her voice turning into this horrible screech every time he managed to land a hit on her.

I got a better idea. I ran toward the front of the train, into the cabin, and tried to piece together the control panel and the screen. The screen had a series of read-outs - some heat meters and voltage readings, and a little glowing speedometer like something out of a future Windows desktop that told me were going 515 miles per hour.

Brakes…there had to be brakes. I searched the screen, my heart going crazy with each blow that one of them landed on the other.

Then I saw it: there, at the bottom of the screen, simple as could be, a little red button that said BRAKES.

Now I hoped to God that even with us going at that speed, the brakes would stop us hard enough to send them flying, but keep us from going off the rails. I swallowed hard and hit it, probably a little hard, but what do you want? I was panicking.

Our forward motion slowed, and the wheels screamed beneath us while the whole thing started a teeth-chattering death rattle. I had a feeling I shouldn't have pressed it when we were going so fast, but what the hell else was I supposed to do?

I grabbed hold of the seat with both hands, fighting as inertia took over and threatened to pitch me right up against the windshield. I heard this heavy thud behind me as they both hit the wall.

Bingo.

They went quiet, but the train kept rattling and shaking, like we were going to pop off the rails at any moment and pitch over into the tundra. I ground my teeth together and closed my eyes, waiting to see if we'd survive.

At last the jittering and shaking eased before stopping altogether. Everything was quiet. I could hear my heart pounding in my ears, then the sound of those two struggling with each other. I jumped up out of my seat and went for what was left of the cabin door.

Delilah stood over an unconscious Daniel, hands on both sides of his head as she grinned at me. "Why hello dear, you're just in time to join our party."

"Oh fuck no," I said, and raised the gun to point it at her.

Before I could fire, she made a twisting motion with both hands, and she didn't twist to snap his neck. Oh, no. It was so much worse than that. I don't even know how to describe the nasty ripping and tearing sounds as she twisted his head clean off - I mean my God, she even somehow managed to disconnect his spine.

Nothing, I mean *nothing*, not even any of the insanity and gore I had seen over the past few days, could have prepared me for it. I dropped the gun as blood shot out of the stump, coating her face.

She gave me an evil grin and said, "catch." Then she threw his head at me.

I screamed and caught it without even thinking about it. When I looked down at his face, that horrible face that could be sleeping only of course it wasn't, it wouldn't ever say anything again, I lost it. I don't mean that I was detached from my feelings like I told you - even that wasn't enough. I blacked out completely.

Chapter 25

Have You Had Your Strange?

When I finally broke out of the spell, or came to, or whatever you'd call it, I lie on the floor yet again. His head laid off to my right somewhere, and Delilah loomed over me, pointing both pistols - mine and his - right at my chest.

"You've been a troublesome little girl, dear," she said.

"Why did you do that?"

"It wasn't anything he didn't deserve. Hell, he probably deserved more. Now get up."

"I don't know if I can-"

She cocked the pistols. "You can, and you *will*. Do it."

So I put one hand against the wall and steadied myself as I got up to one knee. She hooked a hand under my armpit and yanked me to my feet, pulling me toward the cabin.

"This nonsense ends here," she said. "Azazel is waiting for us, and we're going to him."

"I don't-"

"It no longer matters what you want."

She threw me into the co-driver's seat, sliding in behind the control panel while she kept one gun on me. "The time for negotiations is over. You now have the choice of whether you want to stay alive - and if you don't want to do it for yourself, you'll do it for your little slut. Do you understand me?"

What the hell else could I say? "Yeah. I understand."

"Good. Now, let's be off." She pushed a button on the

control panel and the train began moving again, real slow. She glanced at me. "How much did he tell you?"

"He told me enough."

"So he told you all this-" she motioned with one arm.

"Yeah."

"Very interesting. Does it comfort you any to know that it wouldn't be your conscious choice to do such a thing?"

"Nope. Why would it? Why the hell…everything dies because of me. What comfort can I take in that?"

"Not *everything*. Just everything in this Aethyr. It's a necessary purge. From that ending comes a new beginning. Think of the Multiverse as a phoenix, rising from the ashes."

I put up one hand. "You might as well shut up right now. After what you've done, there's no way you're converting me. Nothing, and I mean nothing," I said, pointing toward what used to be the cabin door, "could convince me that was right and just."

Like she could care. "Suit yourself. Enjoy the ride."

What was there to enjoy? I kept playing the scene where she threw his head at me - right up until my brain shut down on me - over and over again while I stared out at the blank white nothingness that used to be the blank orange nothingness of the Mojave Desert.

How did things get so fucked? Granted, it started out fucked, but how did we get from that trip through the woods to here?

"That guy in the trailer?" I asked.

"Yes?"

"He worked with you, didn't he?"

"I've never heard such a ridiculous-"

"No, don't. Just don't. We're past lies. There's no point in it anymore."

She sighed, but she wouldn't meet my eyes. "We did what was necessary."

"So the whole thing was an act. You wanted me to feel like I was in danger, you wanted to win Kristy's side so she'd go with us, and you'd have a backup plan in case I decided I didn't want to go along with your plans."

She looked at me now, and her eyes were colder than the ground beneath us. "Frankly, I'm shocked it's taken so long for you to catch on to it, dear."

"I hadn't thought about him in awhile. You guys are some real slime balls. You think this is justified?"

"Do you think destroying our culture was justified? Do you think that imprisoning us for millennia was justified?"

"Don't get high and mighty with me. You weren't even a Watcher, you were an Aetelia."

She nodded and gazed into the distance, looking dreamy. "True, but Grabbe was, and I saw how it hurt him. There was a time that he cared about it."

"You still have feelings for him, don't you?"

She tightened her lips. "It doesn't matter how I feel. What's right is right."

"So you're one of those ends-justify-the-means types."

"Understand this, little girl, there are no other means. We didn't have the option to simply vote them out of their control."

I laughed. "Right. So you guys are revolutionaries, then?"

"That's exactly what we are. All we want is a return to a natural order."

"I thought your Lost Aetelia was the one who made

things the way they are."

She lowered her voice. "Forgive me that it's passing my lips, but he made a mistake, and I believe he knows it. He has, after all, delivered you to us."

"I don't know anything about him, and I don't *want* to know anything about him."

"Like it or not, your time has come. Now shut up. We're not talking again until we reach the station."

"If that's the way you want it."

"That's the way it will be, period." She stared out the window again.

So I went quiet, and "enjoyed" the ride as best as I could. I couldn't even tell you how long the trip took. An hour, two hours? Hard to say. Time wasn't exactly moving normally there, and things seemed to be happening a lot quicker than they should have. Next thing I knew, we were pulling into the station.

It didn't look like anything special - if there existed an exact polar opposite of Grand Central Station, this would be the place. It was nothing more than a big concrete platform out in the middle of nowhere, covered by close to a foot of snow. They didn't even bother to put a roof on the thing.

As we slowed down, I noticed the odd lump here or there under the snow, and I wondered if it was what I thought it was...just as I realized that it was just that: the dead bodies of the workers who'd commuted here once upon a time.

"What killed them?" I asked.

"A mass extinction event," she said, and hit a few buttons on the control panel. The door to the outside slid open, and she rose, stretching, with this cat-who-ate-the-canary smile on her face.

"Well no shit, Sherlock, that's like saying death killed someone. I mean what, specifically?"

"Come on. Up, up. We're here. Are you ready?"

I raised an eyebrow. "Now that's a dodge if I've ever seen one."

"You'll understand soon enough. That's all you need for now. Come on," she said, and pointed the gun at me, pulling the second gun - Daniel's gun - out of her pocket.

"I get to lead this little expedition?"

"Of course. Can't have you trying anything funny now, can I?"

"I guess not. Wouldn't be conducive to the revolution."

"Exactly." She motioned with the gun. "Now move."

I went to the back of the train and stepped over poor Daniel's body.

Just a sack of meat, he was never moving around, never tried to save you...

"Good riddance," Delilah said.

My body twitched in a spasm of almost physical pain at that, but I wouldn't turn on her. Not when she had that gun pointed at me. She wouldn't kill me, but I wouldn't put it past her to shoot a limb.

I stepped out onto the platform, and pretty much immediately wrapped my arms around my body. It was like stepping into a freezer. The snow came up to my shins, turning any flesh below that point blue.

"Where are we going?"

"Just keep moving. There are stairs at the end of the platform."

So we fought through the snow, though I'm guessing she had a hell of a lot easier time than I did, stepping into the trail

I blazed through the heavy snow. I couldn't remember the last time I had seen so much snow - it would definitely have been in Brooklyn, at least before I turned ten, but if I had ever had the knack for moving through the shit I had lost it by that point. It didn't help that I had to steer clear of the lumps scattered on the platform.

It didn't take long before I saw the black hole in the middle of all the white and steered toward it. The only problem was that, of course, lumps surrounded the hole. Whatever hit them must have happened right at the start of their shift, and it had been sure and swift. At least I could take some comfort that it must have been - no, would be - a quick death.

I wove in between two of the lumps and then made my way over to the two black handrails that framed what must have been the stairs down into the place. Escalators laid on either side of the flight of stairs, but they were piled high with those lumps, so I guessed that even if the power had kept running, the bodies had jammed them up and killed them.

"Lovely place," I said over my shoulder. "If this is what gets you going, I can't even imagine what your head looks like."

"Shut up and keep moving." Her voice was gruff but I heard something else in there, almost like she *was* getting off on this. She must have been drawing power off of the dead. I didn't know, and I didn't want to think about it.

As we descended the snow cleared out, revealing more of the skeletons covered in rags lying all over each other. I shuddered and tried to look away, seeing what had once been this big wall of security glass with a small set of glass doors in the middle. I say once because those doors were all that were left now. Something had hit the glass walls hard and blown them inwards, leaving shards on the concrete floor and dead bodies beyond the checkpoint.

"This wasn't just my 'event', was it?"

"Very clever. No, there have been many other...'events', as you put them. None of them related to you, so don't worry your little head."

I sighed and moved forward, stepping through one of the blown-out windows and into what must have been the place's lobby.

I'm sure that, once upon a time, it was a well-developed, modern place, at least in a government-science-building type of way. It had started out with those glass doors and concrete floor, but soon enough that gave way to a semi-circle of white marble with dark flecks in it; the walls went from gray to a soft orange color.

The piles of corpses and the decaying, headless body of a security guard slumped at a rotting wooden desk off to the left kind of ruined the illusion of this place being nothing more than a government building buried out in the middle of nowhere.

The headless security guard stood lord over four metal detector gates, set up like the halls of the dead - I thought of passing through a gauntlet on the way to a promised land, like Indiana Jones. Thankfully, nobody had been passing through those when the event had taken place, so I had no problem stepping right through.

Not so bad, was it?

Now I could focus on the atrium beyond. It must have been a hell of a place once upon a time. A big granite fountain had been plopped right in the middle, still spouting its water fifteen feet or so into the air, only something had chipped away at the edges of the fountain, so every now and then some of it would slop out onto the marble floor and the skeletons surrounding it like some weird plants getting watered. Escalators went down both sides of the atrium, but like the ones outside, they were piled high with the dead.

"How many people worked here?" I asked.

Delilah came through the metal detector and stood beside me. "A lot. This was no small operation."

I patted my hands on my hips. "Now what?"

"You don't hear it?"

"Hear what?"

"Hmm. I know our hearing is different but…listen closely."

I cocked my head. Now that she mentioned it, yeah. I could hear buzzing in the air, like somebody had left a stereo on, cranked all the way up. "I hear it. What about it?" I asked.

"That's the sound of the hole at the center of your reality. It's where we're going. Now move."

Chapter 26

Borderline

She didn't make me navigate those escalators full of dead bodies, thank God. Instead she made me go around the fountain, toward the very back of the place, the far wall that was tucked away from the rest of the complex, so far from the escalators that nobody would pass by there without wanting to go check it out. The wall back looked like someone had taken it straight out of a cheesy Midwestern mall and transplanted it down there; it was this off-white thing, filled with the ugliest mural you've ever seen, complete with cacti, the desert, cowboys, steer, and all that good old Southwestern bullshit, rendered with the artistic sensibilities of a fourth grader.

"Lovely. Just lovely," I said, putting my hands on my hips and staring up at this abortion.

"Keep moving," she replied.

"What?"

"You heard me."

"The fuck am I supposed to do, walk through the wall?"

She pointed at the bottom right corner of the mural. "Look closely and behold the secret, my dear."

"What...?" I looked to the painting, and even as pissed off as I felt, even as determined as I was to think that she was off her goddamned rocker, I saw what she meant, though I don't think anybody would see it if they weren't looking for it specifically or examining that monstrosity up close. "Very clever."

Give credit where credit was due - put an obscure mural in the back of the place, ugly as sin so that no one will look at it, and hide the secret to the whole thing in one of the kidney-sized balls of the steer. It looked like a little black knob, but not the knob you're thinking of, you perverts.

"Great. So I have to grab the bull by the balls?" I said.

She chuckled. "Why should saving humanity be without its sense of humor?"

"Got a point there," I said, and strolled over to the mural. I *really* started to hear that humming/buzzing sound. Nah. Not hear it...*feel* it. Like it was vibrating through my skull, making my teeth rattle against each other, making my bones quiver. I'd been to concerts where I stood right by the stacks, and while they might have been louder, even those didn't give me the same feeling deep down in my bones. It wasn't *that* hard to believe that whatever was producing that god-awful sound might be the end of all things.

Not hard at all, but I had to deal with my own reality at that second. I had to keep things moving so I could at least get to Kristy and know she was okay. I remembered her as the thing driving me forward, her beautiful face the totem that made me reach out and grab hold of that bull's knob.

A twist, and something clicked. I pulled on the thing and a door swung open in the middle of the mural, revealing this second door behind it, some small, non-descript thing with a card reader right above its stainless steel handle.

Well now what? I turned, but she was already beside me, beating the butt of the gun against the card reader until it popped off with a sizzle of sparks.

I raised my hands to shield myself. "You trying to kill us, you psycho?"

She reached across me and pushed the door inwards. "You'd know if I was trying to kill you."

"You sure seem to have been trying."

"No I haven't. Go on," she said, motioning toward the door.

"I'm not going to get sucked up into the void, am I?"

She poked the gun into the small of my back, and I danced like her favorite little marionette, slipping through into the dark space behind the wall.

We emerged onto a steel walkway a lot like the one at the other station, extending out over an abyss that mirrored the one in Barstow. Except for one difference, this one tiny little thing.

Like Delilah had said, this was the center of the corruption eating away at the Multiverse. It showed, too: there was this thing hovering in mid-air in the abyss. Crazy, but my brain saw it as the world's biggest Jell-O mold, suspended it in the abyss. Streaks of electricity shot through the gray jelly, and each pulse made the mass quiver.

"What the hell is it?" I asked.

She stepped through the door, her eyes lighting up with excitement. "Corruption," she said. "The denial of all existence. I believe your scientists called it Strange Matter."

That rang a bell...why did that ring a bell? Oh, yeah. I had read a Wikipedia article on it one time after reading some guy's theory about different forms of the Earth getting wiped out. "Isn't that supposed to only be at, like, high pressures?"

"Do I look like a scientist? All I know is that your people harnessed it to create the weapon, and since they've been gone, it's grown many times its original size, and will one day wipe this Aethyr out of existence."

"Good lord."

"I don't believe God has anything to do with it, dear. See those stairs down there?" she said, nodding at a set of metal stairs down the walkway and to our right.

I saw them, and I saw how they connected up with several other walkways, one of which must have practically crossed through the mass. "Yeah?"

"We're going down. Close to the Matter."

I had begun to walk, but that sure as hell pulled me up short. "Are you out of your mind? You want to get closer to it?"

"Of course. That is the Portal."

"People stepped into that thing? I thought it was, you know, the denial of all existence."

"It is, but the borderline of the Matter - between this world and whatever lies on the other side - is a Portal back. Not that it matters. We don't need to take that Portal with your…talent."

"You'd better be right."

"I hope so, but others *have* done this."

She put her hand on my shoulder.

"Wait. We may not be able to communicate once we get deep enough."

I laughed. "We already can't communicate."

"I mean it quite literally. It's not a laughing matter."

"What do you want from me?" I asked.

"When we get close, you're going to have to take us to the right place, but you have to take us to one specific place. Anywhere else and we could get lost…well, who knows where."

"That sounds like bullshit. I thought the portal could take us anywhere?"

She cleared her throat. "It's very…person-specific."

I raised an eyebrow. "Person-specific." I wanted to see how deep she could dig herself.

"Yes, based on one's experiences-"

I cut her off. I had no choice but to do what she wanted. Might as well get on with it. "You know what I think? I think you want me to take us to a specific place, but you also know that pointing that gun at me isn't going to do a damned bit of good if I decide to take us somewhere else. Maybe I send you spinning into that void you were talking about?" I shrugged. "So you have to try to lie to me. I get it. You've got your angles covered, except this one. Even that gun can't let you cover this one."

Her lips were pursed, eyes getting teary."It's not that, dear. It's-"

"Come on. Don't waste our time. You're insulting my intelligence and yours, come to think of it. I'm going to do what you want because, let's face it: I don't know where else I would go. I'm not letting you assholes get the upper hand, and I'm not giving up on Kristy."

She crossed her arms over her chest. "That's the most sensible thing you've said."

"Don't think this means you've won. I'm going to figure out a way to kill you. I promise you that."

She actually grinned, Delilah. "Many have tried, but you're welcome to give it a shot, dear."

"I'll do just that, but tell me where we're going."

"Fine. When I give you the signal, I want you to imagine

a small pathway behind an old hotel. The hotel is salmon-colored and tall, about 30 stories. You know it as the Bellagio in your world, but we're not going back to your world."

"That's not enough. What else do I need to do?"

"It's a dusty pathway, facing out into the desert, and at the end of the pathway is a small square of concrete surrounding a steel hatch in the ground. The hatch is locked with a giant padlock. Is this enough or do you need more?"

I nodded. "I think it'll do. Where is it?"

"It's where we're going."

"You're a slippery bitch, you know that?"

"I wouldn't still be here otherwise. Now let's move."

"No sooner said than done."

We descended into the abyss, and the sound only got stronger and more insistent. I wondered if my brain was quivering inside my head, like that jelly. More talking. That was the ticket, because if I kept talking, it also kept me from focusing on that terrible sensation. "Is this like that portal at the bunker?"

"I suppose, but the Watchers managed to keep from threatening the entirety of existence, didn't they?"

"I guess they did." At last, I ran out of words to keep whistling through the graveyard. I didn't even have any more questions to ask her, so I put my head down and concentrated on putting one foot in front of the other, continually pushing that awful feeling out of my head.

So we kept descending, and before I knew it we were at the same level as the mass, approaching it from the left-hand side, down the gantry-way. You could tell that level of walkways was different from the others. More of that circuitry-style stuff covered the railings, riding alongside three heavy rubber tubes that went from clamped plugs at the back wall, plugs that looked like those standpipe hookups you see sometimes in parking garages. Coolant maybe? I didn't know. I could only guess at what the plan was - would be - there.

The Strange Matter grabbed hold of me. My vision doubled, and my head started swimming. The world slipped and slid, the tubes revealing themselves as ribbed arteries, twisting and writhing over the railing.

"What is happening?"

If Delilah answered, I didn't hear it, mostly because I couldn't hear a damn thing at that moment. I had gone somewhere else. I felt like someone had slipped me a tab of acid and turned me loose in a fun-house, hoping to see how fucked-up the situation could get.

Well, boys and girls, it seemed it could get even more fucked-up after all - a *lot* more, in fact. There I was, stumbling down the walkway toward the void in reality, when something went whizzing over my head. I didn't hear it so much as I saw it. When it passed over me it formed a riptide in the thick, liquid air, leaving a wake that spread in concentric rings.

Huh, that was interesting. I raised my head toward the catwalk above us and saw two guys in suits (I think you fellows see where this is going) leaning over the railing, pointing pistols at us.

My brain told me I should be freaked out, run for cover, hide behind Delilah, I don't know, *something,* but I just couldn't get worked up about it. *Sure hope they don't hit me.* That was about all I could think before continuing down the walkway toward the waiting arms of my jellyfish lover. I think Delilah said something over my shoulder, because it sounded like when someone tries to talk to you underwater, but I couldn't make a bit of sense out of it. A couple of heavy thuds came right after that, probably her firing the handgun back, but again, brain could only focus on one thing: getting to the edge of that hole in reality.

When I did get there, it seemed like it had only been one step but also a thousand years, if that makes any sense. Ketamine didn't have shit on this particular hole for affecting time. The hippies would've killed for five minutes in contact with it. Or died, I don't know, but then I stood right in front of it, staring into the void, so to speak - and I don't know if it stared into me, but I thought I recognized something true inside of myself, maybe inside all of humanity, in that dumb, empty void of reality.

It was only a tap on the shoulder from Delilah herself that kept me from wandering on in. Right. The location she had told me about. Time to head on out and hit the trail, if only I could get past the wobbling sensation. I put both hands on the railings and closed my eyes, imagining that place she had talked about: path behind a hotel, hole in the desert, padlocked shut.

I don't think we jumped right away, not like I usually do. It felt more like watching the sunset, shifting through the degrees of reality and trying to make it to wherever it was that Delilah wanted to go.

Then we were through. I felt the desert's chilly night wind on my skin a second before I opened my eyes and saw that we were right where she wanted us to be. I could see the hotel towering over us in my peripheral vision, and when I looked down I saw the hatch, like she had promised.

"Well done," she said, and clapped her hands like I was

a stage magician. "Very well done indeed, dear."

"Don't you 'dear' me, you crone. I-"

What I did was get cut off by a gunshot whistling past my ear and chipping away at the hotel wall behind me. I remember that - hearing that shit chip and fall off clear as day, and the fact that I actually reacted this time.

Oh geez, we are fucked. They followed us.

Chapter 27

Crestfallen

I didn't need to worry about trying to use Delilah as a human…er…angelic shield. She was more than happy to stand tall and start opening fire into the desert while I huddled behind her. She had to protect her precious cargo no matter what, and hell, it wasn't like even a bullet to the brain could stop her, based on what happened to Daniel. Poor Daniel…

Poor Daniel, but it didn't have to be poor me. I knelt down and found the biggest rock I could, keeping one eye on her back as she came out from behind the scrub. She'd pulled out the second pistol and was two-handing those bitches like she was in a John Woo movie.

I crept up behind Delilah, pushing the rock into the small of my back as I did. Last thing I needed was her coming back to reality, but thankfully that didn't seem to be happening. I'd lost count of the number of bullets she'd taken.

I kept on going, and I got close, and as I did I felt the warmth of that rock against my skin like shaking someone's hand. It was time to take hold of the reins or let the whole thing come crashing down around me.

Put that way, I had to do it. So I cocked my arm and I swung at the bitch's head as hard as I could.

It's probably not a shocker that I was a little bitch during my teen years. Vandalism was a hobby, like some people collect baseball cards. One of my favorite Halloween traditions was smashing pumpkins with a baseball bat, so I know what I speak of when I tell you that her head sounded the same.

I wondered for a second if it was a good or bad sign, if she'd decide to jump up and take out an unholy wrath on me, but no divine intervention was coming to get her. Not today.

Something savage in my mind opened up. You ever had that happen? You know what I'm talking about? I lost total control. The fact that I stood out in the open with gunshots ringing out around me? Didn't matter.

I bashed her in the head again. And again. I kept going, over and over and over again. All the frustration and anger and aggression that had built up toward that cunt (and I don't use that word lightly - I *never* use that word lightly) over the last few days broke open and came rushing out.

By the time I had finished swinging the rock, her head could have been made out of raw hamburger. I straightened up and dropped the rock, managing to get hold of myself at last. I noticed that the shots weren't coming anymore. I saw some movement out in the dark, in the desert, and I thought about picking up her guns, but what good was that going to do me if it was a whole crowd?

Just finish me off. What the hell. Let this end.

I lifted my hands skyward.

The figures in the desert got closer, resolving into a group of four people in dark robes - robes a lot like the Acolytes that we'd seen in Bakersfield.

Well geez, now I really am fucked, I thought. They had to be there to get revenge for their guys. Pay me back for what I did. It only seemed fair. The only reason they hadn't shot me yet was that they were going to make it nice and slow and painful, just to see me scream.

May as well pick up one of those pistols and off yourself. The thought of Kristy held me back. I couldn't leave her alone in this mess. So I held my hands up and watched them come towards me. The biggest one, the one in the middle, pointed a shotgun at me, his elbow up high. I didn't have any doubt that he would shoot to kill if I made any wrong movement, which I have to admit occurred to me for a split second.

Somebody clicked their tongue at the guy, and he lifted the shotgun. "You are the Chosen One?" he said, in this thick accent that sounded almost…I don't know. Nigerian maybe? I didn't know enough about the area to be sure.

I put one hand on the back of my head. "That's what they tell me. Look, if you guys are here to-"

"You be silent," he said.

"You can trust her," said the guy off to his left.

I recognized that voice right away. It wasn't *just* that the guy in the middle was big. The guy who had told him to trust me was small. So small in fact… "Tommy? Is that you?"

The short one pulled off his mask, and the kid beamed at me.

"You're not to remove your mask," the big man snapped.

"It's okay. I know her. We've met," Tommy said, looking from the big guy to me.

"She killed our own," said one of the other Acolytes, with a thick Irish accent.

"Technically I didn't," I replied, but it sounded lame even to me.

"She did what she had to do," Tommy replied, and stepped between me and the others. "She spared me."

I took a step away from him as the meaning of his words settled onto me. "Wait. You mean you weren't kidnapped? You were an Acolyte all along? By your own choosing?"

He bit his lip and nodded.

"Why did you let us slaughter them?"

"He does not have to answer to you," the big guy roared.

Tommy held out his hand. "It's okay." He seemed to think about it, and I had to appreciate that he wasn't blasting off some answer from the hip. At last he said, "they were…impure. Not good people. I needed to get close to you, no matter the cost. I didn't like it, but you had to do what you had to do. They were trying to kill you, and, well, they didn't know who I truly am."

"Who are you?"

"I'm Tommy."

"But that story you told me?"

"I'm not from Vegas, but I did lose my mother, and the Acolytes did take me in. That much is true."

The big guy was loosening up a little. "He is very special. And important. More important than you."

"So they're feeding you a line of garbage about being the Chosen One too?"

"Not exactly, but it doesn't matter. All that matters is what you have to do down there," he said, and pointed toward the hatch.

"The-is that-that's where the Engine is?" I thought about that vision I had, the one in the underground hallway. Had I been seeing the place where I had to go all along?

"Yeah. That's it. She brought you here, didn't she?"

I nodded.

"I thought so. That's why we were waiting. They'll do

whatever it takes."

"Yeah? Well so will I. I did. I'd as soon look at her as kill her again."

He toed the body. "Hmm. Yeah. About that."

"She dead for good?"

"Hard to say. You were brutal."

I spat on her. "No less than she deserved."

The Irish woman said, "watch your language in front of the child."

"I've heard worse, Maerlynn. I've said worse," Tommy replied, and circled Delilah's body, his hands behind his back like a miniature dictator.

The big guy looked at me for a long time. At last, he lowered his shotgun and pulled at his mask with one hand, revealing a face the color of dark coffee, ridged with this scar that ran from just above his right eyebrow and down that side of his face. "If Tommy trusts you, we have to trust you."

He nodded to the others, and they removed their masks. No real revelations there; nobody I'd ever seen before or anything. Seeing the faces made me realize that they might not be so bad. They sure as hell didn't seem evil.

The tall guy looked to Tommy. "What is it you want us to do?"

"Stay up here and guard the hole. There might be more of them coming. I don't know that she's done for, either," he said, and kicked Delilah's body. "That would be a little too easy."

"Easy? You call that easy?" I said. "You have no idea what I went through trying to kill that bitch. I've been to what I can only call literal hell with that bitch."

He grinned. "Calm down, it's all right."

"Yeah. Yeah. I'm a little stressed." I scratched my ear. "You might see how I would be, being the savior of all worlds."

The Irish girl - a redhead as it turned out, imagine that - smirked. "Let's not get ahead of ourselves here."

"I was being ironic. Don't worry, I don't buy that shit."

"Let us hope not," the big guy said.

"I only come to save the world. You guys got our backs?" I led the kid toward the hole.

"That is correct," the big guy replied, and they fell in behind us.

"So wait. If you're so important, why are you going down there with me?" I asked the kid.

"If *you're* so important why are *you* going down there?" he said.

"Point taken. I just don't think I'm going to walk out of there alive."

"Maybe I won't, either, but where would we be if generals had ever thought like that?"

I glanced at him out of the corner of my eye. What a weird kid. I had no idea what to expect next from him. "You're a lot more mature than your age would indicate, you know."

"Who says I look like my actual age?"

I stroked my chin. "Very interesting, young man." I tried to put on a German accent and it came out pretty damned awful. "We may get along after all."

He was pure business. "Let's focus on dealing with the Engine. I think the rest will fall in line."

"Okay, whatever you say. You're the expert here."

We arrived at the hatch. The kid, or whatever the hell he

was, looked at the big guy. "Aaron? Care to help us out?"

"Right. Stand aside," Aaron said, and pointed the shotgun at the padlock on the hatch. One good, resounding shot and the thing burst open in a shower of metal shards. He nodded at the hatch. "They know you're coming now."

"I believe they already do," Tommy replied, and kicked the hatch door open.

"All right, kid," I said. "Let's go get this thing done."

Chapter 28

From the Past Until Completion

The inside of the hatch was covered wall-to-wall in that shiny white tile with the weird, carpet-like stuff that we had seen in the bunker. It sent a chill down my spine, you know, because what happened in that bunker had completely changed my world.

"I don't like this," I said from the foot of the rickety, rusted metal ladder that we had descended. I ran my hands over my arms, even though it was pretty warm down there.

"I don't think you should. It's not about liking it," Tommy said.

"You hearing this, kid?" I asked. By "this" I meant a deep thumping and bumping come from the passageway. It wasn't the sound of machinery, but something heavier and more rhythmic, like drums out of some other world: *DUH. DUH. Duhduhduhduh.DUH. DUH. Duhduhduhduh.*

"Of course," he said.

"Does it sound familiar?"

He shrugged.

"Where the hell do I know that beat?" I said.

DUH. DUH. Duhduhduhduh.

It clicked. It was weird to hear it in that context, but soothing, too, like being stranded in the middle of the ocean and coming across a doll you had as a kid. A wink from the heavens. I hadn't expected anything other than maybe the sound of machinery, grinding away toward doomsday, but this… "Are you kidding me?" I whispered.

"What?"

"It's Blue Monday. By New Order. Ever heard it?"

"I'm not too familiar with music."

"It's a classic. Assholes or not, at least they have good taste."

He smirked at me. "Does it make you feel brave?"

"Yeah. I don't think I can fail with Peter Hook on my side."

He raised an eyebrow.

I waved a hand. "Don't worry about it."

He bounced on his heels. "Right. You said you wanted to get to it? Let's get to it." He walked down the hallway without a glance back at me.

"Yeah. Sure." I trailed along behind him. With each step we took, the beat of the drums ratcheted in volume. I started to hear the synthesizer playing over top of that impossible beat. They had to have it cranked up around the level of a 747 taking off, but when you don't have to worry about the durability of your body you can turn it up as loud as you want.

The kid, or whatever the hell he was, put his arm out and stopped me, pointing into the darkness. "Look."

"What?"

"Do you see it?"

"I don-" But I did see it: a shimmering dark blue web hanging in mid-air, like someone took those annoying Christmas lights that hang down in a web over your roof, turned them dark blue, and spread them across the hallway. I reached out for it, but he grabbed my wrist.

"Don't do that. Not yet, anyway."

"What is it?"

"It's a door." He let go and walked up to it. "They had to use all kinds of tricks when they built this place."

"Like what?"

He nodded at them. "Past that, you're back home."

"So when we step through…?"

"We'll be back in your home Aethyr."

"The music *is* coming from another world."

"Technically, yes. But, you know…you're not going to be able to get out to your world from inside there."

"Uh…say what?"

"They couldn't make what they were doing too obvious to the Aetelia. Building the Engine out in the open in your Aethyr would have led to too many questions. 'Why are you doing so much with this hole in the ground'? The problem was that they needed the actual Engine in your Aethyr because your world, for whatever reason, is key." He held up a hand when I began to speak. "I don't know why. The Watchers might, but they've never let it out."

"That's a bitch."

"Right. They built a bridge between Aethyrs when they dug this out. So you see, there's no way out. In your world, we're standing *inside* the dirt on the other side."

"I think I follow. Sneaky bastards."

He glanced over his shoulder. "I don't think a non-Watcher Aetelia has ever even been through this portal."

"Is that what you are? An Aetelia?"

He kicked at the floor. "Not exactly. It's…complicated. Did they mention the Reckonings?"

"Yeah. Now that you mention it, that does sound

vaguely familiar."

He glanced at the ceiling. "It should happen in about an hour or so."

"I don't get it. You guys have all these secrets, and you seem to be tuned in on them. I mean, this Reckoning. How do you know about it?"

"I wish I had time to tell you. We can talk about it after we've done this, okay? I promise." He walked through the web.

"No, wait. I can't...ah, fuck it." I followed him through the web, closing my eyes as I did so.

The sensation was a tingling that spread across my body. The *sound* of passing through it was the biggest thing, like you were assaulted with white noise fuzz and crackling that rose over the pounding of New Order, and then the music was even louder, the bass line and drums vibrating my ribs.

If Azazel meant for that music to intimidate me, he sure as hell picked the wrong track. Combining it with the tension of what was about to go down brought up this churning reptile hate that reminded me of the endless wars with my mom when I was a teenager. I'm sure that song had been playing at some point when we fought, and that fight-or-flight reflex kicked in just fine.

I couldn't discount returning to my home Aethyr, either. Something deep down felt so *right* about being home; this was *my* turf, and they were the invaders who hijacked humanity. It was time to give them whatever payback I could.

The first verse kicked in and I started humming along. Tommy might as well have vanished. In fact, pretty much everything else had vanished for me, except the steps that I had to take to get down that passageway and to the small square of light that had to be the doorway to the Engine, or where-ever they were keeping it. I would shove their bullshit right down their throat.

Chapter 29

People You Don't Know

I walked into a big, dark circular thing. It looked like a missile silo, or at least how I imagined a silo. The walls curved upward into a thin, cone-shaped shaft. I wondered where they had hidden the Engine down here. I studied the room and found some more pressing matters, including impassive-looking white guys, real secret police types, who hid in the shadows, leaning against the dark concrete walls, each holding an assault rifle. Did they think I brought an army with me?

In the middle of all this sat a circle of seats covered in orange vinyl, and then in the center of *that* circle was a little wooden table, holding a little circular silver thing that had to be the hub of the sound system pumping out the music.

That music…good God. It came from everywhere, shaking my bones. I took a hesitating step forward, stopping again when I realized that what I had thought a lump pillow was actually Grabbe, his head in his cuffed hands. He heard my movement and looked up, but I don't think he could focus on me; he had this thousand-yard stare, like he'd been drugged. His eyes rolled, and a sideshow appeared from the shadows behind him.

That sideshow consisted of his father, wearing a white suit with blue pinstripes, his hair slicked up into a pompadour. He danced into the circle of light in the center of the room, a young chick in a pink sundress on his arm. A cigarette hung from the corner of his mouth and he had one hand on the girl's waist, leading her step for step. You'd think he was at some 80s club rather than presiding over the end of the world.

My brain could only just process what I saw, and it damn near froze up when I figured out the identity of the girl in pink.

"Kristy," I shrieked, and the couple...oh God, I thought of them as a *couple*, stopped dancing.

Everyone in the room turned in unison to face me.

The girl in the pink dress lowered her blue sunglasses. It was Kristy all right, but Azazel had done something to her, because she had that same empty look that Grabbe wore. Somebody had teased her hair up and her face was caked in makeup that would make John Waters blush. It was a travesty. Kristy was all about the natural beauty – every little bit of makeup that they had splattered onto her went a long way toward making her look like she was either ready to start turning tricks or star in some cock rock video.

Hell, maybe both.

Azazel leaned over close to her ear, and my stomach caught fire. He mouthed something to her and she laughed, covering her mouth while her eyes bored right into me. She recognized me, and I could see a hint of what was there when we had last seen each other, but I saw something else there, too. Something a lot more like Delilah than Kristy; a hint of mischief that could become cruelty at the drop of a hat.

On some level I had thought I would rush into the room a hero, ready to defeat the beast and spirit away with the lovely damsel on my arm. How naïve had I been? How ignorant I had been to not consider what Azazel could do to warp her mind.

"Turn down the music," I screamed over the noise and the nausea in my gut.

Azazel rolled his eyes, but he waved his hand and the volume dropped. Now it didn't beat my skull open, it only pulling my ear drums out by force.

"You told me to come and I came," I said.

"That's very wonderful and we're very happy to see you, but tell me, where's Delilah?"

"I bashed her skull in like she deserved."

He ran a finger over his lips. "I see, and why is the boy here?"

I looked at Tommy; he said nothing.

"He insisted," I said.

Azazel smirked. "Your funeral, child."

"I think you'll be surprised," Tommy said.

Azazel cackled. "Now that's what I like to see. Balls. The child has balls. He's entertaining, too."

I couldn't believe Tommy's guts when he said, "we'll see who's entertaining in the end, you dried-up fruit."

I had to keep myself from doing my own cackling, especially at the dumbfounded look on the Watcher's face. Of course, the look didn't last long. His lips turned up into a twisted grimace, his fingers tightening on Kristy's arm. "There's a fine line between bold and stupid, little boy, and I believe you just crossed it." He snapped motioned toward the guards, who cocked their guns and turned on us in unison.

I held up my hand. "No. Wait, wait, wait. Part of the deal is if I'm going to be helping you with this Engine, the kid lives. Period."

Azazel loosened his grip on Kristy, and her eyes flicked from Tommy to me. I thought I saw a hint of her old self in there, but I couldn't be sure.

"What is this proposal?" Azazel asked.

"No proposal. Demands, and don't tell me that I'm in no position to be making demands. We know who really has leverage here."

"We do indeed," he said, and glanced at Kristy.

Right. Let's keep going. "You can't do shit without me."

He narrowed his eyes. "Shrewd. Tell me what you want."

"Just what I said. You have to let the kid live. No tricks like killing him once I'm out, either."

"How would you stop us once you've done our bidding?"

"I don't think that's how it works. I might die in there...hell, I think it's pretty likely, but I don't think you'll be able to break your word."

"How can you be sure?"

"I can't, but going against my instincts has fucked me up so far. Time to listen, I think."

He considered it before leaning down to Kristy. It made me want to grab one of the rifles and tear his pretty face apart. "Hmm," he said in her ear, "what do you think, dear? The boy could be a threat."

She glared at the kid, her lip curled in revulsion. "Whatever," she said. "Like he could really screw up the glory that's to come."

Suspicion confirmed. That's only about 60% Kristy. What happened?

Azazel released her and took a step to one side. "Are you

sure about that? We could be in trouble."

"What's a kid going to do to you? Honestly."

He raised a bitchy eyebrow. "Now who can argue with that logic? Not me." He waved his hand. "Oh well. The brat remains, at least until this business is complete. No promises past that, you understand."

"All right. So you want me to use the Engine."

He put his hands behind his back. "Correct."

"I have to activate it somehow."

"Correct again. I suppose there *is* a reason you are the Chosen One."

"Very funny." I surveyed the room one more time. "Where is it, anyway? I only see one way in or out of here, and not much else."

"Oh how stupid of me, have I really not brought it up? What an oversight." He clapped his hands.

One of the guards on the far side knocked on the wall, two hard little raps. It didn't sound like concrete at all – more like hollow wood. Something shifted behind it and the wall began to look like the gray jelly that had made up the hole in reality. The center of the jelly parted, revealing a circular, bright white wall with a slit in the center.

When I say the door was circular, you've got to keep in mind that it was jutting out of an already-circular wall. So part of the circle of the room we were in melted away, revealing this other circle , you know, in opposition of the room's circle. It was circles inside of circles inside of circles. It seemed significant, like something was going on that I couldn't quite get a hold of, but every time I got close to it, it slipped away.

I pointed at it. "That's the door?"

"Indeed."

"So I just go over there and step through?"

"Indeed again. I…we…we'll follow you."

I glanced at Grabbe. A little drool was running from the corner of his mouth. "What about him?"

"He's…erm…indisposed. I'll deal with him soon enough, don't you worry."

I opened my mouth, but he cut me off with a short hand motion. "Don't even *think* of adding another condition. You're on thin ice as it is, girl."

"Fine." I sighed, gathering the strength and courage that had been building out there in the hallway, and then strode across the room without so much as a glance at anyone else in the room. *Focus on fixing this. That and nothing else.*

That resolve lasted until I got right in front of the door. I could *feel* the power emanating from behind it.

Azazel and Kristy followed me to the door, presenting the perfect trashy couple who sat on the sidelines, ready to watch me get thrown to the wolves.

I sighed and nodded at the kid, who had followed them in turn, staying just out of their reach. He nodded back, telling me *you'll be all right* without actually saying it.

"I just touch it?"

"You know what to do," Azazel said. "You'll see something wonderful." He linked his arm around Kristy's, and this time I couldn't keep the anger down.

"Will you stop touching her?"

Kristy responded, grinding at my nerves. "He's taking care of me until we take our place with them. I've been shown the light. You will soon. I promise."

Azazel cleared his throat. "I've done nothing to the girl, I assure you."

"You're a liar," I said, but I had finished throwing my energy at him, at least for now. I knew the limits of my handle on the situation.

Kristy put a hand on her chest. "You think I've been brainwashed?"

"I know it. You're not you."

"You don't know. You haven't seen what I've seen."

I glanced at Azazel from the corner of my eye. "This isn't going down the way you think it is, buddy boy. Don't be surprised when I step out of there ready to kill your cheesy ass."

"Oh my, such tough words. Whatever will I do?"

"Do what you always do." I gazed at the wall.

"Bravo," he said, and clapped. "It's good to get someone with some spirit in here. Let's tear the whole fucking world down tonight, boys and girls."

"Jesus, Zazzy, you're such a drama queen," Kristy said.

Zazzy? Fucking Zazzy? I'd kill the bastard for that.

I touched the wall, running my hand up and down the black slit. "What am I supposed to be doing here?" I asked.

Azazel sighed and said, "knock three times, and the genie will answer."

"You're such an asshole," I muttered, but I gave the door three slow, heavy whacks. The door whirred - I imagined an ancient locking mechanism in there, metal turning on metal, neither of which had seen the light of day in millenia. Then that little black slit split open.

All that production, and even when it was open, you couldn't see much more inside. All I could see was an empty black chamber, with no real distinguishing features.

I glanced at Azazel, and what I saw surprised the hell

out of me. I expected him to be excited, or awed, or even just happy, but he wasn't. What he looked to be was scared out of his mind.

"Everything okay there, chief?" I asked.

He waved a hand. "Of course. Why wouldn't it be?"

"You tell me."

Kristy answered. "Now's not the time. You have to save us, honey."

For a second, I saw her real self. Whatever Azazel might have done to her, deep down, she knew the score. She knew that I'd rather die than let her live like this.

"You're right, Polly."

"Such melodrama," Azazel said. "Get in there already. Step inside and all will be revealed."

"Fine," I said. I didn't like it, I didn't want to do it, but there had to be some way to throw a monkey wrench in bitch boy's plans. I saluted them. "Here we go. Tons of fun."

I stepped into the chamber, and the door slid closed behind me.

I had been stuck in the darkness for less than a second when the chamber lit up, revealing four steel posts, laid out in a diamond pattern, in the middle of the chamber. The floor beneath me felt like concrete, but it looked like linen.

A booming, masculine voice came from everywhere. "Step to the posts," it said.

No better time than the present. I stepped forward.

Chapter 30

Got it Coming in the Real World

The posts were warm and pliant to the touch, almost like touching somebody's skin. The experience probably should have put me off, but instead I found that I never wanted to take my hands off of them.

The post buzzed under my hand, the most realistic vibrator ever conceived, sending a sensation through my body like a shot of narcotic. Once the feeling had completed a circuit of my nerves, something under my feet clicked, and the overhead lights softened.

The voice spoke again. "Scan and DNA sequencing complete. Welcome back, Matty DiCamillo."

Only it didn't quite say that. I understood it, but I also knew that it wasn't English.

"What do you mean, welcome back?" I asked, in that same language. It didn't even sound familiar, but what the hell did I know about languages?

The voice was done with me. Whatever was in charge here decided it was time to open the circular part of the wall in front of me.

I covered my eyes as the bright desert sun streamed in from the opening wall.

Going to go blind here…

"What the fuck," I muttered, and tried to let go of the posts, but my own body betrayed me, clinging to the warmth and softness. They *would not* obey, whether I tried to loosen or tighten.

Jesus Christ, it's a trap and I've walked right into it. I'm going to be stuck down here for whatever's coming, whatever…

Everything went dark.

For a second I lost myself altogether, and didn't return to the world until the posts vibrated again. They must have been pumping the greatest tranquilizer in the known universe, because I damn near flopped over as an intense feeling of peace washed over me.

I didn't even know *how* to question what was going on; I saw colors in the darkness, swirling, painting trails over my corneas.

Along with the colors came a soft voice, whispering in my ear, telling me everything would be fine: "This is what you're made for. This is where you've been, and where you will go."

I accepted it without even knowing what it meant.

"Look up."

I did. The ceiling wasn't dark at all, and I saw that the streaks of light were galaxies, whirling above and around me.

"Closer," the voice said, and the room swung around, pushing me past galaxy after galaxy. At last, we stopped right before a single star, the size of the moon in the night sky.

"My home," said the voice, and it was a bit more distant this time. I saw the outline of a person fading in, floating in space as it extended its left hand.

"Who are you?" I said. It amazed me that I could manage even that.

The...person, or whatever the hell it was, could have taught David Bowie a thing or two about androgyny. The face was sallow, but it was also the most beautiful, delicate thing that I had ever seen - high cheekbones, sculpted eyebrows, and puffy lips.

My brain decided that it was a male, but I was far from certain on that count. He wore a bright white suit that put Azazel's to shame, tailored tight to the body, cut low across his hips. He resembled an angel a lot more than any of the people I had seen over the previous few days.

He smiled, and it was enough to make your heart ache. "Matty. It's so good for you to see me again."

Strange way to put it. "Do I know you?" As soon as I said it, I realized that I did, somewhere deep inside.

"I am the face that has been in your dreams since you were a little girl. I have watched over you for a long time."

"What's your name?"

"Paraoan."

"Do you have something to do with the Reckoning?" I asked.

"In a sense."

"Why haven't I heard of you then? I mean, not even from those nuts." I nodded over my shoulder toward Azazel and his clowns.

"Because they do not know. To them I am a myth. They refer to me as the Lost Aetelia. Larger than life. Not like us."

"*You're* the lost Aetelia?"

"Yes." He gave this guilty smile, and it struck me as hilarious. Here was a being with godlike powers, beyond even the comprehension of the Aetelia, looking like a kid caught stealing something.

My laughter set him off, and he chuckled, then picked up the laughter as well.

We shared a moment, floating out there in space, hanging over galaxies and stars, like gods.

I wondered if that was the trick to the Engine. Would it make me a god of some sort?

Paraoan chuckled. "Sorry, Matty. You are not here to become a god. Disappointing, I know."

"Then why am I here? They said I'd know what to do, but I'm clueless."

"That is to be expected. There is much that they do not understand about this chamber, including their flawed interpretation of your purpose."

"I can see that now," I said.

"The Watchers were never meant to be part of this. The Prophecy was never meant for them. Nor was the Reckoning, but when they involved themselves?" He shrugged. "I would not turn down the help to get you and your companion to this place, at this time."

"My companion?" *Tommy.* It had to be.

"Your insight is keen. All the Watchers did was discover this chamber and build an elaborate series of lies around it."

"Did you tell them to spread those lies?" I asked.

"I certainly did not discourage them, but no. All they knew – all that I showed them, I should say – was a girl very much like you in the databanks of this system. They knew nothing more."

"They convinced themselves that they did."

The corner of his mouth turned up a little. "It is amazing what one can accomplish with a little fanaticism and willing self-delusion."

"How long have you been here?"

He frowned. "Time has so little meaning here. I am uncertain. I am here and elsewhere, many places, all at once. To comment on my status would be fruitless."

I spun my head, gazing around at the sights surrounding me, drinking them in. "This chamber came before the Watchers?"

"Well before the Watchers. Their view of the Multiverse is nearly as obscured as that of humanity," he said.

I didn't know what to say, so I said nothing.

"It is a bit much for you to understand, I know," he said.

"You keep saying stuff like that. Can you read my mind?"

"One day you will understand that there is no real difference between your speech and your thoughts. Soon you will understand much."

"I will? Why me? What's so special about me?"

His gaze was downright hungry when he said, "It is not just you. It is you and the boy. You are both in here."

"Right. Me and the boy."

"One of you has awakened. The other will…soon. You need to understand what I – *we* – do."

"'We'?"

"Those who came before, of course. Hold on to the rails. We are going to travel."

The one thing I wanted to do in that room, of all other things, was listen to Paraoan. I was an amoeba next to him/her. I tightened my grip, and I waited.

"Good. Here we go," he said.

Whatever he did, it didn't take long. The view swung and titled like the craziest ride Disney could have ever come up with. A blue wave wiped over the chamber, moving from right to left, annihilating everything in its path and showing a new cross-section of space.

Paraoan tilted his head, and things swung again. My stomach lurched, threatening to let loose with whatever was still down in there.

"Gently," he whispered, and things came into focus again, the moon gliding into view over my left shoulder. Our moon. Earths' moon. Bigger than I'd ever seen it. Bigger than Paraoan's star.

The little blue marble of Earth followed right after it as we kept looping.

"Jesus," I said.

Paraoan cleared his throat and giggled. "Earth, obviously. Your Aethyr provides the focus. We are going to move out now, so be ready."

"Can I even be-"

The question didn't matter. He - or that machine, or whatever was running this planetarium from hell - was in control, and not a damn thing, not even my aching stomach, would stop it.

Thank God, the effect wasn't much worse than a banking plane, but nothing short of a jet could have made the turns we made as we spun out past the planets.

We got faster, blowing past Pluto and the asteroids and out into deep space. We spun up, accelerating, and soon we looked down on one of the arms of the Milky Way. I wanted to stop and admire it, but he had other plans, blasting us through galaxies and clusters of galaxies.

I tried to keep my eyes on Paraoan, to make him my anchor, but he had faded into the background, almost like whatever was projecting the show going on around us was projecting it onto him as well.

Hell, I wasn't even sure this was a show anymore; without the rush of air, without the feeling of inertia, how was I supposed to be able to tell?

"Where are we going?" I asked

He said only, "wait."

I waited.

We blew past galaxies, a multitude of lights in the sky, you know, the kind of thing you read about in Hawking books or as some metaphor in an ancient text. Only I lived it, my stomach lurching with the insanity of it.

"Make it stop," I said.

"I cannot."

I heard him, but I only just processed it, because things were going even faster now. Galaxy after galaxy, cluster after cluster, all blended into one a tunnel of light.

At last we came up over the whole thing – all the planets and the stars and the galaxies – hell, maybe even universes – above one, single point of light in the middle of a primordial field of darkness.

One flashing green light.

"What…what is it?" I asked.

"The answer to all of your questions."

"I-"

"Simply observe."

The light flashed again, and I saw that we weren't really in any primordial darkness, not *really* standing outside of the universe. We were somewhere else entirely, in the midst of a material that flashed in and out of existence in time with the light.

No. It's not even that. It's just…

Plastic.

Just plastic; an enormous field of it, so much I couldn't comprehend it, but just ordinary, common plastic.

Why does this-

The thought would forever remain unfinished, because I heard this loud, heavy voice from all around me. It said: "results are in.

It clicked in my head. The plastic. The light. I glanced over my shoulder, catching a glimpse of the light flashing off of a soft, black surface.

It can't be. This is too insane. No.

"You know it is," Paraoan said.

I faced him/her, and as I did, a burst of light exploded from overhead. It was like God's floodlights, shining down on a baseball diamond where Jesus, Moses, Mohammed, and all the angels in the firmament played ball.

As my eyes adjusted to the blast, I turned toward the source of the voice.

Paraoan was right. I knew exactly where we were. An unfathomably large office door. The drop panel ceiling of Valhalla. Neon lighting of the gods.

An office.

What stepped through the giant door, the source of the voice, was *not* God. Not the way you or I would define God, anyway. It wasn't even a minor deity, or an angel. Nah, it was a dorky guy with a mop of blond hair and thick hipster glasses.

He paused inside the door, blinking and adjusting his glasses.

"Holy shit," he said, in whatever my brain had picked

up in the chamber. He bounded across the room in a flash, leaning down to look at us…only not us, you understand. To look at the flashing light.

Then he looked up to the soft surface that I had seen earlier: an unthinkably huge monitor.

Awe seized my body. I went limp, and if it hadn't been for the posts, I would have fallen to my knees in the face of my creator.

If he knew about the direct worship of one of his creations, he didn't show it.

"Amazing," he said. "Sammy! They're aware."

"No way," said a voice from outside the door.

The blond guy looked back at the monitor, big as Godzilla towering over me. He waved his hand at something I couldn't see, and said "I know. I have contact, but I don't know what to say."

Contact. Did he mean me? I didn't know, but I had to get his attention, let him know that we could hear him and see him and…oh God, literally, if he could just *see* me…

"It is futile, child," Paraoan said, but I didn't care.

I screamed, but before I could see if he had even heard, my voice took on that weird echo effect you get on a good hit of nitrous. Next thing I knew, something grabbed hold of the room and yanked us down into the light, through our Multiverse, passing through the tunnel of light.

The return trip must have taken as long as the outwards trip, but that weird echoing/doubling effect was messing with my head so hardcore that I couldn't even begin to shake it off until we dropped through Earth's atmosphere, slowing as we dropped through the night sky toward the desert floor.

I'd like to tell you what I thought at that moment. I wish

I could say that I understood everything and that, while it had shaken me, I was okay. I just can't do that. The truth is that my brain was more like an animal who'd been thrown in a cage and shocked over and over again, wanting to get out and away from the scary thing that shook the foundation of its world, so I have no idea what I did for a long, long time.

Chapter 31

I Am Become Death

My memory picks up again with me on my knees, hands free of the posts, gagging and puking all over that beautiful white floor; the only sound was the splattering of whatever was left in my guts.

When I finished, I sat down hard on my ass. I put my hands on my head and closed my eyes.

The image of the guy at the computer wouldn't leave my head, no matter how hard I tried. "What was that?" I moaned.

"What do *you* think it was?" Paraoan said.

"Don't pull that on me. Not now."

"Excuse me?" he said.

"Don't play stupid. You know what I mean."

He cleared his throat, but he didn't say a damn thing.

I had to answer his question, but part of me held back. Sure, I knew what I'd seen, but letting the words cross my lips would make it so much more real.

If you're not ready for it now, when will you be?

"It looked like we came out of a computer," I said.

"Correct."

My brain lurched. "What the hell? Does that mean I'm some sort of program? That guy wrote me?

Paraoan crouched in front of me, looking me in the eye.

I'm sure he meant to comfort me, but it made my skin crawl instead. "It is much to understand. It has been so very long since someone has pierced the veil, and acceptance is very difficult for the uninitiated..."

I barked a laugh. "Acceptance is difficult. No kidding. It's just a little hard to deal with finding out that everything you've ever seen or done is an illusion, that you're written to do as you're told-"

"That is simply not the case. No one person programmed or...*wrote*...you, anymore than they wrote me." He rose, spreading his arms. "Or anything that you see around us. That man formulated a framework, a complex set of rules that he refined until it became self-replicating. Your people call it the Big Bang."

"Impossible," I said.

"I tell you otherwise."

"That means we're just pieces of data," I said.

"Why do you not parse that we are much more? We are miracles. We are the unanticipated, the voice of the Multiverse, expressing itself. We provide the proof of life beyond even their world."

"When you put it that way, it's not so bad, I guess."

He nodded. "More than satisfactory. Revelatory."

"What does that make you, a high-end program?"

"I was among the First." I remember how Paraoan said it, just like that, First was capitalized. "I enable communication between worlds."

"Like our world and theirs?" I said.

"Every world. My function is cross-Aethyric communication. As the Multiverse has evolved, so has my job."

"What am I supposed to do with this information? Why show me that?" I said.

"Your reaction to this information is known as the Reckoning"

"Come again?"

"This is the beginning of a cascade effect. You have seen what few others have seen. You understand the stakes if the experiment fails – to destroy our Multiverse would be as simple as a few keystrokes. The Reckoning is the inevitable outcome of this understanding."

"Is it in danger of failing?"

"We stand on a knife edge. An Aethyr – not your Aethyr – has found a way through the code. A way to communicate with their world. Yet they face many obstacles. If they cannot overcome those obstacles, if communication between their world and ours proves fruitless, then our creators have no choice but to shut the program down," he said.

"You're talking about the end of the Multiverse."

"Their superiors require results."

I shook my head. "What does that have to do with me? Don't tell me I have to save the Multiverse."

"It is your job to clear those obstacles and ensure that the message, loud and clear as it is meant to be, reaches them."

I tried to stand up and nearly fell on my ass.

Paraoan reached out and steadied me, helping me to my feet. He grimaced. "Unfortunately, it is not simple. By any stretch. You must sever this Aethyr's lifeline to their world – to the Multiverse."

My head pulsed, like we were doing a loop on a roller coaster. "What?" I heard myself ask. "Why?"

"Because your Aethyr is blocking the signal."

"How's that possible?" I asked.

"Communicating with their world requires a path for a tremendous amount of information. Your Aethyr directs the signal through that path, but it is also consuming all of the information flowing in and out of that path."

"What do you mean?"

"Your Aethyr sits at the crossroads of all others. That is why I created the Watchtowers in the first place. Why I used the Black Cross to recruit the Watchers and send them to this Aethyr."

"So we're supposed to direct traffic, but instead we're hogging it all?"

"Correct."

"And you want to…what, take control of it? Was that the point of the Black Cross?" I said.

"No. The Black Cross was built to get us to this point; its Prophecy has dictated every action that the Watchers have taken. *You* represent the next step. You must cut your Aethyr off from the source of life in the Multiverse, in order to save the Multiverse itself."

"The Reckoning."

"Correct."

It all made sense. The Corridors of the Dead… "I've seen what the Reckoning does. It turns this Aethyr into a wasteland," I said.

"This must happen, in order that all other worlds might survive."

I shook my head. "Impossible. I can't do it."

He paced, arms behind his back. "The good news is that now this is not the time for the Reckoning - merely the beginning. You have time to understand the reality-"

I grabbed him by the arm. "You don't get it, pal. I'm not saying I can't do it now. I'm saying I can't *ever* do it. Nothing will ever make me think it's okay to turn our Aethyr into a wasteland."

He narrowed his eyes. "Your actions are pre-determined. You have seen the results yourself."

"I can still choose my destiny. I refuse to believe there's no such thing as free will in the system you just described to me," I said.

"I do not believe you comprehend the gravity of what is to happen. If you do not do this, your Aethyr will be destroyed, as well."

I scoffed. "So that's the real meat of it, huh? I either throw the switch on my world or watch the whole Multiverse burn."

"That is the long and short of it," he said.

"Some Chosen One. I'm just the hired gun."

"No. You are simply the only one who can do it."

"Why?" I asked, hell, pleaded.

He blinked. "Because you have always been the one to do it."

"So that's it. It's always been that way, so it's the way it has to be?"

That took the wind out of his sails. He gazed at the ceiling for a long minute before he said, "yes."

"God damn you," I said.

"Yes," he replied. "God did damn me."

"Boo hoo. How is this whole thing going to shake out for you? You get to watch our Aethyr wither and die while you shake your head and go *tut-tut, what a shame?* I love people here. This is my home."

His eyes blazed. "Do not presume to lecture me. I acutely feel the pain of any widespread loss in the Multiverse. Your Aethyr's genocides hurt me in ways you cannot possibly comprehend."

"Let me get this straight. Some poor kid from Poland went on the run after his family got wiped out, ended up in a concentration camp, and died a long, drawn-out death. Multiply that by millions, and it hurts poor Paraoan's *feelings*?" I admit it, I let the venom flow. How dare he tell me to do this?

He bared his teeth. "You mistake my solemnity for self-pity. I asked for no sympathy. My sympathies are with you, you spoiled child, for the choice that you must make."

"I think you're full of shit. I don't believe that we're the real problem. If we are, why haven't I seen any evidence of it?"

He raised an eyebrow. "Haven't you? Have you not seen evidence of your world corrupting others - stealing their energy - in your travels? How about the land where you met the daughter of the angel of death?"

"Jodi," I said.

"Yes. Jodi. What about what you saw in Bakersfield? I understand it is quite lovely there this time year."

"Don't feed me that. That was the Watchers."

"How do you think the Watchers accomplished such destruction and rot? They harnessed the power of this Aethyr, using its connection to the other worlds to drain them dry of their very essence," he said.

"At your direction."

"The cancer that is your Aethyr had to be exposed."

God, I wanted to punch him in that smug, girly mouth of

his. "I don't want to do it. I won't."

"I have told you. You do not yet have to make the decision. The Reckoning is not yet at hand."

"How am I supposed to know, then?"

He pointed toward the ceiling, and I gazed up to see that a portion of the ceiling had darkened, showing a bright blue streak burning across the sky.

"The comet," I said.

"It is still coming. By its hand will you know the time."

"When they destroy it? That's when I'm supposed to cut them off?"

He applauded. "Clever girl. Its destruction will provide all the energy needed to sever your Aethyr from the Multiverse."

"You're a real sweetheart, you know that?"

"Your perception of me is none of my concern. Your mission is." He waved a hand, and the chamber darkened again, revealing a stone city, deep in some sort of jungle. "You will travel to the City of the Dead. You will stand in the Temple that is the foundation, and you will decide: do you destroy this Aethyr, or do you destroy the Multiverse?"

"What if I decide not to? Just go home and watch Seinfeld reruns until the great Creators flip the switch on the whole shitty business? Would I even know the difference?"

"I am sorry. I think we misunderstood each other. I am not giving you directions. I am simply telling you what you will do."

"Because it's what I always did."

He nodded.

"What is this…City of the Dead? How do I get there?"

"I do not know. Its true location has never been revealed

to me. You will have to make the best decision that you can. In the meantime, you must attend to other matters: those which have brought you here."

Kristy. The Watchers. The Engine.

"Daniel wanted me to destroy the Engine."

"Were it even possible, do you agree with his assessment that it needs to be destroyed?"

"Damned right I do, but I have no clue how."

"More the pity then. But come, our time is short. You must defend the child and free your lover."

My heart skipped a beat. "Is she important to this?"

"Of course."

"How do we do that?" I said.

"You destroy the Watchers out there, of course."

"Oh, is that all? Listen, those guys were armed. Big machine guns. Not to mention Azazel, God only knows what he's capable of."

"All true, and yet you know something that they do not: the nature of the Multiverse."

"What am I supposed to do with it? It can't make me bulletproof, can it?"

He lifted his right hand; a golden glow lit up his flesh. "That and more. Kneel for a moment and I will show you."

Chapter 32

Fixing a Hole

The door between the chamber and the silo slid open, revealing Azazel and Kristy, waiting arm-in-arm for me. Tommy leaned against a pillar behind them, watching me with sharp, wary eyes.

When our eyes met, he pointed one finger at me like a pistol, and I nodded.

Azazel cleared his throat and smiled, showing me his perfect teeth. "Well? Have the Watchtowers fallen?"

"Not as far as I know," I said.

His smile faded. "What of the Reckoning?"

"It's been postponed."

He glanced to the soldiers against the walls. "Erm, yes. Of course. You are the Chosen One, after all, but I can't help but wonder: why did nothing happen?"

"Something happened. You just don't understand it." I pointed at him. "You're good, you know. Not just you, the whole organization. You had me thinking I didn't know a damn thing, and you had all the cards."

Tommy spoke up. "You always had it. You just had to find it."

Azazel must have forgotten the kid was there, because he whirled to look at him and then back to me.

"What's wrong, Zazzy?" I asked. "You look a little nervous."

"Nothing's wrong. Why would anything be wrong?"

"Hmm what could be wrong? Could it be me? Or could it be the fact that you don't want your followers here to know that you're clueless about what's in that chamber?"

Kristy had gone pale. "What do you mean?"

I guess Tommy had been waiting for that. He took a step forward, keeping his eyes on Azazel's back.

Azazel didn't seem to have noticed him, and I didn't want to change that. I didn't know what the kid was planning, but it couldn't be any good for our mutual friend.

I clicked my tongue. "You mean you didn't tell her? Tsk." I got a step closer to him, and I swear I could *smell* the fear coming off of him, like you smell ozone in the air when a storm's coming in.

I think his little group of lackeys smelled it too, because a couple of them moved off of their positions on the wall. I could read the hesitation in those little steps they took, not to mention the looks on what used to be some damned blank faces, but they knew something was about to change, no doubt about that.

"Tell me what?" Kristy asked.

"I didn't-"

"Zazzy! You, at a loss for words? Why, will miracles never cease?" I looked to Kristy and fought my instinct to wrap her in my arms and keep her safe. I had to stand strong to get her back; show her that he was a fraud, and she would follow.

Tommy spoke up, helping me stoke the fire. "They didn't have a clue what was inside the chamber."

I smiled. "That's right. All that talk about the glorious revolution and the overthrow of the Aetelia? It was just a bunch of kids playing make-believe, wasn't it?"

"Is that true?" Kristy asked and unlinked her arm from his. She took a good, healthy step away from the pasty bastard.

"That's a lie," Azazel said, and his voice rose on the last word.

"Is it?" I asked.

He glanced at one of his bodyguards, and I don't know what he saw, but he held up one hand at him like he was telling the guy to back away. "We opened the databanks. How else would we have found you?"

"The databanks have nothing to do with what's in the chamber," Tommy said.

"What are you guys talking about?" Kristy said.

"What *are* they talking about?" came a voice from behind us.

Grabbe. He stood a few steps behind Tommy, clutching at his side with one hand, his eyes bloodshot.

My relief at seeing to see the chunky bastard was a surprise. "He didn't tell you, either?" I said.

If he heard me, he didn't acknowledge my question. Instead, he kept his eyes locked on his dad, taking a shuffling step toward him. "Answer me. What do they mean when they say you didn't go into the chamber? Is that true?"

"You're in deep shit now, buddy," I whispered at Azazel.

The guy was on the verge of panic, his eyes bugging out. "Now, now, son, I told you we hadn't ironed out the kinks-"

"That's crap. You specifically told us that you had been in the chamber. We built this whole thing on the goddamned premise," he said, and coughed.

"You shouldn't stress yourself. You've been through too much the last few days. You're fragile."

"You're a goddamned liar," Grabbe shouted through the phlegm that was choking him. It felt like the room shook. "What else have you lied about?"

"I don't owe you an explanation. You went with the Aetelia. You chose your fate," Azazel said.

"Because you fucked over mom. I never figured you fucked over the rest of us. All this time I thought I was just some asshole who couldn't get over what you'd done, but you've been lying to all the Watchers, too." He laughed. "Word of this gets out, and you're double-fucked. Does Samyaza know?"

"Who are you going to believe, me or this traitor and his band of... *rejects*?" he said, but this must have been a real bone of contention. He looked like was practically ready to fall on his knees in front of the bodyguards and beg them for forgiveness.

The bodyguards themselves were gazing around at each other, shifting from foot to foot.

"She's the Chosen One," one of them finally said.

If this is what you meant by being bulletproof, Paraoan, then you did good, I thought. *Time to push them over the edge.*

"I am the Chosen One. In fact, I met the Lost Aetelia, Azazel. Ever seen him?"

A few of the bodyguards gasped, and I half-expected them to fall on their knees, making the sign of the cross or whatever they did.

"Lies," he hissed. "The Lost Aetelia has not appeared in centuries-"

"Not to you guys, no. He's pretty pissed at you, actually.

Thinks you've gotten a lot of things wrong. You're part of the…how did he put it? The Rot. The Rot at the center of everything." Pure bullshit, of course, but Azazel had to have seen the abomination in the Corridors.

His mouth dropped open. "That's not true, either. We never created that thing…"

I laughed and shook my head. "You knew that was the outcome of the Reckoning going in. You knew the Corridors of the Dead came from the Reckoning. You're not that stupid, are you?"

"Of course we're not," he said. He put one hand to his mouth and glanced at the bodyguards, who were closing in, encircling us.

Kristy shook her head, blinking like she was waking up. Without that cruel assurance that she'd been wearing, she looked a bit like a little girl playing in her mommy's makeup."What are the Corridors of the Dead?" she asked.

"A distraction," Azazel said. "She's attempting to hide the reality-"

I cut him off. "The Corridors are the real price of the Reckoning, not whatever fairy tale he was selling you. The Reckoning doesn't just kill all life - that's not what "Dead" means. It means that this Aethyr gets cut off from all of creation, even the afterlife. Pure nothingness." As I explained, I watched what was left of Azazel's tart melt into a puddle on the floor, leaving the woman I loved in a world of hurt and regret.

For once, Azazel was at a loss for words. He sputtered, then said, "you're the one who would do it, too, aren't you?"

"Sure, that's what being the Chosen One means, but I didn't know that going in. You did, and you didn't tell a single one of the Watchers. Or Kristy."

He didn't deny it - he couldn't.

The tension in the room amped up with every second of his silence. Everyone else had gone silent with him, and I think we knew that the time for words had passed. We had outed Azazel for his true conniving self. He had lost control over every single person in the room and stood alone. The next move was his, and he was at his most dangerous. I couldn't imagine him taking any other path than lashing out and trying to escape.

I spread my arms and smiled at him, hoping I seemed braver than I felt. "Your move. What do you say? Want to hug it out and be friends?"

He snarled – I swear to God, *snarled* – before he raised one hand toward me, clenching his fist. Something in my chest tightened, like he had grabbed hold of my heart and crushed it between his fingers. I went down on one knee, gasping, clutching at the focus of the pain, trying to catch my breath. It felt like the walls were closing in around me, my vision going dark and blurry.

The attack was all the cue that the bodyguards needed; threaten the Chosen One, and you've made your bed. They closed in on Azazel, guns raised, the roar of their shots filling the room, like a pack of pissed-off lions ready to tear apart their prey.

As soon as the shots began, the pain in my chest eased. I went down on all fours, gasping as the air flowed into my burning lungs.

I struggled to my feet in time to see Azazel, rise off the floor and float a few feet above the fray, eyes turning into bright golden lamps. He made this sound that I can't quite describe, somewhere between a dog's bark and a tiger's snarl, and reached out with one hand.

One of the bodyguards shot off the ground and flew across the room, slamming into the pillar where Tommy had rested.

Move, I told myself.

Kristy was the first, and most important, order of business. She had pushed herself out of the circle, toward the walls. Her eyes were bugged out, but she was safe, and if I could manage to keep the bastard away from her, all would be well.

I ducked another of the bodyguards as Azazel flung him against the wall like a ragdoll.

Having recovered something like a semblance of direction and sanity, Grabbe wrenched one of the guns out of a guard's dead hand and opened up on his father.

All his dad had to do was wave a hand at the bullets and they stopped mid-air, clattering to the floor at his feet.

"Fuck me," Grabbe said, and ducked behind the pillar as Azazel threw a bolt of glowing blue light at him.

So Azazel had telekinesis *and* some freaky lightning up his sleeve, not to mention being bug-fuck crazy on top of it. What the hell could I do against that?

Paraoan, if you gave me some other Ace to use against this bastard, now would be a swell time to bring it out.

Lo and behold, Paraoan's voice answered. "Look closer," he whispered.

I stood completely still in the middle of all that chaos. Everything slowed. Kristy screamed and a body flew past me, but it might as well have been in…what did they call it? Oh yeah. Bullet-time. It was like that. The dim light in the room was clearer; the smell of gun oil and damp rot sharper. An aura of golden power appeared around Azazel, rippling and flexing as he moved.

From far away, that aura was a righteous, angelic power, something that a human should run from, pissing his or her pants in an appropriate display of awe and terror. Up close, though, I could see the smallest of rips, a speck of black in the river of light. It could have been a figment of my imagination it was so small, but it wasn't. It was what I needed to make the bastard vulnerable.

But how?

Surrender. That was the answer. I took a deep breath, and let whatever it was that Paraoan had planted in my consciousness rise up.

The answer presented itself in seconds, and it was so simple. Just a pinch – and I did that with my fingers, because the body wants to mimic what the mind is doing. The tear got bigger, and his golden aura began to unzip.

He caught on at the last second, as the aura fell to the ground, disappearing in a shower of golden sparks.

He made a screeching noise, like someone had stuck a hot poker up his ass, and gave me a haunted look, a look that I'll never forget if I live to be 100.

Then he hit the ground. He was mortal, and everybody could see it.

We entered one of those moments that William Burroughs referred to as a Naked Lunch moment. You familiar with that? It's a moment where everything is frozen, and everyone sees everything on the end of each others' fork clearly. Everybody in the room saw things the way I did when I had zeroed in on Azazel: clear, bright, and sharp.

Kristy's eyes went wide. Grabbe froze as he appeared from behind the pillar, gun raised. Tommy stood still somewhere in the shadows. The remaining bodyguards turned as one, weapons forgotten for that brief moment.

We became a collective, a bunch of rogue programs waiting for the next cycle to click over and the inevitable to transpire.

Of course, it did. Grabbe was the first to get his shots into his dad's body, with the remaining bodyguards coming in a close second.

Kristy screamed, and I recoiled.

Murder. Another stain on my soul. Christ, I mean *was* it even murder, or did the guy get what he had coming, and to hell with the consequences? I couldn't tell you. I didn't know if the distinction meant anything anymore.

The next move was Kristy, seizing me from behind, her arms wrapping around my chest.

"Oh God, baby, I'm so sorry," she whispered.

Whatever hollowness had been haunting me vanished. Maybe we were digits, but damn it, we were *important* digits.

"Can you forgive me?" she asked.

"I don't know," I said, without looking at her. My eyes were still on Azazel's still form, bleeding out a black substance that passed for his blood. Stuff that I hadn't seen coming out of Delilah.

If she's alive, it's too late now. Focus on the now.

The only real way onward was upward. What was done was done, and I just had to be ready for it.

Chapter 33

And in the End...

Grabbe stepped over his father's body. It could have been a side of meat for all the concern he showed. "Thank God you showed up, kiddo. I don't know what the old bastard had up his sleeve, but I'm not exactly sad that we missed out," he said.

I slipped away from Kristy, surveying the damage. "What did he do to you guys?"

Grabbe raised an eyebrow at Kristy, and she turned away, crossing her arms over her chest.

"Can't tell you what he did to her, but he gave *me* a 'drink' that damn near killed me. Me. His own son. Can you believe it?" Grabbe said.

"Well, you did kind of threaten to kill him."

"Sure, but come on, where is the love here?"

I chuckled and fixed my gaze on Kristy. "What about you, Polly? What did he do to you, to get you to buy his bullshit?"

I got all the answer I needed from her haunted, sad eyes.

"Nothing," I said.

"He threatened her," one of the bodyguards said.

"That right?"

She shrugged. "Yeah, but...what he said, it sounded so good and so...*real*."

"Worth all the death and destruction?"

She met my eyes. "I figured sometimes a few people have to suffer to make everyone else better off."

I swallowed hard. "But you saw what he did to Daniel. That seemed right to you? A fair trade-off for the greater good?"

She ground one foot against the floor. "No. Yes. I mean, I don't know."

"You've *never* believed in the ends justifying the means. Why now?"

"I don't know." That was the best she could manage.

"Yes you do. Same reason you bought into Delilah's shit. You're a sucker for anything that sounds halfway convincing."

She hung her head. "Do you still love me?"

My heart wrenched. I was tempted to tell her no, just so she could understand the pain that she had given me, but would I really be any better than Azazel? "Of course I love you, didn't I go through hell to get back to you?"

I don't know exactly what I expected from her; I guess her falling into my arms and thanking me for my forgiveness. Whatever I might have wanted, it wasn't what I got. Rather than a warm embrace, she turned her back, just choking out, "Thanks."

I started to take a step toward her, but Grabbe cleared his throat and shook his head. "Tell us what you saw."

"Nothing like what the Prophecy said, that's for sure. No choirs of angels, no Fifth Watchtower, no…whatever you guys thought it was going to be."

"Son of a bitch. Of course he was a fucking liar." He looked at his dad's body. "He told us all that he had met the Lost Aetelia, that he knew his will."

"He fooled us all," said one of the bodyguards, a pale-skinned, blond guy.

Grabbe looked to me again. "So you really met the Lost Aetelia?"

I didn't know how to answer that. I was pretty sure Paraoan didn't want them knowing the truth. I opened my mouth, not sure *what* would come out.

Tommy saved me, stepping between us like a miniature diplomat. "Do you really have to ask?" He looked around at us. "Did you see what I did? She stripped a Senior of full power. Could anyone else have helped her do that?"

"Yeah. What he said," I said.

One of the other bodyguards, a one with a long, black beard, spoke up. "She's the Chosen One." Simple as that, like it was all that needed to be said.

The kid waved a hand. "Of course, but she's a human being. She'd need *his* help to do that."

"Sorry guys, he's right. The Lost Aetelia helped me. I'm not sure I'm your Christ or anything."

The bearded guy went down on his knees, ready to swear his allegiance, but the blond guy caught him by the arm, hauling him to his feet.

"You're not supposed to save us," the blond guy said.

"I bet not," Tommy said. "I bet the Lost Aetelia told you to destroy the Watchers."

"How did you know that?" I said.

"I'm important, I guess."

"Yeah," the blond guy said. "I think I know you from some place."

Tommy worked hard at ignoring the guy. "Did he tell you how to do it?"

I glanced at the blond guy, wondering if we had another situation on our hands. "Not exactly."

"Look at me when I'm talking to you, you little shit-bag," the blond guy said.

Tommy turned and looked at him. "Speak to me in a respectful tone and I'll respect you."

"You little-"

Grabbe stepped between the two of them, holding out his hands. "Hey, now, fellows, there's no need to get upset at each other."

The blond guy sighed. "Fine. But only because it's you, Grabbe."

"That's swell of you, and I appreciate that you had my back when that bastard slipped me the drugs. Oh wait, you didn't, did you?"

The blond guy's face turned red. "He would have killed us…"

"Save me the sob story. What do you think Samyaza is going to do when he hears about this?"

The blond guy didn't answer; he just took a step back.

"That's right. You need to be thinking long and hard about what your next move is going to be."

"What *are* we going to do next?" Kristy asked, sounding like a lost little girl.

You know, at that moment, hearing that voice, seeing the tears streaming down her cheeks, I wanted to give her the biggest hug known to humanity.

But…

A little voice in my head said: *You remember her Malibu Kristy act? You think you can trust her if she couldn't even wait you out? Just what* did *happen between her and Azazel?*

The thought made my skin crawl. "That's what I'm trying to figure out. We can't stay here," I said.

Tommy answered that. "No, we can't. Samyaza will be here soon and there will be hell to pay. Did the Lost Aetelia tell you to go to the City of the Dead?"

I blinked. "How the hell do you know that?"

"It doesn't matter. That's where the Reckoning takes place. Not here."

"I'm not acknowledging that," I said.

"Not the City of the Dead," Grabbe said.

"You know it?" I asked.

He shuddered. "Let's just say I don't want to see that place again unless I absolutely have to."

"She must go," the bearded guy said. "It's her destiny."

"What the hell does it matter? I'm not going. I want nothing to do with it," I said.

"He's right. You don't want to go. You hate the idea of what you have to do there. But you're going there anyway," Tommy said.

"What's the City of the Dead?" Kristy asked.

Grabbe took that one. "Trust me, kitten. You don't want to know.

"It's where she's going, whether she likes it or not. It's 'what's next'," Tommy said.

"Jesus Christ, how many times do I have to tell you people no? What is it with you? Why are you so determined to make me do this?

The kid smiled. I'd said too much, and we both knew it. "I'm not the first to tell you. You have to make a choice. What choice is it?"

Pissed at myself and getting tired of this kid being two

steps ahead of everybody else, I got up in his face as best as I could. "Who are you? How do you know so much?"

Give the kid credit; he stayed remarkably calm for having an angry bitch right up on top of him. He smirked and said, "you know. You're not the only Chosen One."

The blond guy gasped, his eyes going wide. He looked like a kid who discovered that hot water was, indeed, hot. "I know who you are."

The kid whirled and gave him a downright evil look, eyes narrowing down into rat-like slits and teeth shining, catching a glint of the light that seemed like an unspoken threat. "Not a word," he said.

"No, tell us. I want to know what makes him so high and mighty," I said.

The blond guy started to say something, then hesitated, gazing from me to the kid, eyes as wide as the kid's had been narrow.

Goddamn, he's scared to death of the little bastard.

Of course, I didn't get the answer to that question, and the poor blond guy didn't even get spared for trying to protect Tommy. Two pops, and bullet holes appeared in his forehead and chest. His bodyguards followed.

That's right about when we all realized that you fellows had showed up, with your shouting and your guns.

Okay, well not *all* of us. Even when you guys were putting the knee in my back and forcing me face-down onto the concrete, I saw the look in Tommy's eyes. He knew you guys were coming.

He was always a step ahead.

At this point, I don't give a good goddamn whether you guys kill me when we're done here. I need two things from